# Hope for Us Yet

## The Collected Stories of Ramsbolt

### Jennifer M. Lane

Cover design by Alia Hess – cultofsasha.com

Copyright © 2019

Published by Pen and Key Publishing

jennifermlanewrites.com

ISBN: 9781733406864

# ACKNOWLEDGEMENTS

Thank you to Essa Hansen, Kali Glover, and Cheryl Murphy.

Special thank you to Alia Hess.

*"I am the Cat who walks by himself, and all places are alike to me."*
*— Rudyard Kipling, The Cat That Walked By Himself*

# CHAPTER ONE

Water spewed from the faucet into the slop sink, battering Adelle's old watering can and spattering the wall. Drops sprayed her green apron, soaking in. She fumbled the cold water handle, and it came off in her hand.

"Not again. Stupid thing." Water shot at the ceiling and rained down on a shelf of spider plants. She ducked beneath the sink for the emergency valve, the knees of her jeans soaking up the lake that formed on the tile. Her brown eyes narrowed as she reached for the pipe in the shadowed corner. She might be twenty pounds overweight, and her knees might be killing her, but that sink wouldn't get the best of her. "I'm gonna be too old for this one day, you know. We have to come to terms, you and me."

The room fell silent as she turned the valve tight. She brushed sweat-streaked brown hair, flecked with early signs of gray, across her forehead and hefted the can from the sink, careful not to slip, then worked her way around the counter strewn with white roses and baby's breath, sprays of statice and eucalyptus, as the last of the water dripped down the wall.

Morning sun flared through the glass of her flower shop, blanketing the wide windowsill and wicking moisture from the soil of her ancient plants. Older than her forty-three years, anyway. Shards of aloe reached from pots and spears of viper's bowstring, what her father had called mother-in-law's tongue, stabbed toward the ceiling. The sun brought out hints of red in the patches of stain that floated like islands on the worn-out floor. Three generations of florists and guests had rubbed the boards raw with coming and going. Refinishing the wood was one more thing that would never get done. Not with money as tight as it was and not with nerves that sizzled and seared when she counted up the cost of what needed patching and mending.

She reached between pointy aloe arms and pressed her fingers to the soil. It was parched and sun dried, ready for water. She aimed gentle water at its earth, a monthly ritual of letting rain fall gently onto the plants that needed it and avoiding the ones that didn't until water pooled in the drip tray. From plant to plant, succulent to cactus, it was a dance, choreographed by generations along the deep windowsill until she reached the end.

"Drink up, little lovelies."

Across the street at the antique shop, Penny had a cat named Jake who seemed a great listener. Some people without people had cars. If you snuck into Jaleesa's garage on the other side of town at just the right moment, you could find her talking to just about anything with a motor. But Adelle had plants. New plants she grew from seed. Flowers she cut into arrangements. Her mother's cactus and the descendants of her great-grandfather's plants. Kitchen herbs and succulents and buckets of tulips and daisies. All of them tucked into, in front of, and behind the shop.

The can empty, she let it fall to the floor and ran the back of her hand across her forehead, scraping long brown hair to her temple where it would stay until it crept into her eyes again, carried by sweat and gravity.

"If you ask me, that air conditioner isn't doing anything at all. But don't tell the air conditioner I said that. My luck, it would stop making all that racket, and we'd have to listen to ourselves think. Right?"

She smashed her fist into the side of the unit, hoping something would happen.

Nothing. "All this thing does is buzz." She turned the plastic knob, yellowed and brittle with age, but nothing came of it. Not even a change in tune. "I can't keep up either, old girl. This summer's going to be the death of us."

She could forgive the air conditioner for its sins, but she couldn't live with the humidity.

"Maybe some air flow will help. What do you say, little aloes?"

She propped the front door open with an antique milk jug as a pack of boys on bicycles turned onto the street from the cemetery, circling in front of the empty stores.

Levering Road was the widest street in town, designed for a trolley that never came to be. It was the scene of most of her happiest childhood memories, buying penny candy at the General Store, finding magic in the toy store, and playing on the sidewalk. Most of those kids grew up and moved away, so there were few people to reminisce with and fewer shops that offered the kind magic she knew. The town was brighter then. Now it was strewn with trash from cars just passing through and dust kicked up by a new generation of kids on bikes with less to explore.

Across the street, Penny dragged an old metal ladder out from the antique shop. Penny's red hair blazed in the sun. She wore old jeans and a fitted T-shirt, and she had pulled her hair back into a tie. The ladder wobbled as she climbed, but she didn't seem to care.

Adelle felt guilty for having resisting Penny's idea of an art festival, even if she'd done so silently. She'd resisted everything about Penny, really. The woman had been new to town as she closed her grandmother's estate. She'd been loud and chaotic, with an air about her as if she faulted Ramsbolt for not meeting her expectations. Once Adelle tempered her own expectations, she was able to accept the woman twenty years her junior. Now she felt bad, watching her neighbor fill her arms with streamers and banners and old decorations.

"I should give her a hand." Adelle pushed the door open, crossed the street, and stepped onto the high curb.

Penny tugged on the ends of streamers.

The sun was bright and stung Adelle's skin, even for the early hour. She shielded her eyes and peered up at Penny. "Want some help?"

Penny dangled the end of a streamer. "Sure. Thanks. I suppose I can save all of this for next year."

"It was a lot of fun. I wanted to apologize, properly apologize, for not being supportive. I'm really glad you pulled it off. I'm sorry I was so resistant." Resistant was an understatement. Even though she hadn't been vocal about her distaste for commotion, the noise and traffic, and the strain on Ramsbolt's dwindling resources, she still felt shame for feeling it. "This town doesn't come together as much as it should. And we definitely don't get many visitors. The festival did a lot of good."

Penny tugged on a blue streamer, and it fluttered into Adelle's hand. "It's cool. I didn't expect as much support as I got, to be honest. Or as many people coming through town. But everybody made some money from it." She tugged on another piece of tape, releasing more streamers. "Hey, thanks again for landscaping the park. It looks really good."

Adelle shrugged and wound the streamer around her hand. "It's just a few annuals, sage and lavender for right now. I'll plant some bulbs that'll be pretty in the spring. It'll take a few years to get things going, but it will be nice when it's done."

Her phone buzzed in her pocket, and she reached for it. Marissa. She only called from the bakery when there was a wedding or a funeral or town gossip too good to wait for. But Marissa was judicious and only spread the good gossip, so it was worth taking the call, even if it wasn't about business.

Adelle waved her ringing phone and held up the bundle of streamer. At least she'd been able to settle her regret. "Do you mind if I take this call? I can come right back."

"Not at all. I'll probably be done by then, anyway." Penny reached down and took the ball of blue plastic. "I'll stop over with coffee later."

Adelle crossed the street, dodging the boys on their bikes, and accepted the call. "Hey, Marissa. What's up?"

"You're never going to believe this. Morgan is going to college." Marissa's rapid words were barely above a whisper.

"What? How do you know?" Morgan never once said anything about going to college. "Doesn't Meldrick pay him enough to be the town manager for him?"

Meldrick Lacey had taken the town manager job from Adelle's father by force, turning the town against him. Once he had the job he fought for, he paid his son to do it instead. He told people the job was so simple a toaster could do it, that he had a new job and no longer had time, but Adelle knew it was all lies. Meldrick never wanted the job. He just didn't want her father to have it.

Marissa giggled. "You know that town manager job doesn't pay. Unless Meldrick threw in some extra for the trouble. Maybe Morgan finally made enough money off his dad to afford college."

"Fat chance." Adelle collected her watering can from the floor and put it back in the sink. "How'd you find out?"

"Meldrick was in here to buy a cake."

"That asshole. I hate him. But Morgan's such a good kid. And smart. Is he going to Orono?"

"No. North Carolina!" The sound of distant glasses scraping tables and forks on plates said the bakery must be busy.

"How is he going to be the town manager from North Carolina?" As soon as she said it, she saw the point in Marissa's call. It wasn't a heads-up about good news or a possible order for flowers. It was bad. All bad.

"That's why we're having an election. Meldrick doesn't have time for the job. It amounts to a resignation, I guess."

"What election?" No one had mentioned an election. There'd been no signs or notices anywhere. There hadn't been an election in years.

"They announced it at the town meeting. Two nights ago. Where were you?"

"I never go to those. I hate being stuck in the stinky library basement with all those people. And I hate all the drama."

Marissa's sigh came through loud and clear. "It's not drama. It's fun. How else are you gonna know things?"

"I know things because you call me from your perfect bubblegum world of cupcakes and cookies and tell me everything I need to know. And then some."

Marissa stifled her laugh. "It's a process, all this perfection. It involves going to town meetings. Anyway, no one is running for office so far, but at least we know why there's an election."

Adelle slumped onto her stool at the counter and pushed aside sprays of baby's breath. A picture of her father, his arms full of flowers, was nailed to the wall by the door. The whole town had loved him as a florist and as the town manager, until the day they didn't. The stress of the job and Meldrick Lacey's campaign to undo him had led to the strokes that eventually killed him. But Morgan Lacey had respected her father's legacy. He'd left well enough alone, hadn't destroyed Ramsbolt's ways of life. He even made it look easy, being so young, with so much energy and natural charm. Without him, who knew what would become of the town. Someone new could do all kinds of crazy things. Tear down buildings she shopped in and played around as a kid. Remove the clock just because it was broken. Her father had kept it safe from destruction for years. They could let Arvil build skyscrapers all over town and destroy the heritage. Everything her father worked so hard to preserve could be gone in the blink of an eye, and Ramsbolt as she knew it could cease to be.

"Adelle, you should run."

She brushed stray blossoms into a pile. "Run from what?"

"Don't be goofy. Come on. You must have picked up a lot about that job from your dad. We need a competent manager. Who else is going to do it?"

Something had to be done to keep the future from becoming even worse than the past. If Ramsbolt got any smaller, she could lose her store and everything her parents worked so hard to save. She'd have to move, but to where? To what? Like nearly everyone else in Ramsbolt, she was paycheck to paycheck.

Her shaking hands ran over the pile of tiny white flowers and scattered them across the counter. Her voice high, she protested. "I can't. I won't. It's not a job I can do. I'm totally the wrong person for it, but someone has to do it. What are other people saying? Are they upset? Are they worried?"

The air conditioner clunked and fell silent, a reminder that she was too poor to fix what she had, let alone move to something better. And Ramsbolt was all she knew. She had no savings, no distant relatives or far-flung friends to seek refuge with if the economy got worse and the store went under. She'd sink like a stone. It felt like the last of her father's days at the helm all over again, being bombarded on all sides by fears she couldn't see or hear. Tossed by waves, she had no control of the ship.

"I haven't talked to anybody. I don't know if people put the pieces together yet. All they said at the town meeting was that they would need an election soon. None of my customers have been talking about." And Marissa listened to everything. "Look, I got a line here. People need cupcakes. I'll call you right back."

The line went dead.

Adelle grabbed a catalog from the stack of mail and fanned herself, sweat dripping into her eyes. It was more than just a flush of summer. It was utter panic.

# CHAPTER TWO

Six hundred and twenty-four steps. That's how far the flower shop was from the newsstand. Adelle counted once when her mom sent her for a spool of receipt paper, and she'd never forgotten. About three hundred steps into her trip for price tags, near the beginning of Main Street, she stopped where a vacant corner store threw shade on the sidewalk. A red-and-blue sign with white lettering, printed on someone's home printer that had been low on cyan toner, announced an upcoming election.

It was the same paper, same font Morgan used to announce town meetings and utility repairs. The sign proclaimed an election on August twenty-third, to be held in the library basement. No mention of candidates.

In ballpoint pen, in the tiny bottom margin, he had written *see Morgan if you want to run.*

The street was papered in the signs. Every shop window had one. The post office, the bakery. There were two at the deli.

Her chest tightened, and her skin tingled with a rush of unease. She shouldn't be bothered by it. She should be happy for Morgan. He deserved a great education. He was twenty, after all, and he'd put off college for two years. On the surface, her distress was certainly the result of not wanting him to leave. She never thought he, of all Ramsbolt's brightest, would go. But the burning in the pit of her stomach came from a deeper ache. The stinging reminder that the town, for all its wants and needs, could be brutal. In a town that small, every defect was personal, and it took a special kind of person to prioritize the demands. Like her father, Morgan was one of those people.

Adelle crossed Main Street without looking and stepped into the newsstand. Behind the counter, Warren sat on his metal shop stool, scribbling on a notepad. Mack and Lewis, the same two men who'd been hanging 'round the counter since she was a kid, kept him busy, so Adelle waved and wound her way to the back of the store.

"What will happen if no one runs?" The keys in Mack's pocket jingled when he hoisted them over his expanding waistline. "I bet the town will get together and appoint someone. We'll hafta."

"That's the same thing as an election, dummy." Warren tapped his pen on the old wood counter.

"But no one's running." Mack cleaned his glasses with the hem of his blue button-up shirt. "If there's no town manager, what then?"

Lewis hooked his thumbs in his belt loops and rocked on his heels. He'd worked at some agricultural agency with the state for most of his life and knew enough people there to keep the town up to speed on political gossip. Eager to hear his answer, Adelle pretended to care about a box of colored pencils.

"The state won't have a choice but to annex Ramsbolt to another town. Probably that fool Adler from over in Bloomburg. Moron. That town's got twelve percent income tax and eight percent on every property. You gotta pay a hundred bucks a month just to get your trash picked up." Lewis said. "He's as greedy as they come. He'll take everything we got and give himself a raise."

"They'd *have* to raise taxes to pay for roads and do stuff Ramsbolt don't want done." Mack shook his head.

Adelle didn't have to strain to hear Mack's voice. Any time taxes were an issue, his voice boomed loud enough to hear from across the street. She heard Lewis loud and clear, too. Her father had hated Adler. He'd called him condescending, pushy with his ideas. From everything she remembered, he was everything Ramsbolt didn't like and didn't need.

Lewis waved a hand. "Lower your voice, will ya. I don't want that Adler man here, but don't ya want the roads fixed, though? Main Street's more holes than street. That clock ain't worked since Reagan was president."

"Adelle should do it." Warren pointed at her with his pen, and Lewis and Mack spun to face her. "She'd be good at it. Probably learned a lot being around her dad when he was town manager."

"No, no, no." Adelle shook her head, and her dark brown ponytail flung from side to side, smacking into her shoulders. "Nope. Can't. Just not possible."

It wasn't even an option after everything her father went through. Running the town was an impossible job that paid so little it didn't cover the water bill. She would never forget what the town did to her father, wearing him down with constant demands until there was nothing left of him. Every unreasonable demand he tried to meet, and each reasonable demand he couldn't, took a little more out of him until he was left with nothing. He spent his last days on earth frustrated that he couldn't solve problems that were never even his, while being attacked by Meldrick for being unsuitable to the task. All the hurt and frustration killed him in the end.

"Why not?" Lewis eyed her with suspicion, his brows creased and eyes narrowed. A burn rose within her. An embarrassment, like being falsely accused, and she rushed to the back of the store where Warren kept the price tags. She pulled the plastic pouch from the hook and under Lewis' glare, pulled her wallet from her purse.

"What do I owe you, Warren?"

"A buck thirty." He pushed buttons, and the old cash register clinked and clanged. "You'd be good at it, I think. You should consider it."

Lewis shifted beside her, his keys rattling. "We all have a duty to the town, miss."

What did he know about duty to the town? Did that duty extend to showing basic kindness to the people who run it? She took her change from Warren with a shaking hand and bit her tongue. Nothing good would come from barking at Lewis.

"It might be nice to have some of your dad's charm back around here." Mack stepped back, out of her path to the door. "Nothing against Morgan. He's a good man. But your dad had a way about it. Easy to talk to. He tried hard."

Adelle met his eye, the sharp edge of the plastic packet digging into her palm. "He tried too hard, Mack. And I'm nothing like my father."

Warren's metal stool creaked when he leaned forward. "You're plenty charming, Dell."

"I don't have his determination, that's what I mean. I wouldn't be any good at that job." It seemed a simple way to close idle chatter, to brush it aside, but it was clear from Lewis' stance, his hands deep in his pockets and his elbows tight to his sides, that his opinion was firm. But so was Adelle's. She wouldn't subject herself to the kind of torture the town laid out for her father. There was a reason she didn't spend time with people.

He lifted his chin and in a slow drawl said, "It's unpatriotic to turn your back on your town."

Adelle stuck the plastic pouch in her purse to avoid looking at him. One glance at him and she wouldn't be able to keep her outrage to herself. She zipped her purse shut and something in the sound of it emboldened her.

"You know what? This is ridiculous. I'm not turning my back on the town. I just don't want to run. Period. Yes, I think someone should, and they will. They'll come along and be great at it. But I don't see why anyone would think I would entertain it for half a second."

Lewis' eyes bulged. "Well, you're making it sound like a terrible job to have. Public service is important."

"Sure it is, but it's not for everybody, or we'd have nothing but a massive government and nobody working. We'd have no farms or delis or grocery stores or flower shops. You wouldn't want me there any more than anyone wanted my dad there. Seems you all forgot what this town did to him. Glossing over the past. Since when is driving a man to his death the good old days?"

"Fine. You just remember how much you hate big government when it comes in here and taxes you to death just because they want to fix the damn clock. Because that's where we are, missy. I ain't saying *you* need to run for office, but everybody has the same *not me* attitude, and this place is going downhill faster than an avalanche on a warm spring day."

Lewis hiked up his pants, and his keys jingled.

Adelle's face burned with everything she hadn't said for all those years, with all her anger at the town. Words swarmed like angry bees, but she couldn't put them into an intelligible sentence.

Warren held out her receipt. "Ignore him. He gets all riled up. Old men got nothing better to do."

"Apparently." Adelle took the receipt. "Thanks, Warren."

She yanked the door handle and stormed onto the street, beneath the clanging bell. Lewis wasn't entirely wrong, and that was only half of what made him so irritating. If no one ran for office, tragedy would be unavoidable. Not having a town tax certainly was a benefit. Even if someone decent did run for office and take the job, there was nothing to stop them from destroying the things that made Ramsbolt great. Her father's legacy of keeping the town's culture intact, of preserving their traditions and way of life, could be the least of her worries. She couldn't even afford to fix the air conditioner. She definitely couldn't afford to pay a cent in town taxes. And what if it made more people move away? Without weddings and births, birthdays and funerals, she'd have nothing left. She couldn't survive on garden herbs and vegetable plants all year.

Mack and Lewis did have a point. There was plenty to be worried about. Her future was out of her control.

Across the street, the town clock was still stuck on 10:35, just as it had been since a cold day in 1988 when it let out a loud clunk and startled Mrs. Griffins, who had just left the market and dropped a jar of mayonnaise. The sidewalk was still cracked from decades of freeze and thaw. Shops were still dark and empty. Her father had tried to keep the people from leaving. He answered every call and sat with every resident to hear their complaints. He tried to act on every one, but there was never enough money, or parts of himself, to give. He tried to fix the cracks and mend the tears, to meet all the demands, so he shed his own late at night, poring over books and searching for answers. Change had never been good. It only brought more bad news, more broken things, and all he could do—and all Adelle could do—was resist what they could and weather what they couldn't.

Reminders were everywhere, in every brick and every window. She couldn't deny the lump in her throat as she slipped between a blue pickup truck and a sedan.

She clutched her purse strap in a shaking hand. Through the bakery window, she could see the counter, relieved Marissa wasn't there. Slipping through the shop and into the bathroom, she let her purse fall to the pink tiled floor before the tears arrived and overflowed, streaking down her cheeks. Facing herself in the mirror above the sink, she dabbed her eyes with a wad of toilet paper.

She loved Ramsbolt just as it was. The way it was when she was a kid, and she could run through town until the streetlights came on. She'd loved Ramsbolt when the streetlights stopped working, and the dim lights on porches and through curtains guided her home, and she loved it when they found the money to fix them in some miraculous happenstance. She loved Ramsbolt for the way it endured and never changed. How cicadas came out in late July, every year, and sounded like the same summer played on repeat. It was hard to say goodbye to some things and some people, but saying goodbye was easier than making a grave mistake and selling the town to the highest bidder. Someone needed to run for office, but it wouldn't be her.

She blotted her cheeks and blinked up at the light, willing her eyes to absorb the last of the tears. With a deep breath of vanilla-scented air, she tossed the tissue in the trash.

There was no one to tell her it would all be okay. Not that she needed someone to tell her, but sometimes she missed her parents and the reassurance of knowing an adult was in charge. Some days it felt like there were no adults left in the world at all. She didn't feel like one of the confident adults she knew as a kid. She felt like she was about to be crushed. There was no money to move, and no skills to take with her. The woman looking back at her in the mirror, with her puffy cheeks and smattering of freckles, dabbing her eyes with toilet paper in the bakery bathroom, wasn't smart enough, strong enough, or savvy enough to weather a change as big as the one Lewis warned about.

If annexing the town was an option, things had to be worse than she thought. Lewis was right. Fixing petty squabbles between neighbors and mending a broken sidewalk or two wouldn't be enough. If it came down to a tax, it would smash what was left of Ramsbolt into smithereens. And if it all went to Adler, Ramsbolt would never look the same again.

# CHAPTER THREE

Adelle was twelve years old, a year too young to run the register by her father's standards and two years too old to play in the street by her mother's. But she was just the right age by her own estimation to repot seedlings, give them names and price tags, and put them under the grow lamps until they were big enough to go up for sale.

She shoved her thumb into the soil of a terra-cotta pot and pressed dirt to the side, making a hole big enough for the transparent stem of a frondy chamomile seedling. Across the counter, her father trimmed the ends off daffodils, making an arrangement for a woman whose admirer was to be kept a secret. Florists, he said, must create with the utmost discretion. Beyond her dad, across the street, a woman in a denim skirt emerged from the General Store with a bag on her hip. Sunlight reflected off the open door, into the store, where it blazed heavenly on the ice cream cooler that had been calling to her all afternoon.

"Can I have a quarter, Dad?" Adelle squeezed the bottom of the thin plastic pot, and a clump of growing medium and delicate chamomile stems fell into her palm.

"What do you need a quarter for? Use tweezers when you do that."

Her father jabbed a daffodil into a cheap plastic vase the shape of a tulip and the color of spoiled milk. He'd been like that lately, jabbing and poking at plants, dropping things instead of placing them gently, and muttering to himself, as if every town battle waged in his head. "And be careful with those seedings, Dell. If you break the stems, we can't sell it. All that time and water to grow it wasted."

"I'm not gonna break it. I have little fingers. All you have to do is be gentle."

Resting the clump of soil on a chipped saucer from a broken teacup, she brushed it away, revealing five thin stems. She lifted one and let the wisps of roots coil into the hole she'd made. With the tips of fingers soiled with crumbs, she pinched the dirt around the stem, closing the hole.

"There, little guy. You'll be making tea in no time."

"Don't forget to water it." He shoved one last flower in the vase and turned his back to her, cutting off a tumble of ivy that crept down from a high shelf.

Adelle clenched her teeth to hold in the sigh. "I know. You don't live in a flower shop and *not* know that plants need water, Dad."

Strand of ivy in one hand, her father reached across the counter and tugged the end of a fraying braid with the other. "Sorry, bug. My mind is on this streetlight fiasco."

"What streetlight fiasco?"

"You haven't noticed? Most of them don't work anymore."

She hadn't. She was never out at that hour. Long gone were the days when the orange glow of the streetlights along Main meant grabbing her bike by the handlebars and making the slog home, and she only heard her father's business in broken bits and pieces. Adelle punched four more holes in the dirt, making room for the rest of the seedlings. "Is it that big a deal that some light bulbs burned out? Get someone out there with a ladder. Can't somebody from the hardware store do it? It's not like they don't have ladders and light bulbs."

"It's not that easy. The wiring is ancient. It's a fire hazard. We had to turn them off last week, and you'd think we shut down the whole town the way people go on about it."

"Is that what Mr. Thorne was in here about?"

Her father spun the vase and adjusted a tumble of ivy. "That and fifty other things that got on his nerves last week. It's like raising four hundred little kids some days." He pushed the vase across the counter. "Put those seedlings under the grow lamp, will ya? And stick this in the cooler. You can take those succulent arrangements outside, too. Cooped up in here all winter. It's finally nice out."

She brushed soil from the counter back into bucket at her feet. "Geez, I thought you didn't want me to do this at all. Now you want me to perform child labor."

"Take a quarter from the register and get a creamsicle. You've had your eyes fixed on the market all day."

Adelle carried the seedlings to the grow racks in the hall behind the stairs. She left the chamomile alongside the dill and thyme she'd transplanted the day before, put the daffodil arrangement in the fridge at the front of the store, and smashed her thumb into a button on the register. With the other hand, she caught the tray of coins and bills before it slammed into her.

"Just one. We can't afford two. Not today."

"I know, Dad." She slid one quarter from the drawer and made a dash for the door.

"Succulents!" Her father waved his pruning shears at the front window, at the row of cups and saucers filled with haworthia that looked like spiny hedgehogs and young jade plants with their paddle-shaped leaves.

"I will. I promise. I'll just be two seconds. They're gonna close soon."

Her eyes fixed on the General Store, Adelle pushed through the door and stumbled into a man in oil cloth overalls stained with grease. By the smell of him, he'd been outside all day.

"Whoa there, Dell." He held his arm out to catch the door before it slammed shut and stepped to the side, out of her way.

"Sorry, Mr. Sommerwill. I got an errand to run."

Her cheap white tennis shoes dug into the back of her heel, but neither they nor the sweltering summer heat slowed her down. She dashed across the street without looking, leapt across the sidewalk, and landed on the tiled entrance to Miller's General Store, sweat dripping down her spine from the short jaunt. Just inside, she slid open the ice cream cooler door and extracted her prize. She knew better than to rip open the wrapper there in the store—her mother had raised her better than that—but the impatience made her fingers twitchy.

Mrs. Miller leaned across the counter with her hand extended. "No need to make you wait in line if you've got exact change."

"Thanks, Mrs. Miller. It'll melt right off the popsicle stick if I let it."

"If the rest of the summer is the scorcher this spring has been, you can count on that."

Adelle waved goodbye and dashed back to the shop. With the wrapper pulled down to catch any drips, she savored the first taste of creamy orange confection. It tasted like she figured food in heaven would, sweet and cold. It wouldn't take long to finish it, then she would put the plants outside like her father asked. But those few sweet moments deserved all her concentration.

She rested her back against the shop window and sank to the sidewalk.

"We don't want no tax here! Period!" Sommerwill's voice boomed through the glass, gravelly in its anger, and Adelle sat up straight, aiming her ear to the window. Her poor father got the brunt of everything. The shop was a fairly steady stream of neighborly complaints and friendly requests for him to do more with less. It had been worse than usual lately. Angrier. Her father said it was because he never set boundaries. Her mother said it was because he was too nice to say no.

"People are leaving town left and right. No one here can afford a tax. You'll run the last of us out. My family's been here for generations. I got nowhere else to go. This place will be like Bloomburg, taxed to death."

"No one wants to make anyone leave town. A tax would do the opposite. It would give people a reason to stay. It's just five percent. You want the lights fixed? That money's gotta come from somewhere."

"I ain't got five percent to give. Take it out of your salary then."

"Sommerwill, you know I don't have that much money to lay down on stuff like that. I can barely keep the electric on in this place. My wife is hemming her old hand-me-downs to keep my daughter in clothes for school. And you think Adler's bad? I got to catch a ride with him to the town managers' meeting in the Augusta 'cause I got no truck. Sitting in that Mercedes, back and forth, while that man tells me everything we're doing wrong. We're not Bloomburg, but we're not doing any better than anyone else."

"People are gonna start to wonder, you taking a town manager salary and having a shop, too. And nothing's getting done. This place is falling apart faster than it's coming back together, and it don't seem right to reelect someone if they're not doing the job."

Adelle held her breath, waiting for her father's words. He never raised his voice in anger, not to anybody. He got quiet when he was mad. Maybe that's what drove people to him, what made him perfect for the job of town manager. He had a seemingly unflappable nature that never lashed out. She could feel his rage smoldering through the wall, though. The kind of anger that he'd hold inside and mutter about to himself at the kitchen table.

"Sommerwill, I have already given up as much of my salary to help others as I can. I fixed Lanice's broken truck last week so she could keep milk on people's doorsteps. I already ration our own food to feed my own family. You can't get blood from a stone."

"So you know where we're coming from then. We can't give a five percent tax, because we don't have five percent to give. Yet somehow you keep making problems."

"I did not cause the lights to break. The wiring is old. I did not install potholes on Main Street in the middle of the night."

"I bet you didn't run people out of town either by not finding a way to keep the farms open."

"Don't use me as an excuse for why the town is a mess. It's a mess because the world changes, and we got to change with it. I didn't ask those big stores to move in an hour away. I didn't ask people to go buy cars and drive there. Or for the farms to go out of business. And if you think I make a fortune spending a hundred bucks a month to water plants we sell for a dollar each, then go on believing that. I didn't ask to give up my own farm, to lose my car and my house, either. I've given up every bit of my time for this town, and all you do is gripe and complain."

"If you gave up so much, how come it's still a mess? How come the town clock's still broke?"

Her father's sigh was audible through the window. "Because it's never gonna be enough. Even if I got out of bed at three in the morning to answer the phone, I couldn't have fixed Melba's plumbing. It never occurred to her to call the dang plumber. Everybody in this town thinks I'm the solution and the cause to every little thing. And they're gonna believe whatever they want, whether they go looking for the facts or not. And it ain't gonna change my day one dang bit, because I've done the best I can for this town. The one thing I can't control is anybody being grateful for it. I'd be happy to give five percent, though, if it meant making this town a tiny bit better. If you got any better ideas, spill 'em. Right here. Spill 'em."

Sommerwill didn't answer. Adelle bit down on the popsicle stick. It made her teeth hurt, but she did it anyway, like she could squeeze the last sweetness from the day. Beside her, the door flung open, and Sommerwill's shoes and greasy pants stormed past her, up the sidewalk toward the park.

Adelle scampered to her feet, brushed pebbles and street dust from the back of her jeans. Inside, her father washed his hands in the deep slop sink, his face red and lined with anger. Through the warbled flower shop window, he looked more tired than ever. Smaller and shrunken. Like every person who walked through the door with a demand took another piece of him when they left.

No matter how hard he tried, how much he gave up of his time or his money, it seemed like no one was ever happy. No one came in to say thanks or offer to lend a hand. It was as if the whole world wanted something better. Those who could leave went in search of it, and those who couldn't stood and demanded change without consequence. Why couldn't anyone be happy with what they had?

## CHAPTER FOUR

With every snip of Adelle's shears, another lock of leggy coleus fell to the windowsill. Vivid purple leaves edged in vibrant green scattered at her feet. That plant had been with her family since her grandfather owned their old farm, but Adelle had never been one for houseplant pruning, and what was once a compact, tidy plant had grown tall and wild. The good news about a plant that needed pruning was the chance to turn the cuttings into profit.

"You've seen it all, haven't you? All the ups and downs." It saw the farm get smaller and smaller. It saw the back of a pickup truck as they moved from the farm into town. For a few years, the coleus had a nice view of the cemetery from the little house down the street. And for the last thirty-five years, it watched the antique store with Eliza's steady stream of furniture and cats until Penny came along.

With a snip, another tendril fell to the floor. Across the street, Penny swept trash from the recessed entry of the old General Store. "Lots of ups and downs. Mostly downs, though, huh?"

Adelle collected the stems from the windowsill and floor. She tossed them on the counter with the rest. She would strip the best ones of their lower leaves, dip them in white powdery growing hormone, and set them in a pot of water until they formed little roots and could be planted in soil. Half the coleus in Ramsbolt had come from her grandfather's ancient coleus. Everyone seemed to love how colorful the soft leaves were, and they were so easy and inexpensive to propagate that they always brought in a few dollars. The ones she couldn't sell were never much of a loss.

"It might not be enough anymore, little coleus. It might take a lot more than making baby plants to save this ship. But maybe you can help me fix this air conditioner."

The swish of Penny's broom on the sidewalk bounced between the buildings, and the sun blazed off her curly red hair. Adelle had grown to love her neighbor. Penny was quiet and clean, cared for the store, and cleaned the sidewalks. She even took care of the entrance to what was once the General Store, keeping trash from the road from collecting in the doorway.

Penny came to town with her own set of challenges. She'd inherited her grandmother's antique store, insisted that it be emptied and sold so she could get back to her life. But Ramsbolt had been too poor to buy back its past and too insulated to take on the plight of a disinterested transient. The deeper Penny got financially, the more tied to the store and the town she had become, until one day, she decided to stay. God knows Penny couldn't afford a tax or extra fees on top of the debts she carried and the ones she inherited.

Adelle knew her neighbors deserved better than that. Especially Penny, after saving the store and all she'd done for the town with the arts festival. If it weren't for her, Eliza's old antique store would sit empty and rot, just like the General Store. If only Mrs. Miller's grandkids had wanted to inherit it, she could still get orange creamsicles on hot summer days.

Adelle tapped white hormone powder into the upturned lid. She stripped the lower leaves from a budding stem, dipped the cut in powder, and propped it in a drinking glass half filled with water.

"Whatcha daydreaming about?"

Adelle jumped, dropping a stem. She hadn't heard Riley enter with the mail. "Honestly? Orange creamsicles. I didn't even hear you come in."

The postman dropped a bundle of envelopes and catalogs on the counter and adjusted his messenger bag. At six and a half feet tall, he towered over most of the town and had to duck beneath the lamp that hung from the ceiling over the counter. "What's all this?"

"I'm making little plants again. It's been a few years since I sold coleus. I figure people are ready to see them again."

"The one in the pot inside the market does pretty good." Riley peered in the drinking glass at the cut stems.

"Hey, do you remember the Miller's General Store?"

Riley leaned against the counter. "How could I forget? She had that big penny candy table."

"And that ice cream cooler just inside the door there." Adelle pointed to the empty store with the budding end of a stem. "I'd steal a quarter from the register and run over there for a popsicle and hide in the alley or sit on the sidewalk and eat it."

Riley dropped his bag to the floor. He seemed to shrink by a foot. "Man, I miss that place. I remember giving the guy who worked there a dollar, and he'd mark down what I spent on Squirrel Nut Zippers and Tootsie Rolls. That last five cents was the most important financial decision of my life back then." He flattened the dog-eared cover of a rose bush catalog. "I guess you heard, huh? What with the stroll down memory lane?"

"Yeah. I figured you had to know. You know everything around here. What do you think will happen?"

Riley leaned down, his forearms resting on the counter. "I'll let you in on a secret. Morgan said if no one runs for election, we'll be incorporated into another town."

"So Lewis was right." Adelle's mouth went dry. She could have pulled the flowers out of that glass and downed it all, but it still wouldn't have quenched anything. "We can't give up that easy."

"You can't listen to those grumpy old geezers in the newsstand. They got nothing to do all day but whine."

"But he wasn't wrong. Why did Morgan tell you and nobody else?"

"Gave me a heads-up so I could put in a transfer with the postal service. It wouldn't make sense for another town to keep the Ramsbolt post office open when they could just run a truck out here every day. He told me to keep it quiet, so no spreading that news, hey?"

A transfer from Ramsbolt. The mere suggestion of Riley, the backbone of town, leaving for some distant field of gold was too hard to swallow.

"It can't be that bad." She wouldn't accept it. Not until the giant neon sign lit up and said *Danger Ahead. You're about to lose everything.*

"I guess he figured I'd rather deliver mail in Florida where no one has to shovel snow off their sidewalk than hang around here and be jobless. I figure it was nice of him to think of me."

"It just feels like everybody's giving up. Am I the only one who cares anymore? I can't be the only one who wants Ramsbolt to stay like it is. Why doesn't he put out a call for candidates or something? It's just a footnote at the bottom of the sign. He didn't even print it on there. He just wrote it with a pen."

"I dunno. There's a lot broken around here, right? Look at the park. The brick walk is all torn up. The curb outside the post office is just a bunch of broken rocks held together with some cement now. Grey fixed it one day when he got sick of parking on chunks of it. You can't blame Morgan, I guess. He's a smart guy, but he's still scattered. He's just a kid. No use being mad at him." Riley lifted his messenger bag to his shoulder. "You should run, though."

The only thing she wanted to run for was her life. Away from this constant ebb and flow of things falling apart and trying to grasp at the pieces to hold it together. If it wasn't the floor it was the flower cooler. Or the slop sink. Or the air conditioner. But her family had downsized until there was almost nothing left. She knew from experience that even if there were a miraculous windfall, money couldn't solve every problem. "People keep saying I should run. I wish they wouldn't."

"You know how to do the job. You saw your dad do it, right? No one else has that kind of experience."

"But I was just a kid. I didn't learn anything from just being around it." The only thing she learned from watching her father do the job was that it was thankless and hard, and everyone hated him for exactly what they asked him to do.

"Osmosis." Riley tapped his head and pushed out the door, a blast of summer air pushing in when it closed behind him.

Maybe it was all a tangle of rumors. It wouldn't be the first time the town got wound up about a half truth or an assumption. She dug in her apron pocket for her phone and texted Morgan.

*Is it true? We could be turned over to another town? Bloomburg?*

His reply came quickly. *Yeah. That's what the state said. Bloomburg's the closest option.*

*If no one runs for office. Automatic?*

*There's some law. You should run for office.*

She slammed her phone down on the counter. It wasn't nearly as satisfying as it had been slamming down a phone receiver back when landlines were a thing. She held in a deep breath and replied.

*No thanks. Too much drama.*

*Don't I know it.*

Coleus wilted on the counter. She fanned out the stack of mail. Bills and ads and useless paper.

Across the street, Penny swept trash onto a slab of cardboard. *She'd* gone off to college and ended up in Ramsbolt, running Penny's Loft. What if Morgan went away for school and came back when he was done. Could they get a temporary hold?

*Hey, r u coming back after college?*

*Maybe. Not as town mgr. I'd rather be an engineer than a therapist. Ha!*

Ugh. She slammed her phone down again in frustration, but it wasn't about Morgan. Unless someone did something, some other guy would be delivering their mail. Adler and his administration full of finance people and lawyers and town planners would come rolling in from Bloomburg with their fancy black sedans and business suits to tell them how inadequate they are. He'd hold a town hall in the library basement to say how perfect their lives would be once they had red lights with cameras, two dozen stop signs, and a fancy police force to keep them in line. New streetlights and smooth road repairs would be a gift with purchase, but the price would be steep. He'd probably close the library, too. They'd be squeezed into oblivion by spine-crushing taxes, and their heritage would be destroyed.

It would all be gone, the life they knew. Riley wouldn't be the only one to leave. Especially with Adler in charge.

The sun had inched across the window and lit up the coleus her grandfather grew, that her parents brought into town when they closed the farm. They didn't have a choice but to sell the land and their ancestral home. Times had been hard, and they did what they had to in order to survive. But they managed to hold onto what they loved.

She picked up her phone and brushed away flecks of hormone powder. *Is anyone talking about running?*

*Nope. Not to me.*

"Shit." She dropped her phone and grasped a coleus stem, running her finger along the edge of the soft leaf. "I don't want all this to change. You don't really care. You'll grow anywhere. But I like the way things are. I like the way things have always been."

She held the leaf in front of her face in a cartoon voice said, "Why don't you run for office, Adelle?"

"Not you, too." The leaf fluttered to the table. "I don't have my father's people skills or Morgan's empathy. What's the worst that could happen? Well, everyone could hate me. They could run me out of the office the way Meldrick did my dad. They could stop shopping here and run me out of a job."

She picked up the leaf again and in her cartoon voice said, "But what's the best thing that could happen?"

She sighed. "Just having a name on file somewhere could delay a takeover. Maybe someone with ambition would see how much I suck, and they'd want to do it instead. Nothing makes people competent and willing like watching someone else take a stab at something. No. The best thing would be if I could keep the town from changing."

She dragged the stack of mail toward her and sorted through it, throwing junk in the recycle box beneath the counter. She wanted to run after Riley and make him stay. To beg people to stop believing all this change was okay. Her whole life had been a series of churnings, like gears intertwined. One alteration causing another in an endless agitation. Her father worked so hard, giving every waking moment, and then some, to keep Ramsbolt intact, and now that legacy was at stake.

She glanced at his picture, nailed to the wall by the door. A fine layer of dust had collected at the top of the frame.

If she ran for his old office, she could make this round of change stop. She could drive a wedge in the gears and bring the whole thing to a halt. Doing nothing clearly wasn't the answer.

She pulled the string of her apron and flung it over her head, letting it puddle on the counter by a pile of wilting coleus. She would have to talk to Morgan in person. Every second mattered.

# CHAPTER FIVE

Morgan Lacey lived with his parents on the other side of town, across Main Street and past the library. Adelle took her familiar route, slipping between buildings and following the wild blueberry bushes that bordered yards. It was the path she took a million times as a young girl, rushing to the Girl Scouts meetings held in the library basement. Barking dogs had come and gone, new cars slumbered in repaved driveways, but the porches and windows and blueberries were much as they'd always been.

It wasn't a leisurely stroll. It was a walk with purpose. And not the *I really need a bagel from Marissa's* kind of purpose either. She had no idea what fueled her, whether it was tension or anger or a new kind of fear. Maybe it was all of those things.

At the foot of Meldrick and Morgan's driveway, she downed the last of the berries she'd scavenged, hoping with all her might that something in them, some native juice, would give her the strength she needed if Meldrick Lacey, the man who had tormented her father so, were the one to answer the door. With a two car garage and an empty drive, the house offered no clues.

She hovered one foot over the blacktop driveway and retracted. Why was she there? Was she actually throwing her name in the ring? She didn't want to run for office. She didn't want to hold the office at all. She wanted nothing to do with offices. There wasn't even one at the flower shop.

There had to be another solution, something other than giving up. Maybe what she wanted was hope, some magic elixir only Morgan would have because town managers knew all the challenges and held all the solutions, just like her father before him. Maybe he had some magical plan in the works that would keep Ramsbolt out of the hands of Bloomburg and that condescending man, Adler.

Hope. That's what she'd come for.

But generations of town managers and countless residents with their own ideas hadn't found a way to mend the broken seams without a tax

It wasn't hope she'd come looking for. It would take a miracle.

*I'll just start with congratulations. Then I'll ask if anyone's talked about running.*

She walked up the driveway in her bright white Keds and knocked. The door was white and dented, with metal showing through beneath the scrapes, as bruised and raw as she felt. It flung open a mere second later, and Meldrick glared at her as he bit into an apple with the sticker still on it. Her stomach churned, and her face flushed hot at the sight of him.

Meldrick's ashen brown hair was swept to one side, hiding the baldness that came with age. His polo shirt wrinkled, and his khaki pants rolled up at the hem. He wore loafers without socks and looked every bit like a man who would have taken her father's job and spent all his time on a golf course.

Of course. She forgot. He worked from home now.

She didn't shuffle, though her feet ached to find firmer ground. "Is

Morgan here?"

"What do *you* want with Morgan?" he asked, one eyebrow arched.

If the emphasis had been on a different word, it would have landed differently in her chest, and perhaps all the hatred she had for the man would have stayed firmly blanketed under years of thinly veiled repression. One downside to life in a small town was that it was far too easy to keep running into old wounds. Like her father had said, small-town life was like trying to heal a stubbed toe in a room full of coffee tables. The upside was that it was entirely up to you to learn where to walk and what not to run into. Adelle wasn't enough like him to have learned that lesson.

While facing the man who destroyed her father because he wouldn't bow or bend to whims and do the bidding of bullies, all the wounds rose, debris caught up in a tornado of torment. But she folded her arms, conjured a weak but plain smile, and kept it to herself.

"I just need to talk to Morgan. If he's here."

"Seems I'm the man of the house here, and I need to know why you're here to see my son."

"He's an adult, and it's not really any of your business." He didn't deserve answers from her, and she'd never answer to him.

"Another Faulkner intent on ruining the town." He rolled his eyes, spun his apple, and took a bite. "You're here to talk about running for office. I guess you think your dad didn't do enough damage to this place."

Meldrick would sling his familiar arrows. He didn't have many in his quiver. Yet Adelle was struck, unprepared, wishing she'd not wasted the walk ruminating on the future, but prepared to battle the past instead.

She shifted her weight, shuffled her feet, expecting relief, but her wobbling knees found no stronger purchase. Any desire to avoid confrontation lost traction, overtaken by the offense, by the need to defend her father's legacy in the face of a man who brought him down, who threatened the town, who clawed and fought and slandered her father and did far more damage than her well-meaning, kindhearted, loving dad who grew plants and ran a flower shop and tried his best to solve the town's problems ever could have done. Meldrick Lacey was full of nothing but bad intentions.

"Why do you hate my father so much? What did he really do to you? He did nothing but love this town and try to give everyone everything they asked for."

"Then why don't we have anything we asked for? He was lazy. Nothing got fixed. He made promises to everyone and didn't keep a single one." Meldrick waved his apple toward the curb and drop of juice flung to the black rubber doormat.

"That's bullshit, Meldrick. He bent over backward for this town. He listened to every unreasonable request, and he spent so much of his energy dealing with stupidity—"

"But he didn't do anything. That easement. He was supposed to fix it so my basement didn't flood, and he didn't deliver, so I had to pay for all those repairs. I had to carry the burden when it was the town's responsibility. This is the real world, sweetie. He didn't live in it."

"He had a breakdown! An actual mental breakdown. He had a stroke, and it killed him because of people like you."

"Well, that's a shame, but if he'd taken care of all these problems they wouldn't have piled up, and maybe he wouldn't have had a breakdown. It took me ten years to pay off the repairs on my house. Darn near destroyed my credit. I'm still paying for it, you know, in that I gotta pay my son to do the damn job your father couldn't do." Meldrick inspected his apple, sticker clinging to the shiny red skin, exposed white meat browning with neglect. He chucked it into the yard with an underhand serve and gripped the edge of the door. "That job didn't kill your father. He unraveled all by himself. Know what, you should take the job. It would serve you right."

"Is that some kind of sideways threat? That's a horrible thing to say about my father. And this town."

Meldrick pointed beyond the houses toward Main Street. "That clock is still broken. All these years later and the park is still a mess."

"It's trash from cars that come through here. You know that. And Sparky can only mow the grass when he has a working lawn mower. He's a volunteer. If you had your way, we'd have sixty park employees who do nothing all day, and we'd be taxed into poverty. I'm doing my best to put new plants in, but it takes some time. I don't see you out there doing a darn thing to help this town. But I do see you complaining and littering your own yard."

Meldrick leaned against the door jamb and folded his arms as if settling in for a fight. "My yard is my business. What I'm saying is all our problems were easy to fix if he'd fixed them when they happened. Now we're in too deep. He spent all his time running around sticking his nose in other people's business and not enough time doing actual business."

"You're wrong, Meldrick. This town insisted my father fix its petty squabbles. It might look easy from the outside, but there were days we had a line of people in the shop wanting him to fix stuff they thought was a lot more urgent than a pothole on the way out of town."

"And now you're here to run for office because the Faulkners haven't inserted themselves enough into the town's problems. Just not content to let progress happen, are you? You gotta slip in there and try to keep us from getting anywhere at all. What are you gonna do about any of it? Nothing."

Adelle locked eyes with her father's enemy, with the man who went from house to house, from store to store, and spoke ill of her father, turning everyone against him until he had no one at all. It wasn't just political opposition that Meldrick Lacey created. It was division and anger and hatred. It was intentional. Meldrick accused her father of discriminating against members of the town by not seeing to their concerns, however expensive and impossible they were, and of intentionally shirking his duties. And they were lies.

A flush of anger washed over her and away, carried off into the air by the hot summer breeze and, for the first time, dissipated into nothingness. She willed the words to come, for some phrase or smart statement to fill the void and make a declaration. She tried to conjure the anger that had seethed inside her for so long to answer his question. What *was* she going to do about it?

Meldrick swung the door on its hinges. "So? What are you going to do about it?"

A fierceness filled the void, a determination to wrest from the man her father's bequest, to take back the town in her father's name. Every landmark, every rash on every curb, every tree and flaw that made the town what it was—belonged to Ramsbolt. Not to Meldrick Lacey.

"I'm running for office. And I'm going to prove you wrong." As the words left her, a lightness and clarity radiated through her. Deep down, she knew that vengeance and retribution made a poor source of determination, but regrets be damned, she'd said it. And even if she wanted to take it back, she wouldn't dare. She set her jaw. "I'll find Morgan on my own."

She spun on her heel, crunching over stray bits of mulch that scattered the walkway. If she walked a straight line, it was a miracle. Inside, she had turned to jelly. The path was a blur from the door to the street, past the mailboxes and between the houses. She felt no more mature than the little girl scout who picked blueberries on her way to the library, and the taste of them lingering in her mouth, mixing with the sour bite of fear, drove the point home: she might be the only person willing to save the town. And she was unqualified and only willing as an act of retribution.

She rushed over cracked sidewalks, past a broken streetlight and an overflowing trash can, and crossed the circular park where she hurtled through the shadow of the stoic sailor statue. Back at her store, she dropped her keys because they shook too much to fit in the lock. She pushed her way into the store and stood in the lobby, where her father once stood and argued with Mr. Sommerwill, where her father slumped when he learned his old friend Meldrick had formed an army against him instead of talking out their differences. She stood where her father listened to scores of neighbors airing their grievances and looking for hope, and she cried.

Her father gave them that hope. He gave them that kindness. And Meldrick had taken it all away for the sake of some invisible, undefinable change. And those people who begged her father for help with every little problem, twenty-four hours a day, turned on him without batting an eye.

"Christ, I've never cried so much." She wiped a damp cheek with the back of her hand. "I'm so mad."

She flushed hot with rage, grabbed her apron from the counter, and threw it at the air conditioner. It fell back to the counter in a clump.

"What is wrong with this damn town?"

It wasn't the town's fault. It was Meldrick's. For wanting all that shiny forward momentum. Like trying to fit a square peg in a round hole. Ramsbolt deserved to stay just as it was. Besides, if fate had wanted all that change, Meldrick wouldn't have hated the job and paid his son to do it in his stead. It was just a shame she couldn't have put that into a snappy comeback and spit it out when she was on his porch.

The only way to get what she wanted, to keep Ramsbolt from changing forever, and to prove Meldrick wrong, was to run it herself. And she had no idea where to start.

## CHAPTER SIX

Adelle's apron lay crumpled on the counter beneath the buzzing air conditioner, surrounded by discarded coleus stems. She'd placed what cuttings she could in cups of water and left the rest. Not all prunings needed to be kept.

The sun was setting, painting the windows across the street with a peachy glow. Adelle sat in the dark on the old work stool, winding the string of her apron in her hands and thinking through every facial expression she'd thrown Meldrick's way, every shuffle of her feet, every word she spat. Like a general studying the movements of her troops after a battle, she analyzed every detail, and she couldn't stop feeling as if the whole thing had been poorly conceived. Though she tried to stand up to Meldrick for disrespecting her father's legacy, she hadn't acted like someone who could live up to it. She hadn't been prepared to talk to him. The result was a spiteful rash decision to run for an office she didn't want to hold, to do a task she didn't want to do.

Following in her father's footsteps wasn't something to jump into, and she'd just performed a cannonball into the pool. There were so many things to consider. What did the actual job entail? All she knew from her observations was that it required financial magic and the patience of a sloth to listen to all those people complain. Did she need a new computer? How was she going to pay for that? Did she have to conduct town meetings herself or could she outsource the public speaking part?

And did she need to run a campaign?

She dug her keys from her pocket, stepped onto the sidewalk, and locked the door.

Helen's Tavern was the only option at that late hour, and a suitable one for deliberation or distraction, whichever the night might bring. She crossed the street at Sparky's Engine Shop and rounded the town park, where fireflies flashed in the shadow of the sailor statue. Couples sat on the benches, newly painted with funds from the arts festival back in May.

Meldrick wasn't entirely wrong. Some change was good. The park did look nicer, but plants and paint had been simple changes. It was an inexpensive beautification project. It was something to be proud of, sure, but hardly worth working into her campaign resume.

*Oh, God,* she thought. *Am I going to have to put my qualifications into words? Are flowers and herbs and tomato plants qualifications? If so, they don't feel like it.*

Adelle pushed open the door to the bar. Its warped yellow panes of glass didn't rattle in the frame the way they had before the fire that burned it to the ground. But the pub had been rebuilt in its former image, with a few windows and some televisions added. It was a great example of the kind of change Ramsbolt could stomach. People liked things as they were.

Half a dozen residents were scattered around the bar. Carol from the hardware store sat by the wall, focused on her phone. Grey, the town plumber, sat by the taps. He'd made the bar his second home since

Logan moved to town and took a job as the bartender. Who could blame him? There were so few women in their twenties in town that anyone new was treated like royalty if they gave any hint they might stay. Logan had earned her good reputation, and Adelle admired her for the way she handled herself and the bar. For years, the place had been covered in grease from Helen's long-shuttered diner. Not only did she purge it of the mess, she turned it into a real bar with a cocktail menu and overcame her own set of traumas when her father made international headlines and went off to jail, leaving her with nothing but a suitcase and a new life to chase. Plus, the woman kept secrets like Fort Knox.

Adelle took a seat by Grey. The wood bar was shiny and new under thick layers of varnish. She tossed her keys at an empty spot.

"What's up, Dell? You look miserable." Grey pulled a coaster from the stack and slid it in front of her. She stopped it with her hand.

"I did a stupid thing." She might as well tell the town. They'd find out anyway. "I'm—I was really upset that no one's running for town manager. I went to talk to Morgan and ran into Meldrick."

"Oh boy. I bet that was something." Grey's eyes widened, and his brow wrinkled beneath his beanie cap. "Was there a referee or an umpire? Did you let him have it?"

"Not the way I wanted to. I told him I'm running for office."

Grey clutched the edge of the bar in dramatic shock. "You're shitting me."

"Nope. I haven't talked to Morgan yet or thrown my name into any official hat, but there's not really any going back. I just got so pissed at him for being mean about my dad and everything he did. I just blurted it out." She shook her head. "So stupid."

"I can't blame you. You might not like what I have to say, but I think you *should* run. You'd be good at it."

Adelle rubbed her eyes with the heels of her hands, trying to form the words for a good response. When she looked back at the bar, Logan was there. Brown hair held back with a rubber band, beer-stained jeans and an old T-shirt. She looked every bit the small-town bartender, but nothing could erase the body language of the heiress she used to be. Hand on her hip, she glared at Grey.

"I see you already have a coaster. Grey's gonna put me out of a job. You want a beer?"

"Sure. Surprise me."

Logan reached into a cooler and pulled out a cold bottle. She popped the cap off and dropped it on the coaster. "Want a glass?"

"No thanks." Adelle took a sip. There was relief in the cold tangy taste of it. "Can I ask a question? What did you think of Ramsbolt when you first got here?"

Logan blinked at the ceiling. "Honestly? I wasn't a good judge of small towns. I had no expectations. I thought it was nice enough. Small. Not enough stores. Not that I had any money, but it felt a little deserted sometimes. And it's a little weird in some ways. The place was being run by a guy barely out of high school, and there's nowhere to get any nachos."

Adelle centered her beer on the coaster. "That's a good point about the nachos. But Morgan wasn't terrible. He's a good kid."

Logan folded her arms, her eyes narrowed in consideration. Her words were careful and measured. "I'm not a good judge of what Ramsbolt needs in a town manager. I have no complaints about Morgan. I wish he weren't leaving, though. Mack and Lewis were in here yesterday, fear-mongering about how we'll be taxed into oblivion if no one runs."

"They're not wrong. But we're in luck! Adelle is going to run." Grey held out his empty glass.

Logan dropped it in a tray with the rest of the dirty dishes and poured him a new one. "Your dad was the town manager, right? Before Morgan? That's what Lewis said. Or Mack. I get 'em mixed up."

"Everybody does." Adelle nodded, her mouth full of beer. "My dad was town manager until Meldrick Lacey ran a hate campaign and turned the town against him."

"Harsh." Logan winced. "What was his beef, if you don't mind my asking?"

Adelle centered her glass on her napkin and wiped condensation onto her jeans. "My earliest memory of Meldrick was a battle over parking meters. He came into the shop complaining that people dawdled too long on Main Street. Said they came in from the outskirts of town in their big pickup trucks with mud on their tires. They talked too loudly and took up too much room. He wanted parking meters to limit the amount of time people loitered. My dad said there weren't enough visitors to town to make parking meters worth having."

Logan folded her arms. "I imagine it would have cost a lot to put them in, too."

"A fortune. And someone would have to collect the change, put it in wrappers, take it to the bank. I remember my mom leaning across the counter and whispering to my dad that Meldrick's real problem wasn't where people parked. It was who was doing the parking."

Grey rolled his eyes. "From everything I know about the man, your mother was right. I don't know why he's so..."

"Divisive." Logan finished his sentence.

"Yeah. Divisive. Like he has to make sure he always has more than everybody else, and if he doesn't, someone's to blame. Your dad shoulda put a cork in him."

"How would he?" Adelle shrugged. "Give him what he wanted and hope he went away? That wouldn't have worked. Men like Meldrick always want more. Dad knew that."

In his last days, while her dad was tied to his hospital bed in Colby by tubes and wires that dragged the life from him, with a soundtrack of beeping machines and muttering nurses, he'd mulled over his regrets. He said he should have confronted Meldrick, but keeping the peace was more important than settling a personal score that wasn't even his. She hated recalling those days.

"Anyway, it was Meldrick who had the problem with my dad. Not the other way around. Meldrick should have been the one to address it like an adult. But he acted like an angry kindergartener, ran around to all the shops telling people my dad was a big old meanie who was intentionally holding the town back from progress because he hated the rural half of town. It was lies. If anybody hated the farmers it was Meldrick. But he got away with acting like that. The people who didn't join in on his hate crusade, turned their back against my dad."

Logan's eyes widened, her brow furrowed. "Nobody stuck up for your dad? At all?"

Adelle shook her head and made circles on her napkin with her glass. "Nope. No one. I remember being in the market with my mom, and a woman said we should ignore Meldrick, that everyone knew he was a hothead. But he did real damage. He hurt my dad, and no one even cared, because they couldn't give two shits about my father. They only wanted to know what he could do for them."

Grey chewed on a frayed fingernail. "Man, that sucks. I'm sorry. I was young then. I don't remember any of that."

"That's the thing. Maybe people don't remember, and I'm just stuck ruminating about the past. It makes me angry about stuff I can't control."

It was a terrible habit to continue if she intended to run for town manager. The last thing she needed was to add more fuel to Meldrick's fire by treating him with any less kindness than she did anyone else. It would become a self-fulfilling prophecy of anger and resentment.

Logan raised a shoulder and gave her half a smile. "Maybe you could talk to him? Smooth things over?"

Adelle shook her head, and her ponytail swished against her shoulder. Until that morning, the worst she'd done was go out of her way to avoid him. As fool-proof plans go, it hadn't gone wrong yet. "No way. I have no intention of hashing it out with that man. I just need to be professional, play it cool, and avoid him."

"That's the spirit." Logan returned a wave from Bern and poured him another round. "I'm not going to give you any of that *everything happens for a reason* bullshit. I don't think life gives us things to rise above just because it thinks we need the exercise. But I've known a lot of men much worse than Meldrick. Like *my* dad. And the universe always gives it back to them. You just have to keep your nose clean. Even if you're running just to spite him, you will do a lot of good for this town, and that's good for your karma."

"Too bad I'm not equipped to do the job." Adelle tightened her ponytail and sipped her drink.

"You are, though." Grey turned in his stool to face her. "No one knows that job like you do. You're perfect for this. You can fix things, prioritize all the broken stuff around here. You can actually get stuff done. Morgan's a good guy, don't get me wrong, but he's disorganized and isn't proactive about stuff. He's never had to make a tough financial decision in his life. But you? You know how to run a business."

"I'm a flower shop owner. I buy flowers, put them in arrangements. The most complicated stuff I do is basic accounting. I'm not a politician."

Logan placed a new beer in front of Grey. "We don't need a politician. I've known politicians, and trust me, this place runs fine without them."

Adelle took in a deep breath of beer-scented bar air and let it out in a laugh. "Oh, I'm not so sure about that. The town needs a diplomat. Someone who never gets frustrated, never needs a minute to themselves. I'm not a hand holder like my dad was. I'm not like him *at all*."

"Nobody needs that." Grey leaned back. "They'll take help if it's there, right? But the town *needs* an administrator, and without one, the town goes kaboom."

"Exactly." Logan smiled and wagged a finger in mock indignation. "Look, if Helen and I lose this bar because you decided you'd rather sell the town to the highest bidder, I'm gonna cry. For real. I've already lost enough, and I'm not losing this bar for the second time. Grey? Talk some sense into her?"

"It's one of those fate things," he said. "You were born to do it. Like Logan was born to end up here."

"Everyone keeps saying that. But they didn't live through those days. They didn't see people lined up at the flower shop ready to take a swing at my dad because he stopped trying to fix their personal problems. And you guys didn't see how sad and hurt he was when it all fell apart." Adelle folded her coaster in half, and the fiberboard cracked at the seam.

She picked at the frayed edges. "You should do it, Logan."

"Me? Hell, no. Last time someone in my family got involved in politics, they ended up in jail. I came here to get away from his karma, not slather it all over myself."

"Good point." Adelle sipped her beer. "How did I get into this? I told Meldrick I would run just to spite him. After everything he did to my dad, doing this job is the last thing I want to do."

"What if you had help?" Logan wiped at a wet spot at the bar and threw the towel over her shoulder. "What if you set some boundaries so it doesn't happen again? You're perfect for the job. The best candidate the town has. You know what to expect. You won't be blindsided by it. I mean, I'm sure there are some surprises, but you know way more about the town and how to run it than anyone else does, except Morgan. Everybody likes you. It's not like you beat puppies for a living or anything, you make people happy with flowers. And honest to God, it could be a disaster for us if it goes another way."

Why couldn't someone else do it? There were plenty of good candidates. Nate ran a great little toy store and kept his nose clean. Warren knew everybody and everything. There wasn't a mean bone in that man's body. Helen had nothing to do since Logan was running the bar. Arvil spent his whole life wanting to rule the world. Someone, anyone other than her, had to want this job.

But they didn't. Because they knew it was a thankless one.

It didn't really matter how she got into this situation. It didn't matter that the only reason she was running was because fear, pride, and anger got the better of her. She was in it whether she liked it or not. And it wasn't worth wallowing or resisting, because she told Meldrick she would prove him wrong, and she was stubborn enough to follow through on her promises. That was the real commitment. In that moment, she had made a promise to her father's memory as much as she had to Meldrick. What mattered wasn't how she arrived at the crossroads. It was the direction she took that would make all the difference, and there was no going back.

"Another?" She held out her empty beer. "So what if I do it? What if I run? What could be the absolute worst that could happen for this town?"

Grey's barstool squeaked when he shifted. "Meldrick could be a dick about it, but who cares? He has no beef with you. He'd just be dragging up old history, and none of his arguments about your dad had anything to do with you."

"But what about the best that could happen?" Logan filled a glass for Carol, who was still sucked into her phone at the end of the bar.

"We won't become an annex for some other town. Even if it wasn't Bloomburg and their big taxes, it would all be bad. We control ourselves and put off stupid changes that no one here wants."

"Right. I can get around a pothole, but I can't survive on less than I'm making right now. The best that could happen is that you reclaim that past. You make it yours."

Those were strong words from Logan, who rebuilt her life from nothing. After everything she'd been through, if Logan had complained, Adelle hadn't seen it.

Logan hadn't even complained when the bar caught fire. She stepped up and reclaimed what she lost. And when the bar came back, it was just as Ramsbolt wanted it, just as it had always been. There were a few improvements, but it felt the same, and that was all that mattered.

And that was what she loved about Ramsbolt. That it never changed in the ways that mattered. The park might get prettier, and the buildings could use a new coat of paint. Some benches could be repaired, and maybe the streetlights could get some new bulbs, but the threads that made up the tapestry had never been broken. Ramsbolt's heritage, its culture and traditions were still visible on the surface. And she had to do everything in her power to keep things the same.

But to keep things the same, *she* would have to change. She'd have to be a diplomat, which was the last thing she wanted to be. Putting her name on a ballot didn't mean that she would win. She had no intention of poking at old wounds to find out, but the town could still bear the scars of the fight that Meldrick put to her father. Even if she did win, there were still plenty of problems to solve and no money to solve them with. Pretending to be a politician while campaigning for the job was one thing. She would have to fake it for a lot longer than that if she served as town manager. And she was banking on winning. She had to win to spite Meldrick.

"I don't know anything about running a campaign," Adelle said, her eyes pinned to the bar.

"Then don't campaign." Grey ran a hand over his head, adjusting his cap. "Just put up some signs."

Logan shook her head. "She should definitely campaign. You want people to think you're serious. You want them to see your face and ask you questions so they have confidence in you."

"You need a kick-ass campaign slogan." Grey tapped his fingers on the bar. "Something upbeat. How about Despair and Stagnancy?"

"Not funny. For real. If I'm going to do it, Meldrick is going to be an ass about it, so I might as well have a campaign and a message. Something he can't argue with."

She could hear Meldrick's voice in her head. Mocking her father for being weak and having a meltdown. Blaming the man for suffering the blows he dealt.

For years, she'd avoided the man, crossed the street, looked the other way, waited for him to leave stores before going in because confrontation wasn't her style, and she hated the way he made her feel as much as she hated the man himself. All of that would have to change. As town manager, she couldn't run away from conflict or avoid Meldrick just because she didn't like him. And while running for the office, she'd face new challenges, things she couldn't foresee. But if she had to change to keep the town the same, it was a small price to pay for the salvation.

"If I have a slogan, it has to be something short and simple. Positive. How about..." Adelle folded her arms and tilted her head back. She squinted at the ceiling. "Fighting for Ramsbolt."

# CHAPTER SEVEN

The truck bounced on its leaf springs and swayed to the side. In the back, Adelle grasped at a crate of fruit as it slid across the truck bed, but her little fingers weren't strong enough to catch anything more than splinter. A drop of blood oozed from around the sliver of wood.

"Ow." She listed toward the open rear window. "Jeez, Dad. Take it easy."

"Sorry. I can't control the road," he yelled over his shoulder.

She shoved her finger in her mouth. There were only a few miles between the farm and town, but the path cracked with each winter and rutted every spring. Overgrown fields towered twice her height, swishing grains, long grasses unmowed. As they passed the old Smyth Farm, her father slowed. The brakes squeaked, and the engine rumbled.

Inside the truck, her mom turned in the seat. She wore a look of mild sympathy. She'd looked like that a lot in those days, when their neighbors were packing and leaving for things better and worse. "Adelle. Look. They're boarding up the windows."

Adelle sat up as high as she could and craned her neck. "I see it." She hadn't missed the Smyth's one bit. Least of all Henry, who chased her around the sailor statue at the park and pulled her hair on the way to school. It didn't matter what path she took, cutting between houses and slinking through shrubs. He was always there.

She took advantage of the slower speed to brush the hair from her face and dig at the splinter. Some classmates she missed, but she couldn't care less about the Smyths. "You think they're coming back?"

"I doubt it, hon. And just so you know, you're already running late for school. When we get to the store, you need to jump and run."

"But I wanna put the potatoes in the baskets." She kicked out a foot in protest, and a basket of blackberries slid aside. "I always put the potatoes in the baskets."

"Don't kick, Adelle. Those were your grandfather's, and we can't afford to replace them."

"I didn't do it on purpose." She sulked. "Are they gonna board up our farm, too?"

The truck picked up speed again. Her mom raised her voice to be heard over the truck's metal body panels slamming together as they went over bumps. "No, our place won't be boarded up. Not like the Smyths. Someone's buying our house."

"I don't want to move into town." She kicked out her feet again, careful not to kick a basket this time.

Her mother gave her one of those sympathetic looks that said it didn't matter whether she liked it or not, the inevitable was inescapable. It was usually followed up with a prediction that she'd understand when she reached an undetermined age. Adelle pictured a giant light switch on a birthday cake that she would flip, and suddenly she'd have to walk around with that fake sympathetic smile telling kids to get over it all the time.

"We'll just be closer to things, that's all. It's cheaper if we move. It's too expensive to run a farm. And it'll be fun to live near your friends."

Her father pressed a button on the radio, and Cyndi Lauper cried out about girls wanting to have fun. Adelle didn't want town fun. She wanted to stay at the farm.

"I want my tire swing. And the creek."

"We can still drive out to the creek. The same one runs through town, you know. We'll just live closer to the store and school."

"I don't want to be close to school. I want fields and plants to play in."

Her mother's clenched jaw said the conversation was over. "There'll still be plants. We'll grow them in the yard and sell them in the store. There'll be flowers and herbs and some veggies. Not as many but some. And listen." Her mother reached through the window, grasping at nothing. "After school you need to come straight back to the store and help, because I need all the daylight I can get to dig up that plot in the back, and your father has to run down to the bank to meet the Eastwoods."

"I don't want to live in the Eastwood house. It's creepy. *I don't want to live there.*" She winced at the rising pitch of her voice, knowing her mother would only tell her not to whine.

"It's not creepy just because it's by the cemetery."

It was creepy, and the Eastwoods weren't nice. They yelled at kids when they went past on their bikes, and everybody knew to steer clear of their yard. Who wanted to live by a cemetery anyway?

She clutched the hem of her gray skirt in her hands. The splinter dug deeper. "It's creepy because it's creepy."

"It's a very nice house. It's just the right size."

Adelle scrunched her nose and shook her head. "But it's got ivy on it, and all those trees. It's dark, and I bet it smells bad."

"We'll clean it up." Her mother shifted in her seat, so she could face Adelle. She was in full-blown explaining mode. "The Eastwoods are older. It gets hard to do yard work when you get older. Just be patient, and everything will work itself out. You'll still have a yard to play in, and you'll be closer to friends."

What friends? All her friends were moving away. Holly went to Florida. Mika went to Delaware, wherever that was.

Her father slowed for the red light outside Helen's Diner, but there was no use stopping. There was never anybody coming. The turn signal clicked, and the truck wobbled right, toward town, toward that horrible house with its spiders and ivy and tombstones.

Her mother spun and faced front, leaving Adelle with her silent hurt. It didn't matter that she'd be closer to the wild blueberries that bordered the yards between Helen's and town. She said goodbye to them all the same. It was practice for saying goodbye to the streams that ran through the fields and the tire swing her father made in the front yard when the tractor got new wheels. If any silver lining rimmed the cloud of discontent it was the hope that her parents wouldn't argue about money so much once they sold the farm. The way they talked about it, selling the only place she felt free and safe was the answer to all their money problems. What was so important about money, anyway?

Money couldn't prevent change. They'd tried that. Her parents bought that new tractor, and it didn't fix their problems. They paid a plumber to fix the kitchen, and the bathroom sink leaked anyway.

Over and over, they'd tried to prevent change. Thrown money at the problems until there was no more to spare. But just like the tractor that needed new tires, eventually everything else broke down, too. Her mother said she had to learn to adapt, and the move would be good for her, but nothing good ever hurt before.

# CHAPTER EIGHT

Tipsy and tired, Adelle shuffled into the flower shop. She thumped on the air conditioner, but it was no use.

The stack of bills sat on the corner of the counter, fodder from the sifting of the wheat from the chaff. She couldn't do anything about the bills any more than she could repair the air conditioner. She ripped open envelopes and grabbed a notebook, adding the bills to her to-do list. Electric. Water. They'd get what she could afford to give them.

Seeking comfort from her pajamas, she dragged her tired body down the narrow hall that led to the stairs. The hallway floor was worn bare, and the wood chipped and creaky. Her father had complained about it just as her grandfather had. Generations of feet and handcarts dragged along, wearing grooves in the wood and weakening the seams. She was no closer to fixing it than they had been. Though she had to admit that there was a certain charm to it. If she did win the lottery and paid to have it fixed, she'd only be standing there wishing it could go back to the way it used to be.

She brushed against a bulletin board in the hall, and scraps of paper fluttered, notes from suppliers, and phone numbers scribbled on envelope scraps.

An old phone, no longer in use, clung to the wall just beyond. Three generations had taken orders there for celebrations and remembrances long forgotten.

Upstairs, she slipped into her bedroom, shrugged off her T-shirt, and threw it on the foot of her bed before climbing into her jammies.

She should feel lighter, shouldn't she? Wasn't the whole point in taking a leap of faith that you'd feel weightless once you were in the air? Her stomach was in knots from the freefall, and she was terrified of the landing.

*Maybe I'll feel better if I make it official*, she thought.

She dug through the pockets of her discarded jeans and found her cell phone. She opened her text messages with Morgan.

*Hey. About the election. Is there a form to enter? Can you bring it by tomorrow?*

Morgan's response was swift.

*You're running???*

*Yes. I need to stop this town from changing!*

But how? Running for office was one thing, but there was no tangible way to prevent change or to keep things from getting worse. There was no way to seal the best parts of Ramsbolt inside the bricks and mortar of the town, to protect it from the changing world. She would just have to wing it and hope her sincerity and sacrifice were enough to keep them from eroding into nothing.

*Yay! I'll come over first thing.*

She replied with quick thanks.

The teddy bear she got for her tenth birthday rested in its spot on her pillow, where she placed it every morning when she made her bed. She moved it to the chair by the window and curled up beneath her comforter. It once felt so small, this bedroom. Her parents said it was temporary, just a way to save money until they could afford another house. She'd sought reassurance in those sad and hectic days that the future would be better. That there would be good change ahead, and they wouldn't have to live in the rooms above the flower shop forever. Little did her mom know that she'd get sick, and everything would change, that Adelle and her father would be trying to fill her shoes while running the shop. But in those early days, there'd been hope that after all they'd lost, there'd be some gains. Back then, all her mother could tell her was that there was no way to know what the future would hold, but it would definitely be bad if they did nothing to make it better.

# CHAPTER NINE

Adelle trimmed the lower leaves from zinnia stems and dropped them into buckets of water, their red, fuchsia, yellow, and orange poofs glowing like alien suns. Her father had hated them. Their petals weren't soft enough to suit his style, but Jaleesa, the town mechanic, loved them for their wild nature, and that's all that mattered to Adelle. Or did it? She tossed a stem in the bucket and second guessed herself. She'd been doing that a lot lately.

Jaleesa's surprise thirtieth birthday party was to be held outdoors in the garden behind Diane's Tea Room. Zinnias would be perfect. Warren, Jaleesa's father, wanted rustic and charming. Adelle knew they were Jaleesa's favorite flower, and there was no reason to reconsider.

"Stupid election has me second-guessing everything." She brushed leaves into the trash. "These containers are all wrong, though."

Every vase she had was glass or plastic, too girly or frilly, not rustic enough. But across the street in the antique store, Penny had mountains of buckets and baskets and pails and never minded if she borrowed a few for arrangements. Adelle always left the price tags on, which often drove people to Penny's Loft searching for them after the event was over.

But Penny's store was closed. Nothing to do but watch finches scavenge for food in the street while she ripped leaves from zinnia stems.

Old memories floated up in the quiet void, teasing at the edges of her Meldrick conundrum. She pushed them aside and brushed more leaves in the trash.

"It's a useless endeavor dwelling on the past and getting all riled up about nothing." She dropped a stem into the bucket. But she had a vision frozen in her mind of Meldrick's shadow stretching across the flower shop floor as he waited, hands on hips, to throw outrage at her father.

Movement across the street caught her eye. Jake, the small orange cat, hopped into the window as Penny unlocked the front door. Adelle left the zinnias and crossed the street in the warm morning sun. At least small talk with Penny could serve as a distraction.

Jake greeted her at the door, winding through her legs and wrapping his tail around her calf in a cat hug. Penny was out of sight already.

"Penn? You around?"

"Back here." Her voice floated out from the kitchen, carried on the stream of morning sun. "Is that you, Adelle?"

"Yeah. I need some rustic flower containers. Buckets and stuff like that. Can I look around?"

"Take anything you want. I got an old brass pot back here. The kind you'd put fireplace ashes in, I guess. Too fancy?"

"Probably. I'm thinking aged steel pails. That kind of thing."

"I have a bunch of those out back." Penny emerged from the kitchen, drying her hands on a tea-stained hand towel.

Adelle wound through rows of shelves, to the back wall where Penny kept wicker baskets. "Thanks. I'll slink around there and take a look. Some of these might work, too."

"I saw Morgan this morning." Penny leaned against the wall that framed her tiny office beneath the stairs. "Down at Marissa's. He was all giddy. Said he was coming by to see you later."

Adelle wished she could melt into the floor. She should be excited to share the news, eager to tell the whole world. Instead, she hid behind wicker baskets hoping for Penny's approval like a teenage girl running for homecoming queen.

"Hmm." Adelle pulled two baskets off the shelf. They weren't even dusty. They'd look gorgeous lined with bowls, filled with foam, and stuffed with tumbling, colorful flowers. "Can I borrow these?"

"Sure. What's the occasion?"

"Jaleesa's surprise birthday party. Don't tell anybody. Her dad will kill me if it leaks."

"Oh, I got an invitation from Warren when I ran down to the newsstand for batteries for the kitchen clock. I meant Morgan, though. What's up with him? He never comes this far past Main Street."

"Oh." The baskets crackled as she carried them farther down the aisle, further from Penny's reaction. Once she started blabbing, and once Morgan showed up with the forms, there'd be no turning back. She took in a deep breath. It smelled of dust and old wood. "I'm running for town manager."

It felt weird saying it out loud. And uncertain. They were unnatural words in an even less natural meaning. She'd never run for anything, never aspired to anything other than a home and some security. She expected Penny's reaction to be incredulous. *You? Don't you have to be outgoing, smart, funny, diplomatic, a strategic thinker, and charismatic to be town manager?* It didn't matter that everyone kept telling her she'd be great for the job. She felt like the last person qualified for it.

Hooks on the wall-mounted peg board jiggled when Penny shifted her weight and folded her arms. Her eyes grew wide. "Well, that's great news. I'm not political or anything, but Nate was saying how much it would suck if Ramsbolt got annexed by another town. We need somebody local. You'll be great at it. Oh! I have the perfect thing."

Adelle dropped the baskets by the door, and Penny disappeared into the kitchen. The first reaction hadn't been so bad. It was almost a relief not to be bombarded with questions or burdened with requests. The sound of cabinet doors opening and closing, and the clattering of pans rang through the store.

"What are you looking for back there?" she asked.

"I have this little red toolbox. I know it's in here somewhere," Penny yelled out from the kitchen. "Anyway, I am so glad I got involved with the town because of the festival and all. I really enjoyed being a part of something, you know?"

Adelle scanned the room, looking for more containers. It was a lot cleaner than it used to be, more open. Furniture rested on the floor instead of being stacked four tables high. Small items were contained on shelves instead of being crammed in every nook and cranny. And there were new items. Decorative throws and pillows were scattered about, and next to the door was an old coat rack, the tall lanky kind with hooks made from antlers. Shawls and scarves fluttered in the breeze that puffed through the gap in the door. A cream-colored scarf with little green clovers caught Adelle's eye. It was soft to the touch, a little silky but not too formal. Clovers. On this, of all days. Of course she'd find a clover.

Penny returned with a small red toolbox, rusty at the hinges with a black plastic handle, and set it on the counter, but Adelle was transfixed by the scarf. "You can use this if you want. Might be cute with some flowers in it. Or maybe people can put their birthday cards in there."

Adelle unfurled the scarf from the rack. "That is cute. And very Jaleesa. I like that idea. How much do you want for this?"

"I just put those out yesterday. Haven't even had time to put the price tags on yet. Five bucks?"

"Perfect." She would have paid five times as much. Adelle dug in her back pocket and handed Penny a five.

"Thanks. I'm trying to add gifts to the store. Hopefully it will bring in more repeat buyers. That looks perfect for you."

Perfect. She'd always had a knack for finding four-leaf clovers. As a kid she would sit in the tire swing beneath the giant oak in the front yard, the hard rubber warmed by the sun, cutting into the backs of her legs, and her eyes fixed on a patch of green. Clinging to the pendulum, she'd scan the sea for extra petals, and when she found one, she'd pluck it, run for the house, let the screen door slam behind her, and race up the stairs for her books, where she'd tuck it safe between the pages of *Anne of Green Gables*.

It had been a long time since she'd stumbled upon one in the pages of her books. And it had been even longer since she stood in the grass long enough to find a clover.

"Speak of the devil, there's Morgan." Penny nodded toward the flower shop. "I can keep looking for you and make a pile if you want."

Adelle wrapped the scarf around her neck. Part luck and part armor, she felt stronger for it. "Thanks. That'd be great. I'll be right back after I talk to Morgan. I'll definitely take the toolbox, though. I'll bring it back good as new."

Penny waved a hand. "Don't worry about cleaning it. It's older than dirt anyway. Grey gave it to me with some tools in it to keep under the sink."

Adelle snagged the toolbox from the counter. "Thanks. I'll take good care of it."

She rushed across the street, scarf streaming behind her, and caught up with Morgan just as he reached the flower shop.

"Hey." She skidded to a halt at the door and tugged it open with a shaking hand. There'd be no going back once they stepped inside, once she filled out the papers. It felt clandestine, like a shady rescue operation performed by spies in broad daylight. "After you."

Morgan slid past her into the shop. "Not much cooler in here than it is outside."

"Tell me about it." Adelle rested the toolbox on the counter.

He dug a folder, thick with papers, from his messenger bag.

"I have all the forms you need here. It's stuff that goes to the state and something for the town files. I'm really glad you're running because no one else even hinted at it, and I don't want to be the end of the line."

She wiped her arm across the counter, clearing a space for the folder. "That whole legacy thing. It bugs me, too, sometimes." It had bothered her father a lot.

"I don't want to be the guy who killed the town." He opened the folder. "This looks more daunting than it is. The instructions are on the state website. There are rules about campaign finance reporting and that kind of thing."

"I wasn't going to spend any money. Not that I have any to spend. I wasn't even going to raise any."

Morgan shook his head. "That's what you think. Were you going to put up a sign?"

"I don't know. Do I need a sign? Can I make one?" Being a

candidate was more complicated than she thought. And their meeting was less clandestine spy get-together and more anxiety inducing and overwhelming than she expected. She thumbed through the papers, head spinning at the columns of tiny type and complicated rules.

"You can't spend a penny without reporting it. All the rules for tracking money are in here. You have to follow them to the T."

"Okay. They want me to keep track of every penny that comes and goes. I can do that."

Could she? She did it for the store; it couldn't be that hard. But the six page document about campaign finance was double-sided and, in a very small font, used complicated terms like Election Cycle Limits and Independent Expenditure Requirements, and none of it made any sense to her. She didn't have time to learn all those laws. No wonder her father sat at that counter late at night hunched over books and reams of paper. And what about all of the other rules she didn't know about?

If pride and fear hadn't handcuffed her to the idea of being town manager, she'd have closed the folder, put it in Morgan's bag herself, and changed her mind. She unfurled the scarf from her neck and balled it up on the counter. Was the store getting hotter?

"Not to look incompetent or anything, but I've never run for an office before, and I've got this big event to plan for—"

"Jaleesa's party."

"Right. And I don't know anything about running a campaign. I don't have the money to open another bank account. I don't have donors or backers or whatever they call them. Is there anyone I can ask about this stuff?"

"The state has some resources. I know this looks like a lot, and it sounds scary, but it's mostly background information you don't need.

The rules are pretty simple. It's all in there."

Adelle plucked fading petals from a zinnia. "I'll have to work on this later."

"Look, please don't panic on me. Please don't pull out of the race." Morgan's eyebrows pinched as he pleaded.

She didn't need to be reminded of the stakes. "I'm just overwhelmed today, that's all. I'll figure it out." Her father had. Meldrick had. Of course, her father had no customers, and Meldrick was unemployed at the time, but she wasn't going to let Morgan or anyone else think she was so incompetent she couldn't get past the campaign finance hurdle.

Morgan clutched the strap to his bag. "Once you get set up and have a system, it's all easy. The hard part is getting people around here to accept change. Remember when I set up that website?"

Adelle forced a smile. "Yeah. Whatever happened to that?"

"Arvil threw a fit at the bar, and one of the church ladies freaked out and said it was a bad way to get news because no one would know where to find it on the internet. I mean, it's a website. They're afraid, that's all. Afraid they won't be able to keep up with a changing world. What they don't realize is that the world is changing anyway."

"Well, they'll be thrilled about me then. My whole goal is to prevent change, the bad kind. I mean, big town-altering change that destroys our way of life. Like some other town taking over, making us pay taxes and follow a bunch of stupid rules."

"We don't even have a cop here. We don't *need* one. We only have, what, two hundred people?"

"Two hundred and twelve, to be exact." She hadn't thought about the possibility of some other town forcing them to pay homage to a police officer. "Remember that state cop who used to set up a speed trap, up by the tavern on the edge of town? Got so bored he'd sleep in the car?"

Morgan laughed. "I forgot about him. Nothing ever happens here. But I can picture Adler and his men running around town, making their own trouble. We don't need that."

A police force from outside town ticketing cars and pulling people over for going too fast would be the quickest way to discord in a town that was mostly harmonious. "I just want the good parts of Ramsbolt to stay like they are. How we all know each other and how the bakery is the center of town. I don't want to lose Riley or anyone else. I don't want to lose Ramsbolt."

The older she got, the faster time seemed to move. More pieces of Ramsbolt slipped away every year. People left. Stores closed, and the signs slowly faded. She couldn't bring those things back, but if she could somehow stop the clock and keep time from taking more of Ramsbolt away, she could keep people from suffering the same fate her family did, squeezing and downsizing until all the juicy parts of life were gone. Until nothing was left to make lemonade from but the bitter rind.

"The good news, as far as your campaign goes," said Morgan, "is that the town doesn't trust outsiders all that much."

"Neither do I. I was so mean to Penny when she first came here. I didn't mean to be. It's just that she swooped in here from Otley with her city ways, throwing Eliza's store all over the sidewalk. She was adamant she was not staying here a second longer than she had to. It wasn't her I had a problem with. It was the outsider mentality. I'm glad she ended up liking it here, and she's a really good neighbor. The festival turned out great, too. It could have gone another way."

That was an understatement. When Penny first ran around town trying to get support for an art festival, Adelle had nearly flipped her lid.

The town couldn't support the traffic, the parking, or the trash. There were no public bathrooms, either. But she'd been wrong about all those things. The mountain of objections she'd conjured from thin air evaporated the moment people arrived. Somehow, it all worked out. It was a lesson she'd have to hold onto, especially if she became the town manager.

"It brought a lot of business. A few more festivals like that, and we can fix every clock in this town. We could put clocks on every corner."

"A few more people like Penny and we'll have more solutions than problems."

"That's the truth." Morgan cinched his messenger bag and inched to the door. "I gotta run. If I can do anything, scream. You can file a lot of those forms online to get started. You could be officially in the running in less than five minutes. But the one with the little Post-it on it, you have to sign and give back to me for the town files. Don't forget. I can grab it from you at the party."

The door closed behind him, and she was left alone with a folder full of papers and a million zinnias to prepare.

It felt real, the papers in her hands. Something about the tiny type and the little lines where her initials should go made it feel even bigger, more consequential. She'd never bought a house before. Never bought a new car or signed a large contract. She'd just rolled one success into the next challenge and managed to stay afloat. Maybe it was the grown-up feeling to it, the newness of the experience that made it seem so intimidating.

"Five minutes, huh?" She drummed her fingers on the folder. "Time's wasting."

She pulled her old laptop from a shelf, flipped it open, and pressed the power button. Waiting for it to come to life, she grabbed a flower from the bucket and trimmed off its lower leaves.

The computer pinged. Initializing updates…one of thirty. She rolled her eyes. "If Morgan's right and filing the forms is the easy part, then I'm going to need a lot of patience."

A bright yellow zinnia fell into one bucket, and she picked a pink one from another. "To bad there aren't shortcuts to everything in life online." She snipped off three lower leaves. "Lord knows I could use a shortcut to telling people there's just not enough money to do everything they want."

The town had put up resistance to even the smallest of Morgan's proposals, even the ones that didn't matter. A website wouldn't strip the town of its heritage. Painting the fire hydrants a new color so you could see them better in the dark wouldn't have done any harm. But she saw Morgan's point. No two opinions were the same. One person's life-altering, heritage-destroying website was another person's blasphemous and devastating fire hydrant color, and she couldn't make any of them happy. Not about small things, and definitely not about the cost of snow removal, municipal trash collection, new sewer pipes, and buried electrical lines.

Meldrick's voice from years before echoed in her head, blaming her father for things that never got better, saying her father had put up a wall and kept the town from progressing.

There were no shortcuts to managing expectations, especially in a small town where every voice could be heard, and every speaker wanted something different. And as the modern world inched closer to tiny Ramsbolt, it would be hard to resist the kind of change that showed up on their doorstep. Soon, Arvil would be demanding free Wi-Fi, and

Lanice would want public transportation.

The only thing the people of Ramsbolt had in common was their desire to keep Ramsbolt...Ramsbolt. They just couldn't agree on what that meant.

The laptop pinged, and its screen went dark as it rebooted. The pile of snipped leaves grew around her.

Ramsbolt needed to prioritize, make a list of small, attainable improvements, changes that the town could stomach without losing who they were. As for the rest, they needed to resist systemic metamorphosis. There was no telling who they could become. And to do that, the town needed someone who knew how Ramsbolt had always been. Maybe Adelle wasn't the right person for the job, but she had to try.

If opening a new bank account, tracking receipts, and making some signs would keep Meldrick's kind of change from happening, would protect her father's legacy, and save Ramsbolt from becoming just another suburb, then it was the least she could do.

The laptop pinged again as it restarted. She put down her clippers and grabbed a pen. On the back of a scrap of paper she started a list.

Button. She would need buttons to hand out at the market. Candy to give to the kids. Pencils or nail files or something. Maybe that was too much. She scribbled through the list and started over. Something small and nonconfrontational. Signs.

"I'm not much of a fighter, little flowers. I won't even fight with an obstinate stem. How am I supposed to fight for an entire town?"

She pushed the list aside.

Hope wouldn't be enough to keep the world from crashing down, to keep the town from going bankrupt, people from hating her. She had no idea how it would feel or what she would say if someone challenged her faith in what Ramsbolt could be. She knew she couldn't be as mean to them as she'd been to Penny when the woman wanted more than Ramsbolt had to give. She would have to fake the politician game until she made it.

What did they say? Dress for the job you want, not the job you have? Maybe passion was enough. Maybe people were right, and it was her fate. Fear didn't have to be a bad thing, did it? She was afraid to run this place, and it all worked out. Sometimes fear kept her from making the wrong decisions.

She trimmed the last zinnia, dropped it into the bucket with the rest, and scooped all the leaves into the trash.

Her new scarf sat in a knot behind the laptop. She unfurled it and wrapped it around her neck, then spun and faced the ancient mirror mounted to the far wall. That scarf really did look good. Her laptop pinged and loaded her desktop, one icon at a time. She opened a web browser and launched a tab into the unknown.

# CHAPTER TEN

Adelle brushed sandwich crumbs from the folder she brought back from the bank. In it was a thin checkbook, a debit card, and a brochure about reverse mortgages that she dumped in the recycling bin. She'd put two hundred dollars from her shrinking savings account into it. She'd been saving it to fix the air conditioner, but the town seemed so much more important. Cooler days were coming, anyway, and there would always be next year. She could use the two hundred bucks to buy some signs for the shops downtown. Kim at the bank said they'd put one in the window, and Marissa said she would take a dozen for her yard and at the store.

She ignored her chicken salad and scrolled through free templates on her phone. Plenty of websites offered them with cheap printing. She was looking for something simple, red, white, and blue, and debated between a sign with some stars or one with a swoosh when the door opened, and hot summer air bulldozed through the store. With it came Christina, a bastion of faith and a stalwart of the church. It was rare to see her far from the end of Main Street, where the road terminated at the steps to the sanctuary. When the church needed flowers, they usually called. Adelle glanced at the calendar tacked to the wall by the counter. There were no religious holidays coming up.

"Christina. I haven't seen you since…"

"Church. When you were six." The woman smiled, disarming the fear that she'd be chastised for not attending the only church in town. "I'm kidding. I saw you in the market two weeks ago. But I'm here about the church."

"Is there a function? I didn't think there was a religious holiday in August. Or is it a birthday? I'm pretty good with remembering—"

"No, dear. No. I'm here about Diane."

"The tea shop? Is she okay?" Her mind reeled. Why would the church need flowers for Diane?

"It has nothing to do with arrangements, dear. Diane is fine. We're having a wee bit of a conflict." Christina pulled a stool up to the counter and sat, her hands folded in her lap. "I'm hoping you can help."

Adelle slipped her phone into her apron pocket. "Help with a conflict with Diane? She's so nice. What could be wrong?"

"Diane has changed vendors. For years, she got her tea and honey from a specialty service in Bangor. But back in February or so, she started getting it from some operation out of Portland."

"I'm not sure what I can do about that." Adelle wished she hadn't asked. She tried to keep the conversation light. Maybe Christina would get the hint that she had no intention of intervening in personal disputes. "The tea tastes just as good to me, whether it's from Portland or not. I had tea there last week. I mean, I wasn't sure how I'd feel about lavender in earl grey, but it really was nice. Still, I don't know what I could do about her tea coming from Portland."

Christiana gave her a look that would have stilled a hyper Sunday school class. "That's not what I'm here about."

"I'm confused, Christina. How is Diane's choice of vendors a problem? And what does this have to do with the flower shop?"

"It's the timing of the deliveries. The women's prayer group meets on Tuesdays at four. We always have. It's hard to pray with all that noise. First, the idling truck, then the slamming door and the ramp raising and lowering." She glanced over her shoulder as if the last accusation would offend the Lord. "And he plays the radio."

"You're kidding me." Adelle studied the woman. She tried to soften her look, so her brow wasn't furrowed, and her gaze wasn't narrowed, so she didn't look perplexed or burdened by the chat. She had signs to order, arrangements to make for Jaleesa's party, the crippling anxiety of running for office she didn't know how to hold in a bankrupt town she didn't know how to save. "What am I supposed to do about any of this, Christina?"

"Well, the minister would never say anything to Diane. He's far too nice for that. And it would be way out of line for one of the ladies to approach her, especially because we have tea there all the time. You know how it is." She shook her head like she'd just encountered a bad apple at the market and couldn't fathom the shame of it all. But none of it had anything to do with Adelle.

"And you're just venting? I mean, I can see how frustrating that would be."

"It's heavy metal, Dell. Heavy. Metal. You can't expect the women to pray over all that grunting and screaming."

"Definitely flower shop territory then. Has anyone talked to Carol? Diane and Carol have been a couple forever. She'll understand. Just mention it to her, and it'll work itself out."

The woman shook her head, and light glinted from her tight silver curls. "Oh, we do not want to get in the middle of a relationship. Morgan always fixed these things."

Adelle folded her hands in her lap and squeezed until her knuckles were white, trying to wring out the disappointment. She never asked Morgan; it never came up. She'd hoped the town had treated him better than they'd treated her father, that lessons had been learned. Apparently not.

Christina gazed expectantly, her head tilted and eyes wide, like Adelle was a cashier who owed her change, but Adelle didn't owe her anything. The town had beat down her father's door looking for answers to basic human problems like this. They demanded he carry their burden, then beat him while he suffered under the weight of it all. And when they were done abusing her father's kindness and destroying his sanity, they turned to Morgan for answers to every little problem. She was not about to run a gauntlet of Ramsbolt's predicaments.

If the town's idea of the status quo was having someone on the books whose task was to get embroiled in every tiny dispute and shield people from the uncomfortable truth of life in a small town, some things would have to change. Fast.

Adelle raised an eyebrow. "Morgan always fixed these things? He's barely old enough to drink." He wasn't a therapist. Or a hostage negotiator, for that matter. He shouldn't be asked to intervene in the town's personal problems. But she didn't want to say that to Christina.

"It's a small town. Feelings get hurt. No one wants to make a scene. Sometimes it's easier for someone to pass on an anonymous message. Do you see what I mean?" She wrinkled her nose.

"And that someone is me because..." She just wanted Christina to say it, that she expected Adelle to do her bidding.

Christina laid her fingertips on the counter, as if explaining algebra to a child. "Well, your father always did, and if you're the new town manager…"

She painted on a smile. "I see. But I haven't even submitted all the forms yet. How did you know that I was running?"

"From Jaleesa. Morgan's mom was at the garage this morning with their old Saab. It needs a new thermostat. She told Jaleesa all about how you told Meldrick you were running for town manager, and Jaleesa mentioned it to me in line at the deli, so I thought I'd swing by, because we don't want to bother Morgan. He's got college coming up, and I know how close you are with Diane."

Adelle pulled her apron onto her lap and smoothed it across her knee. "I am friendly with Diane, yes. But perhaps there's a simple compromise here that doesn't involve intervention. Can't you change the time of the prayer meeting? Does it really have to be—when was it?"

She regretted asking while the words left her lips. Christina's head shook with vehemence. The woman pounded her finger into the counter.

"Four. Always at four. There are far too many schedules to coordinate to change the women's prayer time."

An entire group of women so dead set against change? So meek they wouldn't ask Diane to have the delivery guy turn down the music? Prayer didn't exactly require equipment bolted to the church floor. Why couldn't they meet at a house or at the library?

Adelle cracked her neck. "Look. Just this once. I have to talk to Diane about Jaleesa's party and another event at the tea shop in October anyway. I'll casually mention it to her when I get a chance. Not as official town business or even as campaign business but as a favor to you all. Only as a favor, and because I know Diane."

"Bless you. We'll give a prayer for you, too."

"Any time but Tuesdays at four." Adelle smiled and tried to commit the feeling of it to muscle memory. Something told her she'd need that smile again.

Christina shuffled off the stool, waved, and left. As long as the woman didn't run off to some invisible town network and tell them she was open for business to solve every dispute they could conjure, Adelle was glad to see her go. Getting involved in other people's business hadn't served her father well. He cared too much and took on their concerns. It was fulfilling to him to better people's lives and save them discomfort until they took more from him than he had to give.

But that was just the emotional part of her brain, the part that watched her father fade and decay as he lost his self-worth. The rational part of her, the part that heard her father when he told her not to blame the town, that they were just doing what they'd always done and didn't mean any harm, couldn't blame Christina for asking. To the people of Ramsbolt, seeking help from her father was just a series of moments. The full gravity of the situation was only tangible to her and her father, and only after it snowballed. All the energy she put into believing him, to not holding grudges, gave her plenty of practice for navigating Christina's request.

It was a simple appeal, barely a squabble among friends. Christina wasn't wrong to ask; it's how the town had always been. It was hardly setting a precedent if she passed it on to Diane. Besides, all she had to do was ask if Diane could change the delivery time. It was flattering, in a way, that Christina saw her has a succession of her father.

Her father had always said that keeping the peace was the town manager's job. If it meant upending her own peace for two seconds, she'd just have to compromise. God knew, drawing boundaries and asking the town to make a change like that would take a little time.

Besides, sometimes you had to cause a little change to prevent it.

# CHAPTER ELEVEN

Adelle pulled her little red wagon down the cobblestone walk that led to the back garden of Diane's Tea House. The last shop on Main Street before the church, it was the ideal location for everything from baby showers to funeral lunches, and that night it was the setting for Jaleesa's thirtieth birthday party.

Zinnias, snapdragons, and miniature sunflowers fluttered and waved as the cart bumped over the stone walk, beneath a trellised arbor that dripped with wisteria in the spring and popped with deep purple clematis through the summer.

The garden was dotted with tables. Lights were strung overhead in a haphazard crisscross. The dessert table was strewn with sticky and sweet pastries, all thanks to Marissa, and each table was covered in off-white linens and Diane's elegant mismatched place settings. The only thing missing were the floral arrangements Adelle lugged in her red wagon, carefully arranged in containers scavenged from Penny's Loft.

She parked the cart by a table under a string of lights and pulled her ponytail tighter. Disheveled from the walk, she smoothed her favorite black skirt, straightened her new clover scarf over her yellow top. There were only a few hours to set up, between the day's teas and the evening party, but from the look of the garden, Diane was ahead of schedule. There were only a few finishing touches left to put on the garden before the crowd arrived.

She extracted old paint and oil cans, toolboxes, and spark plug boxes that hid tiny glass vases stuffed with zinnias, snap dragons, and chamomile stems for Jaleesa. To the side, for Diane, she set a dozen old jelly jars filled with white daisies and gaillardia, with little red petals with golden tips.

A wooden door slammed, and Diane spilled from the tea house onto the tiny porch, a tray of pastries in her hands. Adelle waved, and Diane lifted her chin in a greeting. She dropped the tray on the dessert table and made her way to Adelle.

"These are gorgeous." Diane lifted an old antifreeze can and sniffed at the vibrant colors. "These big ones don't smell."

"Nope. But they still attract plenty of bees and butterflies. Not at this hour, though, so we're safe. They're Jaleesa's favorite." Adelle lifted a jelly jar. The flowers were as much for her as they were for Diane's tea tables; she hated asking people for things. Maybe seeing, through her father's eyes, how much everyone needed made her want to give more than she took. "These vases are for you. For brunch tomorrow. I figured they'd be nice to have around."

A few arrangements made from scraps were the least she could do. Diane, for all her gentle high teas and graceful Saturday brunches, was a shrewd businesswoman who drove a hard bargain. She was kind, but she had to be strong to run a profitable tea business in a tiny town like Ramsbolt. Adelle admired her for it. In fact, she'd have to take a few lessons in Diane's brand of toughness if she won the election. Managing

Ramsbolt seemed to be all about bargaining with people in lieu of actually meeting their demands. It required a lot of heart to listen and a thick skin to say no so often.

The string of lights picked up silver glints in Diane's bright purple hair as she bent to inspect the small arrangements. She grasped a small jar, stood with her back rigid, and raised an eyebrow. "Nice to have around, huh? Nothing's free, Dell. Spill it. What do you want?"

"I don't want a thing." Adelle turned her back to hide her wince. This was the hard part, asking for something she didn't even want. She couldn't care less when the women's prayer group met or when the delivery driver showed up. She only cared about Diane's friendship, and the business that Diane threw her way. It had crossed her mind more than once that anyone with a few containers could throw some flowers together.

She carried two arrangements to the furthest tables and placed them gently, feeling guilty for lying. But it wasn't a lie, really. She wasn't the one with the request. She was just the one who agreed to make it.

"It's the ladies prayer group at the church."

"Since when did you join a prayer group?" Diane arched an eyebrow in mock inquisition. "Has life gotten that bad?"

"Me? I'm not in the prayer group. They…" Adelle placed a last arrangement in the center of a table. It was a shame the decorating was going so quickly, because she could really use a distraction. "I'm sorry, Diane. I hate to ask you this, but they meet at the same time your delivery guys shows up, and he plays his music loud, and they just want to know if you can change your delivery time. That's all."

"You brought me flowers because a bunch of church ladies bullied you into confronting me about the guy who delivers my tea?"

Diane's voice dripped with something. Derision, perhaps. Or sarcasm. Adelle couldn't face her. Instead, she adjusted a sprig of chamomile. If she couldn't ask Diane such a simple thing, how was she supposed to run a town? She needed to be braver than that, bolder, more confident and self-assured.

She turned to face Diane, reassured by the sarcastic smile spread across her friend's face. At least she wasn't offended.

Adelle shrugged. "They didn't bully me into it. It was just a request, and it seemed harmless since I'd be here anyway." She pulled a lint roller from her wagon and collected stray pollen from the cream-colored tablecloth.

Diane rolled her eyes. "And, clearly, it would have been impossible for them to walk all the way next door to ask nicely. What with you being all the way over on Levering Road like that."

"You said it, not me."

Diane waved a hand. "I'm just giving you a hard time. The guy's route and delivery times aren't up to me, but I can ask them to pick a different day. God knows those prayers might be the only thing holding this town together some days."

Adelle couldn't argue with that logic. She was just pleased Diane didn't put her foot down. If Diane had taken offense and refused, she'd either have to go back to Christina and try to prevent an outright war, or she'd have to avoid the woman and hope she never followed up on the request. Adelle stifled a laugh and tucked the wagon behind the plants that bordered the garden, where it could hide until the party was over.

"But since you asked..." Diane crossed her arms. Behind her some early guests had started to arrive.

"Oh, here we go. I knew it wasn't going to be that easy."

"I've been asking for years for someone to do something about the sewer. The sinks back up, and it's really annoying when we're doing a lot of dishes."

On the verge of protest, Adelle opened her mouth expecting words to fall out, but nothing came. No single objection rang out any more than any other. There was no money? It wasn't her job? Call a plumber? She had expected Diane to ask for something in return, she just expected Christina to be the one who had to deliver. Why couldn't she ask for flowers for her mom's birthday? That would have been easy. And she wouldn't have had to find a way to say that she couldn't deliver on a promise because she wasn't town manager, and even if she were, promises were expensive. She had no control over the sewers. She didn't even know where they were, except for the occasional storm drain. Were they the same thing, storm drains and sewers?

From the corner of her eye, she saw Morgan drop a card on the gift table. She seized the opportunity to deflect and learn what defined a sewer.

"Morgan!" she called across the garden. "Can you answer a question? What's wrong with the sewer?"

He spun from the card table, shoved his hands in his pockets and approached like a scolded school child. Behind him, Logan and Grey were arriving.

Morgan ran a hand threw his hand. "I don't know. What *is* wrong with the sewers?"

Dianne rolled her eyes. "Don't give me that. I've been complaining about this for years." She gestured toward the building. "It backs up all the time and floods my basement. My kitchen sink overflows."

Morgan's face contorted, like it was a struggle to find the words. He lifted one shoulder in a shrug that looked as strained as it was apologetic. "It's been like that forever. It backs up at the street. Grease and stuff get in there. Tree roots can cause it. We had a guy out here from some state works crew, but he said he didn't think that was the problem."

Diane threw her head back and let out a deep sigh. "Why didn't he fix it while he was here?"

"The price tag. We can't afford that. People are gonna have to chip in if they want it fixed. That's all there is to it."

She made claws from her hands and scowled, pretending to reach for Morgan's neck. He stepped back, eyebrows raised. It wasn't a threat, but her anger was tangible.

"It's not my job to fix the sewers," she said. "It's the town's job, and you're the only employee the town has so it's your job to do something about it. Not mine. I just get to mop up all the slop when it comes spewing out of my sink."

"I'm not messing with the sewers, Diane. Don't you get it? We don't have any money. Period."

Adelle took a tiny step back and waved at Logan and Grey, willing them to come over and break the tension with weak clumsy smile. None of this had anything to do with her, though she did have a million questions. If the sewer was really broken, wasn't it a priority? Fixing a sewer had to be cheaper than flooding the whole town. How much could it possibly cost? There had to a fund somewhere with money for emergencies. Right?

Was this how the town manager was treated every time he left the house?

Diane stood firm, hands on her hips. "You always say that other things are more urgent, but I don't see anything else around here getting any attention. And the only thing more important than making water go away is keeping the whole town from catching on fire. Am I wrong?" Diane's head was tilted, the corner of her mouth pinched, and her eyebrows arched. To Adelle, she looked like she was dropping accusations.

Morgan fidgeted, picked at his thumbnail. In the distance, Logan and Grey stopped to talk with Penny and Nate. They were of no help. Adelle could feel the outrage sizzling off Diane like heat from tarmac on the hottest summer day. If she didn't defuse it, the whole party would sense it. "I'm sure that if Morgan says there's no money for it..."

Diane brushed it off. "I'm not suggesting he's lying. Just that maybe we could reprioritize in the future. If you know what I mean. All those plants at the park are lovely, but we could use some infrastructure."

"But the park improvements were paid for by the art festival. Never mind." Morgan shook his head. It was the exasperated look of a man who knew there was no use explaining.

A line of guests had formed at the appetizer table. Nate and Penny snagged tiny wedges of cucumber sandwiches, placing them on dainty plates, Logan and Grey behind them.

Morgan turned to her. "Trying to fix one problem only uncovers more. It's always like this."

Was everybody down the line going to want something from her? What could the delivery driver possibly ask for? And how did Morgan know who to call about a broken sewer? Was there a phone directory somewhere, tucked in the back of a town manager handbook? Worst case scenario, she could call Morgan at college. Or Adler over in Bloomburg. He would know. The thought made her shiver.

Maybe the town manager job needed a suggestion box, an email address with an automatic reply that said *Sorry, we're out. We probably can't afford any of this, but someone will read it and get back to you if it sounds feasible. Also, if you'd like to volunteer to do something without charging money for it, please add an importance flag to your next email.*

Nate and Penny stepped up to greet her, with tiny plates of tiny croissants wrapped around tiny sausages. Logan and Grey were right behind. They exchanged greetings with Diane, Penny and Logan gushing over Diane's hair, and Grey slapping Morgan on the back.

Diane's phone chimed, and she silenced it. She stepped away, whistled for everyone's attention, and shushed the crowd. Warren would be arriving soon with Jaleesa in tow. She expected a quiet dinner in the garden with her dad. Warren expected plenty of drinks.

"That sewer is hanging on by a thread, and we can't afford to fix it. Seriously." Morgan whispered in Adelle's ear. "I'll explain after the party."

* * *

Drinks created by Logan with Jaleesa in mind made for lovely bookends to one of Diane's lavish dinners. The night started with a sidecar made of cognac, Cointreau, and lemon juice, and finished with a Silver Mercedes, made from chilled vodka and cranberry topped with champagne.

As lovely as it was, the chorus of voices Adelle loved to hear from people she loved to see faded behind static. It was as if someone threw a colored gel over the lights, painting everything a sad blue. She'd never been one for crowds, but she loved the people of Ramsbolt. In trying to save the town, was she isolating herself from it? The stream of people who'd entered the flower shop to chat with her dad had only grown more demanding until they took all he had to give and stopped coming altogether. She didn't want to live that life, for the people she knew to stop coming around, to start hating it when they did.

Long after the sun had set, the guests began to retreat, and Adelle collected the flower arrangements, transferring the colorful blooms to cups and stashing Penny's containers back in her little red wagon.

After being bombarded about a sewer she couldn't control, she made it a goal to avoid more demands. She'd stayed planted at her table with Nate, Penny, Logan, and Grey, taking mental stock of all the things she'd heard over the years. All the times Dan and Bern sat in the bar and complained about potholes on the way into town. Mack and Lewis hated weeds in the curbs. Marissa wanted streetlights. Riley wanted new sidewalks. Whether her dining companions sensed the storm raging in her head, or they simply had no demands to add, she took comfort in their laughter. She was already starting to question whether people valued her for who she was instead of what she could do for them. If she didn't put a stop to requests like Christina's, it would only get worse.

She couldn't blame the town, though. They only had these expectations because her father and Morgan had met them in the past. All she had to do was roll with it until she could figure out how to get them to stop asking for petty things and fix their own personal problems.

She filled her wagon with the last of Penny's containers, tucked newspaper around them to keep them safe from bumps and bangs and paused to say goodbye to Jaleesa.

"It was a lovely party. I'm so glad your father invited me. How's it feel to be thirty?"

Jaleesa was a hugger. Problematic as she was often covered in oil or had grease smeared on her top. Adelle flinched internally out of habit before giving into the tight squeeze.

"This has been a perfect night. I'll remember it forever. Thank you so much for the flowers." She motioned to the street. "Dad put a bunch of them in the newsstand for me, and I'll pick them up tomorrow. I'll be the only mechanic in Maine with a shop full of zinnias."

"You're more than welcome. They'll look great with your wrenches."

"Oh, and I think you'll make a great town manager. Mr. Faulkner, your dad, I mean, was always really nice to me. I don't know what the job entails, but I think you'll be great at it." Jaleesa jiggled her wrist, and two bracelets made of zip ties clicked together.

Adelle smiled, though she didn't mean it, and glanced at her shoes. She would need a better response than the one that always seemed to surface. *Lord, I hope you're right—for all our sakes* didn't have the grateful ring that a proper response ought to have.

"Thanks. I like your bracelets. Very creative."

"It's so hard to accessorize, but I do my best." Jaleesa waved as she turned to leave, and the bracelets wiggled on her wrist.

Adelle grasped the wagon's handle and gave it a tug. It lurched over the cobblestones. Main Street was teeming with people, walking to their cars and their homes on neighboring streets. On the sidewalk outside the tea house, Christina chatted with some ladies from church. Adelle left the wagon under a dim, flickering streetlight and approached to offer a report of Diane's willingness to silence the delivery driver. She hoped it would bring the request to a close, and that she'd find the words to draw a boundary, but Morgan stepped beside her.

"Hey. I didn't want to ask when people were around, but did you finish filling out the forms? Do you have the one for the town's files?" His voice was barely above a whisper.

"I have it here in the cart for you. I filled the rest out online. You were right. It's all pretty easy. I even ordered signs this morning. They're white and have my name with a little swoosh and some stars. I only got twenty-five of them because the town's so small, and I figure a few downtown will be enough. Plus, I don't have much cash."

"Great. Look. You want to know how bad the sewer problem is around here? I have something to show you, and you're not gonna like it." Morgan nodded in the direction of his house and stepped onto the street.

"Ew." Adelle wrinkled her nose. "I don't need to see inside a sewer. I'll just take your word for it that the town is full of crap."

"It's not just the sewer that's full of crap. You should see the finances. Come on."

<h1 style="text-align:center">CHAPTER TWELVE</h1>

Morgan made no mention of whether Meldrick was home or not, and Adelle was too embarrassed to ask or seem impolite or intimidated. A confrontation with the man who'd occupied her thoughts in the worst way for the last few days was not on the top of her list of weekend chores. Besides, she'd had a few drinks at Jaleesa's party and would probably say the wrong thing. She could picture herself standing in their kitchen with her hands on her hips saying something like "Yeah, well, you're just a big meanie."

She followed Morgan onto a dark path that led to the back porch. She left her wagon on the walkway and followed Morgan up the steps of their back porch, through the sliding glass door, and into the dining room. She fully expected to see her enemy there like the villain from an old movie, sitting in the dark, twirling the ends of his mustache and muttering "Well, well, well." But Meldrick wasn't lurking in any of the shadowy corners.

Morgan flipped a switch, and the dining room and kitchen filled with light. Everything was immaculate. No hint of dirty dishes or boxes of cereal. No apple cores on the floor. Of course a guy like Meldrick would litter everything but his own home.

Adelle dropped her purse on the kitchen table and dug out the signed form. She held it out to him. "Here's the paperwork. Is this appropriate? I mean, maybe I shouldn't be here. There's your dad, and if people talk…"

It had been a very long time since she followed a man into his house. Following Morgan into his wasn't the kind of town chatter she wanted to generate. He took the form from her.

"Don't worry about it. The town's financial reports are available to anyone who wants to see them. It's just no one ever asks."

Morgan hadn't caught her meaning. It saved her some embarrassment, anyway.

He rounded a wood-paneled wall. She followed him down a darkened hallway and paused at an open door on the left. It smelled like gym socks. Like someone worked in the yard all day and left their sweat-soaked clothes on the floor to ferment. She had no intention of stepping into that room with food stuck to bowls and open cereal boxes on the floor. No wonder the kitchen was so clean. But for as professional and efficient as he'd been as a town manager, as well-liked and amenable, you'd have thought he'd been doing the job for decades. It was nice to know that despite the very adult task of being town manager, he was still a young man at heart.

Morgan turned on a desk lamp and opened a filing cabinet drawer. He dropped the form into a folder and opened his laptop. When the screen lit up, he logged onto a web page. Adelle clung to the doorway until the last possible moment, hoping he would take it to the kitchen table and save her a trip into the dump, but he waved her over. She took a last gasp of hallway air before slinking into the room, around piles of clothes and shoes.

"This is our bank account." He jabbed a finger at the screen, and little waves of color rippled out from the bottom line. "That's our balance."

"What? There's no comma. We should at least have a comma. How do we not have a comma? Three hundred dollars?"

"We have no steady stream of income. That's our general fund. This number over here is what we made from the arts festival. It's specifically earmarked for fixing the park. But this little number is where the money comes from to keep the lights on downtown. This is how we fix the clock. And the sewer. And everything else."

"So where does it come from? Where do we get our money? And when?"

"The state. We get a thousand dollars every few months. That's it. All the details are in here." He patted the top of his filing cabinet. "Plus, we get a subsidy to pay for the school because we don't have a local school tax. The great news is there are more kids in school than in the past few years, because people who grew up here decided to stay. The bad news is that more kids in the school means we're about to outgrow our subsidy."

"Geez. A thousand dollars doesn't go far. And all this time, we've been talking about people leaving, but they aren't?"

"Not as fast as they used to."

"That's a good thing. But not if we outgrow our budget."

"Which is why we can't afford to fix the sewer. So now you know. Also, something will have to be done about this."

"About what?"

Morgan clicked his mouse, and a spreadsheet opened. Adelle hunched over the desk, careful to avoid a cup of flat soda, and squinted at the column of tiny numbers and letters. She recognized the address of the space next door to Sparky's Engine Shop. The place at the end of Main Street with the windows that looked out at the sailor statue. A bunch of buildings between her and the end of Levering. All empty real estate. Peeling paint and dirty windows.

Adelle stood, hands on her hips. "Most of that stuff has been empty for years. What are we supposed to do about it? Someone somewhere owns it, right? We could offer to run an ad or something, to help people sell it. Not like there's money for that. But what's the hazard of having empty real estate? It's just sitting there. Why do we have to do something about it?"

"Oh, it's a hazard. A huge hazard. The town owns all of it." Morgan closed his laptop and stood. He slipped around her and around the pile of shoes and went into the hall. Adelle followed. Where was he going? Was there more bad news hidden in their basement? The second she was out of the line of scent, she took in a deep breath. The rest of the house smelled like cinnamon apples and filled Adelle with empathy for Morgan's mother.

"What does that mean? Morgan, stop and tell me why this is a problem. How does the town own it? What's wrong with empty real estate? Other than it being empty?"

Morgan paused at the dining room table, clutching the back of a chair. He looked for all his youth like a tired executive, staring down at an empty place setting on a conference room table.

"We're hemorrhaging money. We have to pay the real estate taxes on it. All the money we get from the state? We have to give it right back to them in property taxes."

Morgan pulled on the chair and let it wobble back into place. He went to the kitchen, flung open a cabinet, and grabbed a glass. "Want one? Water? It's filtered, and we have the good ice."

Her mouth parched with the heat of her anger. She stepped back against the wall for stability. She could melt all the ice in Morgan's fancy fridge with the fever that rose in her, with the anger and ire. But she wouldn't dare take a drink in Meldrick Lacey's house.

"No thanks, I'm good. How does Ramsbolt own all that? Did we just go around buying up properties? There's more real estate on that list than Arvil owns. What the hell, Morgan?"

"It's an old law. Five years after a property is abandoned, the town takes over the deed." He shoved his glass against the lever on the door of the fridge. Ice plunked into the glass, then he filled it with water. It had to be the fanciest fridge in Ramsbolt. It had a screen on it with the weather. Cloudy. Overcast. Who needed to know that while making dinner? "All those deeds were automatically transferred to the town, and we're on the hook for the taxes. They give us a discount, but it's not good enough. Worst part is, we're on the hook if a brick falls off and smacks some kid in the head. It's a ticking time bomb, and we either have to implement a tax of our own to make ends meet or go to the state and tell them we need help."

She clutched the back of a chair. "But those options aren't good enough. They're hardly options at all. No one here can afford to pay income tax or a property tax to Ramsbolt. And if we go to the state and ask for money, won't they start digging around in our finances and see how bad it really is? Won't that be a bad thing?"

Morgan shrugged. "I don't know if they would punish us for being a tiny poor town, but they could roll us up into another one."

"Bloomburg. They would tax us to the hilt." She hung her head, and her eyes fell on her purse. Her empty purse with not enough money to fill her own fridge.

"Right."

Either way, whether Ramsbolt taxed its citizens or subjected itself to Adler and his greed, the result would be the same. Everything in Ramsbolt would change.

She shook her head. "No. We can't do that. There's gotta be another way. This is not inevitable."

"It is, Adelle."

"We can't tax these people. Look, you have fancy water that comes out of a hole in your refrigerator, and it's telling you the weather. Do you go to other people's houses? Have you seen how people live here? We don't have these things. My fridge is older than both of us combined, and my air conditioner is doing a better job as a heater. We can't afford to pay one penny more just to breath air. A tax will destroy households and drive people out and worse—"

"They'll revolt. They'll turn against you. They'll drive you out of town. I know." He swirled the ice in his glass.

"So what, then?"

"Maybe it wouldn't be so bad to let Bloomburg take over. If you approach them, and you can prove our worth to them, maybe the changes can be phased in so they won't be so hard to swallow. But you'll have to think of something quick, because people are gonna want to know what you propose next week."

"What I propose?"

Morgan had run the town for years, and he'd never proposed anything? Now was this her problem to solve? And what value would Ramsbolt bring to the table that would make Adler become a decent person all of a sudden? Meldrick would have a field day. She could hear him now, running around town telling everyone how two Faulkners conspired to bring down the town, as if he hadn't jumped from the saddle and left his son holding the reins of a runaway horse.

Morgan could have done something about it, too, for that matter. He did a good enough job of laying it all out in less than five minutes. Surely he could have spent just as much time thinking of a solution. He could have used all that time he saved not cleaning his room to think of a way to save the town from itself. Now it was her job?

Morgan set his glass on the counter but didn't let go. "Next week. You didn't read the form? As each candidate announces they're running, they have to show up at a town hall meeting to propose their platform or whatever. Then four weeks before the election, which is just five weeks from now, there's supposed to be a debate. Not that there are any other candidates. So you could just talk about your plans. The election is the day after the last town hall meeting."

"I have a week to make a platform? I don't even know what that means. And of course I didn't read the whole form. There were so many tiny words. I assumed it was about not having outstanding parking tickets and promising not to be a bad person. I didn't know I had to prepare a statement or go to a meeting."

To top it off, town hall meetings were in the library basement. It was one of her least favorite places on earth. She even avoided the stairs to that dungeon every time she visited Sandy, the librarian, in search of a book. It reminded her of being a kid, the unwanted girl in a circle of her peers. Every time she went to some meeting or function there, it was because some big change had come. Someone had died, and their family held a memorial lunch there because it was the cheapest place to rent in town. Or something was broken, and Ramsbolt had to meet to talk about how to live without it. She never came out of that library basement happier than she was when she went in. And now the clock was ticking on a town hall meeting, there were only five weeks until the election, and everyone would want to know what she intended to do about a disaster they didn't know was coming. And Bloomburg, however easy, was not the answer.

She grabbed the strap of her purse and slung it over her shoulder. She had to run, before she got sick and puked all over Meldrick's perfectly tiled floor. At least that horrible man wasn't there to see her squirm.

"Thanks for everything, Morgan. I'm gonna run. It's late. I'll think about that meeting. I guess you'll let me know when it is?"

He swallowed a sip of water and threw his head back while he crunched an ice cube. "Yup. I'll schedule it tomorrow and let you know. I'll print some signs and let Riley know so he can spread the word. Good old Riley. Don't know what we'd do without him."

"Don't I know it. And can you email that spreadsheet to me?"

"You got it. I'll go do it right now."

The sliding glass door moved easily in its track, and she was off the porch, grasping the handle to her wagon, in seconds. The trip across town was a blur. It was just a few blocks down the street, across the circle, and back to the shop. It took six minutes on a clear cool day, but it went so fast her stomach hadn't settled by the time she got through the door. She would need a solution to come just as fast. Her mind was blank. All she could think of was going to bed and not getting out of it for a week.

The town was in far worse trouble that she thought. All that procrastinating had only made things worse, and it all landed square on her shoulders. Pulling out of the election wasn't an option. She would look like a fool, like a traitor for running away from the town's problems. And Meldrick would only run around blaming her father for the state of everything.

She would have to come up with a plan. A way to save the town before it ate itself alive.

# CHAPTER THIRTEEN

"Are you sure you want a pony for your birthday? That's a big present for a twelve-year-old girl."

Adelle's mom snapped the red tie around the neck of her Girl Scout uniform and spun her around to face the mirror on her closet door. The sleeves of her white shirt with its row of green trefoils held the seam she'd ironed into it. She ironed that uniform every week out of respect for the club and as part of the Girl Scout Law to respect authority. Not that it was much of a troop. Everyone she'd have considered a friend had moved away and gone on to other towns. There were younger girls, Brownies, who she barely knew, and two older girls who were intimidating, not for their knowledge or wit but for the language they spoke. It was almost foreign. Half the time Adelle couldn't tell if they were being mean or just talking the way older girls do. But they were the closest thing to peers she had and her only regular contact with people who weren't classmates or adults who came into the store wanting plants and flowers.

Adelle adjusted her wool beret. "I was kidding about the pony. I'm too old for a pony, anyway."

Behind her, her mother folded her arms. "You have to want something."

A trip? A party? Who would she invite? Everyone she'd ever thought of as a friend had left. And where would she go? Adelle didn't want for much. She knew better than to have expectations. "How about a cake, some new sketchbooks, colored pencils and markers?"

"That sounds like something we can do."

Adelle grabbed her sash from the hook inside her closet door. "I can come up with other stuff on my way to scouts."

The dryer buzzed in the bathroom, muffled through the wall. Her mother turned away, back to the laundry. "Sounds good to me. Don't forget about the Sommerwills' new dog. Steer clear of their yard in case he bites. I don't know for sure, but Mr. Newsome said he looks mean."

"Shoot." Adelle muttered under her breath. Barking dogs were one thing. Biting dogs, if it were true, made the trip across town even longer. She grabbed her sash, rushed down the hall, pushed out the front door, rounded the cemetery, and flew down the street, along driveways, between houses, through a yard where she knew there'd be no barking dog who might snip or bite. She threaded the needle of an alley off Main Street, slipped between cars parked at the curb, and crossed the street to reverse the trip across the mirrored side of town. Between stores, down an alley, through another yard, along the houses, and down the driveway, and before her stood the Ramsbolt Public Library.

She loved the library. Its shelves were full of adventures and fantasy worlds and happy places with cottages. Within those walls, she'd met Peter Rabbit and *Anne of Green Gables* and a group of *Little Women*. She'd been to marvelous places and distant times. There had been reading competitions and ice cream socials and Halloween parties where she dressed up like Strawberry Shortcake. And within those walls, the Girl Scouts met in the basement every Thursday night.

The troop of twenty-some girls had dwindled down to five as the economy crumbled, farms closed, and big box stores opened up outside town dragging away the work. Adelle was the only one in the dusty-green uniform worn by girls too old to be a Brownie in their brown sack dress and too young to wear bright green. Too young to sit and gossip about boys and sing songs from the radio, and too old to play pretend.

She tugged on the handle of the library door and closed it tight behind her. The small library lobby smelled like books and ink and old paper. Mrs. Bakewell glanced up from her book, one eyebrow raised and an approving grin lifting one corner of her mouth.

"Thank you for closing the door, Miss Adelle."

That was all there was to be said between them. The keys to pleasing Mrs. Bakewell were to close the door, walk softly, and not touch books you didn't intend to read. Adelle slipped through the library as quiet as she could and made for the stairs in the nook by the bathrooms.

The stairway smelled of damp, like old rags and slick concrete. A light was on in the kitchen to the right. Most of the basement, however, was a wide open space with columns here and there holding the books above them. In the center of the room, chairs were set in a circle. There was no usual bustle. No rushing in and out of the kitchen with a tray of snacks and cups of juice or soda. The two older girls were lost in a teen magazine with a foldout poster of a boy from television, and she'd beat both of the Brownies to the meeting that night. The two scout leaders sat on metal folding chairs opposite the gossip queens, huddled. It looked like a funeral.

"What's going on, Mrs. Thorne?" Adelle shimmied her sash into place and sat in an empty chair. Sitting with the sash on was an awkward endeavor. It either bunched up around her neck or pulled too tight when she sat on it. "It feels like a wake in here."

Mrs. Thorne smoothed her skirt, thin lines furrowing her brow. "The library is asking us to make some changes. They can't host us after tonight."

"But I love coming to the library. Is it closing? Mrs. Bakewell didn't say anything." Not that she would. Mrs. Bakewell only spoke to tell them what to do—and what not to do.

The door at the top of the stairs slammed, and two sets of feet scurried down the stairs. Giggling voices and girlish squeals swirled with the ringing in Adelle's ears. She lost focus, her eyes falling on the toes of her Keds. How could the library close? There were no other places to get books. And despite the strict policy for quiet, there was no other place to socialize.

"Don't be sad," Mrs. Thorne said. "The library is staying open for now. But they're running out of money. Girls! Come in and sit down. We have some news."

The girls scooted onto their chairs, their toes dangling above the floor. A solemnity took hold. The older girls separated. One closed their magazine and tucked it beneath her butt.

Mrs. Thorne shot a glance at Miss Lawson, like the ones her mother shot her father's way when she tried to break bad news or the way her father shot a quick look in her mom's direction before he told everyone he couldn't fix what was broken at the town hall meetings. Adelle was starting to think the only adult who could who could deliver a message without a support system was that Dan Rather guy on television.

Mrs. Thorne smoothed her pristine skirt. Again. "The library can't host us anymore. The town can't afford to keep funding the library, so they're cutting back the hours they'll be open. They're also trying to conserve resources, and it costs a lot to keep the lights on. Without money from the town, the library just won't survive."

Both the library and the scouts? Everything seemed like it was falling apart lately. The town clock broke. The pharmacy closed, and they smashed all the cereal into the pasta aisle to make room for all the bandages and itch creams. She couldn't find anything in there anymore. All around her, everything seemed like it was changing so fast. The people coming into the store to talk to her dad were getting angrier and louder. Mr. Sommerwill had been just the beginning, like the early bird who came hoping for his worm.

Adelle picked at a stray thread at the end of her sash. The problems only seemed bigger every day, and her dad more tired. He wouldn't be taking money from the library if he didn't need to.

Steph Sommerwill, one half of the giggling teenage troop and daughter of the man who nearly tripped over her on the sidewalk when he came to scream at her dad, smirked and shot a squinted sideways glance at Adelle. "Why does *her dad* have to keep screwing up the town? It's because of him the pharmacy closed, and now my mom has to drive all the way to Colby to work every day, and I never get to use the car."

"Hey!" Adelle leaned forward, looking past Cora, whose eyes were fixed on her friend. "My dad didn't close the pharmacy. Your dad barged in and started being rude."

How was it her father's fault that the pharmacy closed? She wanted to argue, to wag her finger at the girl the way Mr. Sommerwill did in the store, but she didn't know enough to debate the topic. All she knew was that rage filled her up and made her ears ring, so she missed anything

Mrs. Thorne had to say. She slumped back in her seat with her arms folded across her stomach, mouth clamped shut so she wouldn't make things worse.

It wasn't very often anyone mentioned her father's job around her. Probably because it was adult stuff, and adults never talked about their stuff in front of kids. Maybe it's because she was getting older, but it seemed like adults talked more about their stuff lately, and none of it was very happy.

"Girls." Mrs. Thorne sat up in her chair, her back straight and shoulders stiff. "The library has offered to let us keep meeting here, if we can move our meetings to Saturday mornings. I know that cuts into a lot of your other activities. We can make this work, we just have some decisions to make. And because this is the Girl Scouts, we thought we'd let you girls make the decision. Would you like to meet here on Saturdays? Find another place to meet? What would you like to do?"

The Brownies fidgeted. The older girls made faces like someone asked them to do math. It was all slipping away. The older kids were never around on the weekends. They piled into cars and drove an hour away to hang out in places where things happened. Younger kids went to the park, ran around the statue, and played in the weeds. Adelle always worked in the shop or in the gardens, helping her mom harvest what was ripe and planting seedlings. But Saturday was better than nothing. It was better than having no friends at all.

No one would want to meet on a Saturday.

"Don't everyone talk at once now." Mrs. Thorne relaxed as much as one could in a folding metal chair. "Kaitlyn. What about you?"

The Brownie with a yellow-ribboned blond ponytail shook her head. "I can't come on Saturdays. My mom drops me off so maybe Thursday is still okay if we go somewhere different, but I have to ask."

The other Brownie, Charlotte, stammered, her short brown bob bouncing against her jaw. "I don't think my mom would let me. She works at the market, and my dad is at the farm, and there's no one else to drive me."

"So that's forty percent of you that can't do weekends. Adelle?"

She wanted to meet on Thursdays, like they always had. Or Saturdays would be okay. All she had to do was slip on the uniform and slip through town like she did on Thursday nights. Her parents wouldn't care. They'd be at the flower shop anyway. But she liked meeting on Thursdays, darting home as the sun set. It made a week of school and homework less like work. The words were as hard to form as an opinion, though, and it wouldn't matter anyway. There was no way the older girls would give up a weekend morning.

There was a hopelessness in knowing it didn't matter what she would say. Her chest was too tight, and her throat too clenched to let the words out anyway. No one cared half as much as she did. Looking around the room at the six of them, she realized it was just a habit, all of them ending up there once a week. It wasn't affection. They weren't friends. None of those people cared about her. And the moment they all parted ways, she'd be forgotten.

Adelle shrugged, hoping it would shift the lump in her throat. Her green sash brushed against her ear.

Steph crossed and uncrossed her legs, and the chair beneath her creaked. "I can't do Saturdays. Sorry. And Thursdays are getting to be a hassle, too, to be honest. I have a ton of homework and college applications, and I'm leaving after next year anyway. Whatever you decide to do, it if works with my schedule that's great. If not, I'm sorry,

Mrs. Thorne."

Mrs. Thorne leaned forward, reaching across the divide, and patted her knee. "We don't want to keep you from homework or college. We're both very proud of you."

Legs crossed, one foot flicking the air, Cora used a magazine as a seat cushion and folded her arms. "I don't see the point anymore, to be honest."

Miss Lawson's glare softened from its instant of savage. "Why not, Cora? You loved being a Brownie. If you don't enjoy Girl Scouts anymore—"

"That's not what I mean. I mean we know each other already. I see Steph every day. We all go to the same school. What's the point of trying to find another place if it's just gonna be a hassle for everybody?"

"So it's a no for you on Saturdays, then." Miss Lawson faked a sad smile and didn't try to hide the imitation.

"Miss Lawson?" Kaitlyn raised her hand. "If it's a hassle to find another place, we could probably not meet. It gets hard in the winter sometimes 'cause the car doesn't start, and Mom always says it's hard to fit dinner in."

Adelle cleared her throat. "Can't we vote?" It was slipping away, her Thursday nights at Girl Scouts, rushing through town with her sash in her hands, collecting badges and sewing them on. The handbook and tasks and the camping. They hadn't been camping since she was a kid, though. It was just one of the childhood joys that had quietly slipped away.

A slow crescendo of chatter rose around her. The more dissent fluttered through the room, the further all the joy seemed to be. The innocent amusement of childhood was slipping into the past, and the future was being torn away.

She raised her hand and started talking without waiting for anyone to acknowledge her. "What about the bakery or over at the church? If we vote, we can ask around, and then we can just meet somewhere else. We don't have to give up. It doesn't have to change!"

"We can still get together and do things." Steph tilted her head, and her voice dripped with condescension. "If you *really want*."

They had no interest in hanging out with a twelve year old girl. They had magazines and boys to drool over. All they wanted to do was get out of there and not go back. Adelle wouldn't seek them out any more than they would her.

Cora shot a hand in the air. "Who votes we disband?"

Two other hands shot into the air. Steph and Kaitlyn. Adelle had never been good at math, but there was no arguing with the majority. If Miss Lawson and Mrs. Thorne called it, that was it—the end of the Girl Scouts. The end of friendships, if you could call them that.

A shame started to form around the abandonment like scar tissue. Like the onset of pain after hitting her finger with a hammer. It was hot and made her tremble. She was the only one who cared. It wasn't cool to anyone, even to Mrs. Thorne or Miss Lawson, to want to be a Girl Scout anymore. The world had changed around her. Everyone but her had grown up, moved on, evolved. And she was still the same kid who just wanted to be liked. But no one wanted to be around her enough to make the effort. Everybody kept leaving, and no one ever came back.

"Who votes for finding somewhere else?"

There wasn't any point in raising her hand. There wasn't any point in staying in the room. The metal chair scraped the floor when Adelle stood. She tugged her sash off over her head and balled it in her shaking fist. Mrs. Thorne would think she was mad, that she was being defiant.

Miss Lawson would probably yell at her and tell her to come back, sit down, and talk about her feelings. But it didn't matter anymore. None of it mattered anymore. No one cared what she thought, so why should she care about them?

Adelle cared, deep down. Her knee bumped the chair as she made for the stairs, into the library, and through the lobby, her sash tight in her fist. She paused at the door, tears thick in her throat, and her eyes glazed. She couldn't look at Mrs. Bakewell. She wanted to cry and beg and plead for everything, for something, to stay the same. But if she started, if she let a single tear fall, she feared she wouldn't stop. For the rest of her life, she would blame that librarian for taking away the one thing in her childhood that felt like friendship, even if she knew in her heart they weren't real friends.

"Thanks for everything, Mrs. Bakewell."

She ran across the street and between the houses, and to the line of blueberry bushes, where she crumbled on the ground at the spot where all the legs grew wild and untangled, reaching for the sun and rain. She unsnapped the red tie from her neck and tugged it off, cursing it for being annoying, but wincing at the lie. It wasn't annoying or hurtful. She actually enjoyed it. At least she used to.

How would she tell her mother? What would she say? How would her dad feel if she came home with tears running down her cheeks because something he did, if Steph were to be believed, caused the scouts to disband? She couldn't go home like that, gasping for breath between sobs. It would be one more grievance in a list that made him sadder the longer it got.

It would be better to sit beside the wild blueberries, old friends who never left or let her down. She pulled a few from a stem and bit into the sweet, tangy harvest, letting the taste of home wash over her tongue. All around her, the ground was covered in clover. While the sun died down and made its slide to the horizon, she scanned the patches of trefoils. There wasn't a four-leaf clover among them.

"You win some, you lose some," she said to herself.

# CHAPTER FOURTEEN

"You have got to be kidding me." Water thundered into the slop sink, ricocheting off the tub and spattering the wall. It soaked her shirt and hair. Adelle dropped the vase she was filling, thankful it was only plastic, and fell to her knees to turn off the water. The knob came off in her hand and water shot across the floor like a fire hose had been turned on. "Not again."

Tension welled within her chest.

She crawled away from the pool, stood on slipping feet, and stumbled down the stairs to the emergency shut-off valve. Overhead, the water trickled and dripped to a halt. She grabbed a trash bag of old towels that she kept around for the occasion and went back up the steps.

While the towels performed their magic, she called Grey.

"It happened again. It's worse. I had to shut off the water to the whole place."

"I hope you don't have to pee. Good news is, I can redo all your plumbing for a six pack." His voice was light, like he was trying to make her feel better. She wanted it to work.

"Imagine what I could do with a hundred bucks. New roof. New windows."

Grey laughed. "You could pick it up and move it to a whole new town for that kind of money."

"Can I get a beachfront view for a crisp fifty? I'd rather pick it up and move it back to 1989." Water dripped from the ends of her hair. She should have saved a towel for herself. "So what will the real cost be?"

"Hard to say without looking at it. A few hundred. That's my best guess. I can be over after lunch and give you a few options."

Adelle squeezed her hair over an aloe plant. "That sounds good to me. I'll take the six pack option, please."

"Maybe you can recoup your money from the town manager job." A loud bang came through the phone. Grey cursed. "Ow. Hit my thumb."

"I wish. That job pays in pennies. Literally. The only thing that job will do is take up a lot of time."

"I gotta run. I need a Band-Aid."

"That sounds bad. Are you okay?"

"Nah, it's just a nick. I'll swing by this afternoon. You'll have water before dinner."

The phone went dark when Grey hung up. It reset to her home screen image of colorful flowers, not cheerful enough to take the edge off the bill. Or that fact that she would have to pee soon.

Her old pink towels grew maroon as they soaked up the disaster. With nothing to do but wait and let her hair dry out for a bit, she opened her email app and unread mail loaded, bold subject lines vying for attention. Tucked in among the spam was a new message from Marissa, two hours old.

*FYI. Maybe you don't have to be town manager if you don't want to!*

"What is this?" She scrolled down to the bottom, to the earliest email.

> Melba Hahn
>
> 8:33 a.m.
>
> To: <Main Street Shops>
>
> Hey! Does anyone know anything about these Bloomburg signs? They just showed up overnight? Nobody asked if they could put this in our window at the outdoor store.

Bloomburg signs? In the middle of the night? What was Adler trying to do?

Her heart thumped in her chest. She could hear it in her ears. Her skin flushed so hot she expected steam to rise from her wet hair.

The past came rushing in the door and swirled around her. Hints of her father trying to pretend like it was all okay while people whispered around town. No one would look her in the eye, and when they did, their expressions seemed pasted on with a dollop of sympathy. Poor Adelle. Has to live with that horrible man no one likes. Is that what Adler was doing to her, picking up where Meldrick's hate campaign left off?

> Warren
>
> 8:35 a.m.
>
> Adler's always wanted his hands in Ramsbolt. Ignore it.

She let out a snort. "You can say that again." In her father's day, Adler had put just as much effort into looking down his nose at both her father and the town as he had into snooping around in town business. But Morgan hadn't said anything about him recently. She hadn't seen him cruising around town in a convertible, pretending to shop like he used to. Clearly he was up to something, if he made signs. What did they say?

Diane Chowdry

8:42 a.m.

Would it be such a terrible idea? Nothing against Adelle, but I need some immediate help. This sewer sucks. Rather, it doesn't, but it should.

Adelle frowned. Her heart and lungs squeezed, and a tightness filled her chest. Diane did need relief from the wonky sewer, and she didn't deserve to wait for it, but did it have to come at the sake of the whole town? Jaleesa wouldn't fix a broken car by dropping a house on it. Why should Ramsbolt just give up?

Something within her snapped, and her heart broke. Diane had to know what a horrible man Adler was. Everyone did. At least she'd always thought so. If even Diane, who she'd always considered a friend, thought Adler was a better option than her, then there wasn't any point in running for office. All the tension inside her chest evaporated, leaving behind a hollow place that throbbed and ached.

It had to be Meldrick, conspiring with Adler to upset her. Ramsbolt was poor. What could Adler possibly want with it?

Barbara

8:51 a.m.

I would love some public transit. It's hard to get outside of town. Maybe a light rail system? And a dog park. Our school needs a lot of work. They need new computers and school lunches and a bus.

The words swam on the tiny screen of her phone. A dog park? A school bus? Computers sounded good, if she were being objective, but there wasn't enough money for those things. And a train station wasn't going to solve their problems. If they would just give her a chance to try to fix it, maybe they could get some of those things with their own merit instead of selling their souls to Adler and becoming a second Bloomburg.

Warren

8:57 a.m.

How are they going to fix things w/o charging a tax?

Finally. Someone with reason. Her pained heart eased a little at Warren's logic.

Barbara

9:03 a.m.

Bloomburg has plenty of money. Always has. Maybe they think with more infrastructure, people and businesses will come to town. Adler is a smart man. I'm sure he has a plan. I'd love a train station.

"You can't just build some train tracks and throw up a train station unless you have some money. And there's no money in Ramsbolt. Adler never gives anything away for free."

Even if he did build a train station, someone would just complain about the noise. If Bloomburg was making grand promises like that, they were lies. Was Meldrick fueling them? Anyone with sense would know that dog parks and train lines aren't free. And anyone who'd met Adler would know he'd already have a steep price in mind. The man probably had a tax law written up, ready to be signed.


Carol

9:07 a.m.

I hate to say it but maybe the job really is too big for one person. It might be worth considering.


Her breath hitched in her throat. Tears welled in her eyes. She closed the email and plopped the phone on the counter. How could they even think that? Why wouldn't they want to save the town? Barbara was almost twice her age. She should know as well as anyone that what they had was precious and worth saving. Diane had to know the sacrifices they'd make for a quick fix. They'd lose neighbors, shops, their history. Were a few shiny baubles so attractive that they'd throw away everything they knew and loved?

She wanted to reach through the phone and yell at them to stop. To stand in the street and let out a primal scream. Anything.

Her blue T-shirt soaked with water and her hair dripping wet, she grabbed her keys from the counter, locked the shop, and pounded the sidewalk on her way to Main Street.

Bloomburg? Adler had always been a horrible man. He would pull up outside the shop, raise his convertible roof, and click a button on his key fob. The alarm would chirp, and he'd straighten his hair in the side view mirror. Dad would tell him he didn't have to lock his doors in Ramsbolt, not in those days, but Adler thought it was a lawless Wild

West with no police officers. He strode through the shop nudging things with his fingertips and wiping his hands on his pants. He'd go from shop to shop, pointing out flaws, inspecting the streets with a white glove as if Ramsbolt were failing some grand inspection.

Adler had always hated everything about Ramsbolt. Maybe to him the town was a clean slate that he could fashion in his image, but his image wasn't attractive to Adelle at all. For him to take over would be the death of their culture. Everything she loved, the feel and the charm would be painted over with stainless steel and industrial veneer. And worse, her neighbors welcomed it.

She had to see it for herself. She rounded the corner at the end of Main Street and faced an empty storefront. Taped to the window was a blue sign with white letters.

Think Bloomburg

Tax-Free Annex

Hassle-Free Amenities

She shielded her eyes from the late morning sun and squinted down Main Street. Blue signs with white letters, all the way down.

# CHAPTER FIFTEEN

Adelle nudged the little red wagon with her foot, and it rolled under the stairs, bumping against the boxes of papers that were once her father's files. The only way to stem the restless tide of dread within her was to keep busy, keep moving. With Jaleesa's party cleaned up and put away, and with nothing on the calendar for the next few days, she tried to fix her mind on the coming spring. It was always a gamble, trying to guess at germination time what plants people would buy two seasons in the future. It was even harder with a head full of static. At least her seed bank gave her a jump start. The same stash of seeds that had served her grandparents kept plenty of options at her fingertips. And as long as she planted them every three years or so and stashed new seeds away, Ramsbolt would never want for heirloom plants.

She took a plastic bucket from the dark corner of a shelf in the hall. Amid silica gel packets to catch any offending moisture, were little mylar bags with descendants from plants much older than her. She carried it to the counter and pried the lid off to take stock when the front door flung open. It was definitely a year for marigolds.

"Bit early, isn't it, Riley?" She snapped the lid back on the bucket.

Riley heaved a cardboard box into the shop and leaned it against the wall. He held out a scanner with dozens of little buttons. "You gotta sign for this one."

She took the thin stylus and scrawled her name. Why did it never look on those little screens like it did on paper? "What is this?"

"I was gonna ask you." He tucked the scanner back on his belt and shifted it into position.

She glanced at the box. "Oh, I bet these are my signs. I'm running for town manager, so I ordered a bunch of yard signs, but I didn't expect them this soon."

"I heard about that. That you're running." Riley leaned against the counter. "I'm glad to hear it, 'cause I do not want to move to Florida. Do you know how hot it gets down there? And humid. Alligators all up in the mailboxes. I ain't got the nerve for that."

"I doubt the folks in Florida want all our snow, so the feeling is probably mutual." Adelle threw the box on the counter. She grabbed a box cutter from her apron pocket and slit the tape. "Can I ask a question? What do you know about those signs that went up overnight?"

"The ones about Bloomburg?" Riley shrugged. "I have no idea. They just showed up. Someone went around and took them down, though. Ripped 'em right off the windows."

"Really? They're all gone? All of them?" Whether it was a show of support for her or Ramsbolt didn't matter. The fact they were gone was a small relief. "But who?"

Riley shook his head. "Couldn't tell ya." He slapped the counter. "Glad they're gone, though. Anywho, I saw you at the party. Was gonna say hi and tell you the flowers looked nice, but Morgan had your ear. He looked intense. More than usual."

Riley's raised eyebrow and tilted chin said his statement was more of a question. As much as she loved him, Riley was the hub of the town rumor mill. Though most of what he spread came from seeds of truth, his fodder wasn't always good. She didn't want to fuel anything that mill would generate, and she wasn't so sure the town was ready to know what kind of trouble they were in.

Riley shifted his weight against the counter, and her coleus babies shimmied in their cups. "Something up that we don't know about?"

"It was just election business." Nothing in Morgan's tone had said that the news about their financial trouble was a secret. In fact, he'd said that anyone could see the finances, but no one ever asked. It hardly seemed right, though, to blurt it out at Riley's request. Saying it out loud would make it feel real. Riley would want to know what she intended to do about it, and God knows she was no closer to plan than anyone else had ever been. It would only shine a spotlight on Adler's campaign to annex the town, if that's what the signs foretold.

She took a deep breath and ran a hand across the back of her neck. There was a lot more pressure to being the only person running for office than she thought. She never dreamed she'd be running against the abstract notion of annexing their town into oblivion.

Riley inspected his nails. "So there's no news?"

"I had to fill out a form and give it to Morgan. You know, there's a lot of paperwork that goes into running for town manager. It's crazy how many times they want you to sign your initials." She deflected and hoped he would let it go. She pulled a sign from the box and flipped it over. Two-sided, just like the website said. "What do you think? I ordered the one with the swoosh and stars. It just felt right."

"Swooshes and stars are good. People won't have anything to

compare it to, so they'll just judge it on its own merit. I don't think people really judge yard signs, though. Do they? They're just kind of *there*. Not that they won't notice. They'll notice."

"You can't put one at the post office, can you?"

She held the sign out, and he shook his head. "Nope. Federal law. No campaigning. Not that I don't want to. Anyone taking over that job is better than nobody. Or that creep Adler."

She deflated with a sigh of relief. "I'm happy to hear you say that, because I—"

But Riley was still on his own path. "Back to Morgan, I figured he was telling you some big secret only politicians know, like just how much trouble this town is really in. The way people tell it, it sure sounds unfixable."

It figured he wouldn't drop it. Once Riley latched onto chatter, he didn't let go easily.

She put the sign back in the box and folded the cardboard shut. "Everything in life is fixable, isn't it? There's always a way if you look hard enough." She wasn't sure that was true, but she did her best not to let her doubt show in her grin.

"I can think of plenty of things that aren't fixable," Riley said. "Broken dishes. Broken promises. Like the ones Meldrick threw around town."

Adelle shrugged. She didn't want to open that floodgate. She'd only end up saying something she'd regret. "Well, Morgan fixed that, right? He kept us afloat for quite a while. A big feat for someone as young as he was when his dad handed him the job like it was a summer internship."

"That's the thing, isn't it?" Riley stood, and the counter shimmied again. He took a step toward the door. Another small wave of relief washed over her. She hated to feel relief that Riley was leaving; she always enjoyed chatting with him, but the shorter his stay, the less likely she'd be to let something slip that she might regret. For now, everything Morgan had told her needed to be kept confidential. At least until she knew what Adler was up to, and she had a plan.

Riley hit the door with his hip, and it inched open. "Morgan took over when it was too much for Meldrick to manage. Happens in the post office all the time. Something gets too big to manage, they break it up and get someone else to take it over. If we're not careful, Ramsbolt will be broken up, too." He shrugged and swung the door open. "Some people around town say that's not a bad thing. Good luck with your signs. I mean it. They look good."

# CHAPTER SIXTEEN

"Thanks for putting up a sign, Carol." Asking had been brutal. She hated needing help from people, even when she knew it would come easy. Walking around with a bunch of signs tucked under her arm felt self-serving. Like she was seeking attention she didn't really want. In a town so small, it seemed pretentious and narcissistic to print your name that big in bright red and ask someone to stick it in a window. She only asked at stores where she knew people would say yes, so she wouldn't have to face rejection, and she'd gone to Marissa first, for the confidence booster. Diane was easy to forgive; she only wanted her sewer fixed. But Carol's suggestion that the job was too big stung a little. She was pleased when Carol agreed to put up a sign.

"You're welcome. It's the least we can do. It's nice to have someone from town running. You sure you don't want a bag for that?" Carol held out her change. "You'll look awful suspicious walking down the street with a giant rope and a spool of duct tape."

Adelle dropped the coins into her wallet and shoved it in her purse. "Nah, I'm good. Save some plastic. Besides, there's no keeping secrets in this town."

Carol laughed. "That's the truth. Those flowers the other night were amazing, by the way. Diane and I have a bunch on the dining room table. You're so creative! I loved the toolbox for the cards. What's all this stuff for?"

"The toolbox was Penny's idea. I'll tell her you liked it. This rope is for some new display pots. I'm going to wind this around one of those massive planters out front and hope it sells. People are into nautical things right now. The duct tape is just for around the shop." Adelle smiled, pulled the rope into a coil and slung it over her shoulder with her purse. "Just kidding. I gotta run. Got a body to bury."

"Don't worry," Carol called after her. "I won't tell a soul."

Adelle slipped outside, and the bell above the door clanged, the sound echoing off the buildings. She waved goodbye through the window as she passed and stepped carefully on the uneven sidewalk. Two doors down, a hand shot out from the doorway of an empty storefront and latched around her arm.

"Hey! Get off me." She swatted at the offender only to find Arvil at the other end of the grasp. "What do you want? Don't grab me like that. You're lucky I didn't punch you."

"You need to come with me. You have to see something."

"I've got rope and duct tape, you know. If you've finally gone off the deep end, and you're trying to kill me, I'm more prepared than you are."

"Hardly. Weren't even watching where you were going."

Arvil was harmless, except for his greed. He owned storefronts, homes, and apartments that he rented out at the highest price he could demand. He charged interest on anyone ten minutes late with the rent. And he could often be found at Helen's Tavern, at the end of the bar, listening to town gossip. The man absorbed everything, bending it to his advantage, and barking at anyone and anything that stood between him and his money. If he was trying to get her attention, it wasn't for anyone's benefit but his own.

He pulled her through the doorway, into an empty store. Everything was coated in thick, white dust, and it was so dark she could only see a few feet ahead. Her mom used to gawk at jewelry in the displays when she was little, but it had been vacant for so long she could barely remember the layout. Just to the left, though, was a wood door that had always been a mystery. Arvil grabbed the white porcelain doorknob and flung it open. Grit flew into the air, and Adelle covered her mouth with her hand.

"What the hell, Arvil?"

"Well, are you gonna come down here with me or not?" Arvil barked. "You're not gonna see anything standing up here complaining."

"I'm not gonna see anything down there in the dark either."

Arvil pulled a flashlight from his pocket and turned it on. He rolled his eyes and trudged down the stairs, one at a time. The stairs were old, plain wood, and they rocked back and forth as he descended. Adelle brushed filth from an old metal folding chair, dropped her purse and the rope on it, and waited until he reached the bottom before she added her weight to the rickety steps. When she reached the bottom, Arvil scanned his flashlight across the darkened basement. Cardboard boxes thick with humidity slumped on shelves, and plastic tubs with masking tape labels were stacked in towers. Adler's ripped posters were piled in the corner.

"I always wondered where that door went. What's this got to do with me? And you were the one who took down his posters."

"Of course I did. He put them on my property without permission. Put them everywhere without permission. Spreading lies. Anyone with a brain knows annexation wouldn't be tax free. He might fix things, but we'll pay for it in the end. I got those signs off too early in the morning for anyone to see, I reckon." Arvil propped the light on a stair, so it shined out at waist height. "You're doing the right thing. Just so you know."

There didn't seem to be enough air in the basement to allow for a sigh. If Arvil were praising her decision to run, and if he were as anti-Adler as she was, she was either on the right track or on a very wrong one. And there wasn't enough oxygen in that dark damp cellar for her brain to fire on all its cylinders.

Squinting in the light she could make out the shape of tinsel garland falling out of an old trash bag. Better that than a snake.

"Why do you think Adler put up those signs? We're too poor to be worth anything."

Arvil tapped his head with his finger. "Think about it. Legacy. He wants to be the hero. Probably heard about it from Meldrick. All you gotta do is be smart. Run for office and state your case. No one really wants to be taxed. Not like he would once he turns this place into a bureaucratic nightmare."

"So what the hell am I down here for?"

"This." He jabbed his flashlight at a black trash bag.

"I don't understand. What is all this stuff?"

"This is where the town stores all its old decorations. I charge ten dollars a month which Morgan hasn't paid me in forever. Christmas is over here. Halloween in the back." He pointed to a dark corner. "All that garbage over there, your father used to hang from the light posts. There's a Santa suit in there somewhere, but the sucker who used to wear it moved someplace warm."

Her eyes began to adjust to the light. She could make out the shapes of boxes on shelves and lumpy plastic bags knotted shut. "What do you want me to do about it?"

"Get rid of it. Put it in your damn flower shop. I'm not a free storage unit, lady." Arvil rolled his eyes. "Look. I'm not trying to be an asshole about this, I just want it gone. You're gonna have enough problems without me on your case. I know what it takes to run this town."

She pulled her hand away from her mouth long enough to speak. "Why don't you do it, then?"

"I didn't say I wanted to. I said I know what it takes. You already know the town is worth saving, and that's more than half the battle won. The rest of the war is a damn bloody nightmare. But it's absolutely essential that you win."

Maybe it was a good thing to have Arvil on her side. He might be grumpy and demanding, but he had a certain gravitas for knowing his way around the financial world. But he also had his own reputation for avarice. It made sense he'd support her. Arvil wouldn't want strict land use laws, high taxes, and a man like Adler with his large committees making demands. Arvil liked the last word. She took in a shallow breath of basement air and nodded.

"The election isn't far away. I need a plan."

"Then you know what you gotta do." He flung his head back, eyes shut, mouth pinched in a scowl. "I'm not paying homage to that man with one single penny of my money. I don't want him near this town. He'll ruin everything."

"Don't I know it. But just playing devil's advocate here. You know the town's finances are terrible. If the town were a person and their bank balance was almost zero, and the bills kept coming in, would you say it would be smart of them to let someone else take over the bookkeeping? I'm flattered so many people are against the idea of annexation, but some aren't. The clear argument in favor of it is that we could get some fast repairs. How do I argue with that? People won't care if we have to pay through the nose if Adler makes it sound all shiny and simple. And what if our finances are unfixable? What if this is rock bottom?"

"There's no rock bottom. There's no line in the sand to tell you that it's time to quit. But it's definitely a good idea to get some expert help before you file for bankruptcy. I would say it would be an absolutely stupid horrible thing to turn this town over to Adler. Or anyone else, for that matter. You have to figure it out."

Adelle leaned back against a shelf of ornaments, packed in a damp cardboard box and labeled in her father's hand. Funny to think there was a day, probably a freezing, biting January day, when he packed that box for the last time. She'd been in high school the last time the town had decorated for Christmas. No one was willing to go out in the cold to take it all down, and it was too depressing to leave it up until April. It was even more depressing seeing it all packed away and labeled a burden by Arvil.

"Listen. Do you make enough money to pay a fifteen percent property tax on that store?"

Adelle rolled her eyes and folded her arms. "Not even close."

"That's what it'll come to if we turn it over to him. Or anyone else. Taxes are used to pay for crap that's needed. They're for the greater good. The greater the number of people, the more good they need, and the more of your money they will take. What happens if they take your store away because you didn't pay the tax bill?"

She didn't want to think about it. She had no place else to go. Her family had downsized until there was almost nothing left, and she wasn't about to lose what remained. "I'd need government assistance, that's for sure."

"Right. More taxes. If you don't take control of this town, God knows how many other people will. Ramsbolt will cease to be if something good doesn't happen, and we need to keep it between us. Inside this town, I mean. Small dollar signs for a small group of people. I support you, and if I can do anything to help you win this election, let me know. Not saying I'll do it, but I'll think about it."

Her mind reeled. She never expected Arvil's support. Not that he hadn't supported her father. Arvil hadn't been outspoken about anything political, not that she could recall. She'd always considered him selfish, complacent until he were imposed upon. Perhaps that's why he never complained to her father. It just wasn't worth it to him.

She decided to start small. "Can you put a sign in your store windows?"

He tilted his head back, looking at her beneath his bifocals. "Yes. But you have to put them up. And come get them when this is over."

"It's a deal." She stuck out a hand. He didn't accept.

"Look, I know who I am. I'm greedy, and I want what's mine. That's it." He turned to the stairs. "This stuff has to go. Figure out what you want to keep. Leave the doors unlocked when you go. You can leave the flashlight on the windowsill."

"I'll go through all this stuff, but I can't do anything with it until I win."

"Atta girl." He climbed the stairs.

She couldn't blame him for wanting his space back, even if no one was using it. She would want all that muggy cardboard lying around. It was probably full of spiders. Alone in the scary cellar with the crickets and centipedes and God knows what else, she grabbed the flashlight and scanned the boxes. A carton labeled Old Parade Supplies was filled with tiny American flags and Uncle Sam hats. There were boxes and bins of garland and streamers and noisemakers. Leprechauns of painted plywood edged in golden glitter. A wrinkled giant pumpkin costume was shoved in a ripped trash bag, complete with a little stem hat and green shoe covers.

Most of it was familiar, if only vaguely, from childhood memories. Her mother had carried their metal lawn chairs down to Main Street, where they sat with a box of sparklers and waited for the parade on some Fourth of July. Her father wore one of those Uncle Sam hats and threw candy to kids. One Christmas, a man dressed as Santa went from door to door with candy canes. She'd been very small then, and he was big and scary.

Beneath a box labeled Christmas, packed full of fake snow fluff and strings of old lights, was a box labeled Girl Scouts. Adelle tugged on it until the side ripped, and the contents spilled onto the damp floor at her feet.

She clutched a familiar brown tablecloth. It smelled like basement, but the fabric was as soft as she remembered. One snowy Saturday, she'd sat in the library with a dozen other Brownies and sewed pieces of felt in the shape of the emblem onto the front. Then late winter weekends, they'd toss it on a table and sell cookies in front of the market. There were old Girl Scout handbooks with brittle plastic covers and a few stray badges that never made it to their sashes. She hadn't thought about those little badges in years, how hard she would work to earn one then rush home to give it to her mom, so it could be sewn on.

She'd lost that uniform ages ago. Gone to time. Lost in the shuffle between adolescence and adulthood. Not enough room to hold onto the past. She'd lost so much that way. All of Ramsbolt had. Stores had closed and families left, taking with them their skills and their kindness and humor. Piece by piece, the colors faded, and it all ended up in one of Arvil's basements, rotting away. A Fourth of July parade came and went for the last time, uncelebrated. Someone stepped out of the giant pumpkin costume, bagged it up, and never came back. And the girl scouts grew up, moved away, and moved on. Without Adelle.

Her father couldn't have prevented any of those things from fading. He couldn't have grabbed those people and made them stay or kept the stores open with no one to run them or shop there. She couldn't blame people who listened to Meldrick and decided her father was bad at the job. All around them things were changing, and he was the only one holding the reins. It was the kind of change that fell on a town and strangled it while it gasped and choked for air. All she could do—all anyone could do—was hold onto what they had because once it was lost, it was lost forever. Into the bags and boxes it went. Out of sight and out of mind.

She gathered the embroidered badges into a stack and stuffed them back in the envelope they'd tumbled from. The box wouldn't hold anymore, so she folded the tablecloth and the sashes, used them to cradle the books, and climbed the stairs, back to the dust and grime. Those things didn't belong there. They didn't belong in the dark. They belong with the people who held onto the memories.

Her purse and the rope were still heaped on the chair. She dropped her treasures on top.

What if Arvil was wrong? Just wanting to save the town wasn't enough. Meldrick had thought he was saving it before he abandoned the job entirely. Morgan thought he was keeping it afloat. Her father thought it was the only thing in the world worth keeping. If wishes made things come true, Ramsbolt was proof that all the want in the world was still lacking. She was glad to have Arvil's endorsement, but it wasn't worth much, not with bad change hanging overhead, ready to smother them all.

There was a town hall meeting looming on the horizon, and she had to present a plan. There was an election only a few short weeks away, and she had no ideas at all. The only solution the town would see was annexation, and she had to admit that it sounded a lot better than "Let's keep Ramsbolt from changing." The worst kind of change was on their doorstep. Inevitable and irreversible.

She set the flashlight on the windowsill, like Arvil asked, with the chips and flakes of old lead paint and broken bits of ceiling tiles, then gathered her purse and the rest of her stuff from the chair. Her arms full, she stepped onto the sidewalk, squinting against the bright sunlight.

# CHAPTER SEVENTEEN

Adelle clung to the edge of Jaleesa's garage, safe in the shadows thrown by a stack of tires. Across the street, people flowed into the library for the town hall meeting like strings of ants drawn by some inherent joint fate. She felt it too, perhaps even more than they did. She needed to go inside with everyone else, pretend to be confident, and state her case. Not that she had one.

Her insides shook like she'd contracted a stomach virus. There was nothing to be afraid of. They were the same people she made arrangements for all year, for birthdays and weddings. But her fingers were stuck, clenched in tight fists at her sides. She felt like a teenager girl again, afraid to pick a lunch table for fear of being rejected.

Her throat was dry. Why was she so scared? The numbers had kept her up all night, etched into the ceiling by creeping shadows. She'd drowned in all of them, searched the shadows and moonlight for answers, but came up dry. No plan. The election was still a month away, but a month would go by so fast. And she had no plan. She might as well get up there and dance a jig.

She swallowed to unstick her mouth, praying her vocal cords would work when she needed them and scolding herself for hiding behind tires like a terrified child, but something about the smell of rubber and metal was comforting in a *life goes on* kind of way. Even if she died from fear and anxiety in the basement of that library, Jaleesa's garage would live on. It might be in Bloomburg's zip code, but it would live on somewhere.

She flushed with a sense she'd forgotten something and checked her pockets. Keys. Notebook. Pen. Maybe it was all the meetings she'd been dragged to as a kid, helping her parents carry signs and flyers. For years, on the second Thursday of every month, she'd followed orders and sat in the front row, hands in lap and her mouth shut. The whole family went to show their support, but by the time she reached her mid twenties, it felt more like a united front against a common enemy. After her father retired, so did she. She hated those meetings.

*You have to go in there. You can't hide behind a bunch of tires all night.*

She ran through the presentation in her head but couldn't get past the start. *You all know me,* she figured she'd say. *I'm running for town manager. Someone has to do it.*

Warren slapped her shoulder from behind. "Wake up."

Adelle jumped. "Warren. Thanks for the alarm." She wiped her sweaty palms on her jeans.

He narrowed one eye. "You look like cattle being led to slaughter."

"I was just wondering what's going to happen once I get in there." She felt for her little notepad again. It was empty, like her thoughts, but it grounded her to reality. At least she could write down an idea if one was presented.

Warren nodded toward the library, where yellow light pooled on the porch. A small cluster of people had formed by the steps. "It'll be the same shit that always happens. Morgan says he can't fix the sidewalk, there's still a discount at the hardware store for anyone who wants to volunteer to fix something that's broke, and please don't drive too fast around the circle 'cause it scares Sparky. Arvil will make a grunting sound about something, and he'll give Morgan the shakes."

"Same old, same old. I haven't been to one of these in years."

"So what's your speech about?" His gaze was expectant, but she had no secrets to reveal. "Morgan says you're presenting your plan."

Her shoulders rose and fell with her sigh. "Honest to God, Warren, I have no idea."

A weak smile crossed his face. He looked like a teacher on the verge of letting her teach her own lesson. She hoped so, anyway. "Procrastinating, huh?"

He nodded toward the street and inched toward the puddle of dim light from a flickering streetlamp. Adelle followed.

"Hardly. Mom was the world's best procrastinator. She hated to open the mail and face the bills, but dad would tear into them. He always said that the clearer the problems were, the clearer the solution would be. You couldn't take a pill for a headache you didn't know you had."

"Has that helped you at all?"

"Not one bit. The more I know about the problems, the harder they seem to solve. I guess that's why we still have them. I have a giant headache, but no pills."

The closer she got to the library, the harder it was to move. It felt like walking through pudding. They took the stairs to the library door, their footsteps echoing on the wooden porch. Inside, people clustered in groups, talking about their kids and the weather.

A group of men waved and called Warren over. He inched away.

"Well, you just remember there's nothing to be nervous about. Everybody knows you're the most qualified person. And no one else is running, so it's smooth sailing."

She returned his smile and slipped silently through the crowd, leaving Warren with his pack of curmudgeons and went down the stairs, to the same dank basement that was never the scene of anything good. At least not for her. Mack and Lewis laid in wait at the bottom of the steps clutching Styrofoam cups of steaming coffee. She gave them a small wave and slipped past.

"Looking forward to hearing what you have to say," Mack yelled out to her.

She waved over her shoulder. "Have a good night."

Her face fell. What a stupid thing to say. Luckily, both of them were nearly deaf. They could barely hear each other, let alone her.

The people who needed to hear her the most were swarming around in the basement, buzzing about kids and the weather, smiling and laughing. If they were half as worried as she was—as Arvil, Mack, and Lewis were—they didn't show it. Even the smallest towns were like that. People lived on, absorbed in their daily grind of making do and getting by. The butterflies in her stomach trembled into a new turmoil. These people wouldn't know she didn't have a plan. Most of them didn't know they had a problem. Maybe this wouldn't be so bad, after all.

The sooner she could get it over with, the sooner she could go home, drink a glass of wine, and find something soothing on television.

She scanned the room and found Morgan in a metal folding chair near the lectern, sucked into his phone. She took a seat at the end of the front row as the room filled in behind her. Morgan had the right idea, diverting his attention from the chattering crowd. The endless to-do list on her phone needed mending, so she unlocked it and edited while the meeting started, but her heart wasn't in it, and her hands shook too much. She didn't notice when Morgan started the meeting. She gained focus somewhere around his explanation for the clock being broken, and his reminder not to trust it to tell the time. Everyone laughed. Then Morgan stammered through the purpose of the meeting. He introduced her without saying a word about Bloomburg or Adler or the mysterious signs that popped up in the night.

Her mouth went dry again. Sahara desert dry. Not enough water in the world dry. She welcomed dehydration and hoped it was a quick and painless death. Somehow her legs, detached from her consciousness and walked her to the podium. Her shaking fingers fumbled with the hem of her shirt, and she approached the lectern like it was a feral cat stuck under the porch, in need of her attention but also apt to bite. There was no microphone. The room was small, anyway. She wouldn't need it.

What was she doing here? What was she supposed to say?

She forced a swallow, and her throat unstuck.

Hands shot into the air.

*Thank God.* Answering questions was better than scraping together whatever thoughts she could find on the floor of her brain. She nodded at a woman in a floral shirt who looked familiar.

"Adelle, what are you going to do about all these kids leaving town for college? No offense, Morgan."

"Well." Her voice echoed off the concrete walls. She wrestled her wince into a smile. "You can't do anything about people wanting to look for jobs."

"But they don't come back."

"Sometimes people leave. You can't force people to stay. We can't make them want to be here or stay with us or want things that we don't want. We can't make Ramsbolt into the perfect place for everyone."

A man in the back raised his hand and stood. "I have to pack my kids' lunches every morning because my wife took a night job, and it would be a lot easier if the school served lunch. And had a bus. Why do my kids have to walk to school."

"The school has never served lunch. That's just…I don't know." It would certainly cost a lot. And there would have to be a kitchen. And staff to cook the food. And a bus? They'd need health care and benefits. Ramsbolt's kids had walked to school for generations. What was so wrong with a brown paper bag?

"Everything costs a bundle." Cheryl ran a tanned hand with perfect nails through her sleek dark hair, brushing it out of her eyes. "What are we going to do about that? Prices keep going up and up."

"You're right. We don't have a great economy. I can't fix my air conditioner. We all need more than we can afford. The town's finances aren't great either. We're not a massive city, and even if we were, no place has perfect finances. We're just going to have to see how we can spend what we have differently. We have to reprioritize our issues and be reasonable in our expectations."

"Schools are important if you want kids to stay," said a disembodied voice from somewhere in the back.

"What do you want her to do? Give them a worse education so they can't go off to college?" Diane sat with her arms folded, her legs crossed, flicking one foot in amusement.

The voice shot back. "Yeah. Then use the money to fix the damn sewer."

She shot a glance at Morgan, hoping for silent instruction. For as long as they talked among themselves, she was off the hook, but if things got out of hand, she would lose her sanity fast. Morgan was no help. His eyes were fixed on his phone. She raised a hand to silence the crowd. "Guys. It's a creative solution, but not educating the kids is probably not in the best interest of kids. Or the town."

If only they knew how much financial trouble the town was really in. But telling them wasn't her job. It was still Morgan's.

Mack rose to his feet and clutched the shoulder of the woman in front of him, his knees wobbling. "What I want to know, young lady, is if you plan to enact a tax. Because I ain't paying no taxes. Period. I broke my back keeping these farms running, fixing broken trucks and tractors twenty-four hours a day for years. Ramsbolt wouldn't be here but for those farms, and I never made enough to live on." He pointed a shaky finger. "I don't deserve to be punished with a tax, and neither do these folks."

She cracked her knuckles. Shifted her weight. She couldn't promise anything. Not a single concession. Especially not to men like Mack who would interpret every blink and nod and hold her to every promise she never made. She couldn't blame Mack for not wanting to pay a tax. Avoiding a tax was half the reason she was running. The other half was to avoid having to answer to people who never came to Ramsbolt and knew nothing about the people. What was she supposed to say?

She shrugged and shook her head. "I'll do my best, Mack. I promise that my goal is to keep Ramsbolt—"

"Oh, dammit!" Arvil's voice boomed through the basement. "Mack. You know nobody in Ramsbolt wants a tax. I'll tell you what the problem with high taxes is. People who pay a lot in taxes think the town makes so much it's gotta do everything for them. There's no personal responsibility out in the world anymore. People can't shovel their own damn snow. Want everything handed to them. You just be glad you got broken stuff to worry about."

"Arvil." Barbara spun in her chair to face him, her wavy gray hair swirling around her shoulders. "The clock has been broken since before my kids were born. Citizens can't take personal responsibility for that."

"I don't need a clock." Dawn held a sleeping baby in her arms, a pacifier over her finger like a ring, at the ready. "I have a phone to tell the time. But I need to push my stroller over the sidewalk, and it's like Dresden after the bombing out there."

Finally, tangible issues that could be addressed. "These are all really important, and I know Morgan is aware of the sidewalks. It definitely will be prioritized. You're right, Dawn. It's really rough. It has to be a priority."

"What about fences?" Lewis stood this time. "The Campbells put a fence on their property up against my yard, and now I can't mow behind my trees. Like a damn jungle back there. The town needs to enforce these things."

Adelle sighed, but it was unfulfilling. *Why am I spending so much time in damp basements?*

It wouldn't be easy to tell them they couldn't have it all. Or anything, for that matter. Words were cheap, and she could promise them the moon and stars, but unrealistic expectations could cost her the election and the town with it. A sidewalk was one thing, but code enforcement? Were there even rules about fences and trees? If Lewis demanded they be enforced, if he held her to the letter of the law, she'd lose her mind. Dealing with requests from the ladies' prayer group seemed much easier all the sudden.

They simply couldn't have it all and stay the Ramsbolt they'd always been. No one had ever run through town with a clipboard, looking for transgressions. First it would be trees and fences, then it would be an all-out war.

She opened her mouth to form the words, to warn them about the consequences. To beg them to hold onto the things that made Ramsbolt so good, else they lose their town to Bloomburg and Adler, and they find themselves living in their worst nightmares, but her subconscious had better judgment. Bringing up the finances would lead to mentioning annexation and Adler. It could start a battle she didn't know how to finish. There was no way she could go toe-to-toe with his resume.

In a flash, she pictured the room devolving in battle, throwing chairs and hurling cups of mediocre coffee. Sandy would have a fit.

She smacked her hand down on the podium. "Lewis. I don't know the specific rules about fences, but I know that if you work with your neighbor, the two of you should be able to figure it out."

Penny stood, her hand on Nate's shoulder. At least someone other than Arvil had her back. "Guys, let me tell you, Ramsbolt has it pretty good. No one here runs around telling you what the rules are and forcing you to follow them. We don't have a police officer. Isn't it great that you don't have to file petitions and stupid paperwork to get things done? We should hold onto that with all our might. Let me tell you, after the red tape of medical school, Ramsbolt is a breath of fresh air."

"But we need rules so we don't get trampled on." Mack pointed his finger in the air, his face red. "We need a town manager who will be a lawyer, judge, and jury!"

Is that what they'd expected of her father? Was that the motivation behind all the petty squabbles they threw at his feet? They expected him to play judge and jury? Putting down her foot now might cost her the election. And it might cost the town their identity. But the rising heat and her speeding pulse got the better of her.

"Since when, Mack?" She stepped back from the lectern, hands on her hips. "Maybe if the town manager had more time to spend on business because you all solved your own personal problems, then things that needed to be fixed wouldn't be put off all the time. I saw all of you—all the time—down at the shop, pestering my father about every little thing, and he jumped and ran for you. He kept the peace in this town by doing everything for you. He found someone to fix your fridge when it broke, Barbara! That's not the town manager's job. And when he needed help, you all treated him like shit. He was in the hospital! Not a single one of you showed up for him. Except you, Lewis. Everyone else treated him like he was your personal problem solver, and it killed him. When he died, not a single person said a word of gratitude. I stood at his grave alone. The game in this town has to change because we're too damn small for you not to take care of yourselves. I will work hard to fix the actual problems, but we need to have a big come-to-Jesus about what *problems* really are."

Adelle's knees wobbled. All her energy was sapped. Drained of the outrage that filled her for so long, she slumped. She felt no lighter for offloading the burden, but heavier instead. As if all that was left of her was loose skin and hollow bone. She took a wide step from the lectern on shaky legs and back to her seat. Dropping into the chair, she folded her hands on her lap to stop them from shaking. The room spun.

She'd never raised her voice at anyone, let alone the whole town at once.

She fumbled for the pen and notepad. If she didn't make a note of their actual suggestions now, they'd get lost in the firestorm igniting within her. She jotted down school lunches, buses, and property boundaries and shook her head at the list. None of those things were her vision of the future at all. All she wanted to do was keep the good parts of the town intact while keeping the worst of the changing world at bay.

She glanced over her shoulder. People chattered and whispered, their heads ducked. The room seemed muffled beneath a blanket of shock, but it spun too much for her to pick up any reaction. Her eyes fell on Penny, who gave her a big smile and a thumbs-up. The support was nice, but Penny was the kind of person she'd expect to be elated and proud of her outburst. Penny always stood up for herself. Adelle offered a sad smile back as the fire within her faded to a cloudy, smoky, smothering heartache.

Her father would have been appalled at her behavior. It was no way to talk to the town she wanted to manage. She'd be surprised if the town didn't pack up all its belongings to the next town by dawn.

# CHAPTER EIGHTEEN

Adelle yanked the handle of the little red wagon, and it flew from its spot under the stairs and rolled into the hall. She dropped to her knees and clawed at a box, one of five her father had stashed in the cubby. Over the years, he'd filled them with papers and journals. Farther and deeper into the nook they'd gone, out of sight and out of mind. She had never bothered them. She never needed to, and she'd never been inclined to peer any further into his mind than he'd allowed her during his lifetime.

There had to be clues in these boxes, some scribbled notes in her father's hand that gave away his secrets. How had he managed for all those years to navigate a feisty town? How had he coped? After decades of fighting and whining and demanding, he must have learned some tricks. Sure, he grew frustrated and angry, and the job had killed him in the end. But it was worth a shot.

She dragged each box across the hardwood floor and pushed them against the wall where she sat among them, inspecting the contents.

It was mostly receipts and old business files. Folder by folder, page by page, she found answers to questions she didn't know she had. Warren had given her father a discount on office supplies. Dad had donated his own money to the pet-store-slash-veterinarian to help neuter and spay the town's strays after a woman complained about the rising cost of feeding feral cats. But Adelle wasn't finding the answers her heart needed. As the years progressed, the receipts got longer, the ink less faded, but there was no hint about how he felt. If his frustrations rose, and if he lashed out and screamed at the whole town and had to apologize, he left no hint on the pages. There was no indication at all that he fought against the tide and searched for coping mechanisms of his own.

"Nothing but crap." She closed a yellow folder and stuffed it back in the box. "It would have helped if he'd have labeled these things. A hundred folders in here and they're all the same. Who needs receipts for paperclips someone bought in 1998?"

The lid didn't fit back on the cardboard file box. She pushed it aside and dragged the last box closer. It was heavier than the rest. She peeled the lid back and tossed it to the side. In it were ancient notebooks with coffee stained covers and pages aged the color of tea, so jam-packed there was no room for air.

Her father's journals. She hadn't thought of them in ages. She never had any intention of cracking open a single cover, let alone reading one. They were mostly just old to-do lists and reminders, grocery lists and notes from phone calls. Right?

He'd always had a notebook of some sort that he wrote in: composition notebooks, the spiral-bound rejects from her old classwork, thin little journals, and large bound logbooks. They kept him organized and sane, he'd said. But he was a man of few words, and she expected nothing more than phone records and schedules. And now that she'd managed to insult the whole town while vying to fill his shoes, skimming ancient to-do lists, it seemed worth going through them, even if she stumbled on some deep dark secret. She'd take any advice she could get, no matter the cost.

She extracted notebooks, a few at a time, and spread them on the floor. Her father's handwriting crammed the pages. Their covers were dated, some in ink, some with scraps of paper taped to the front. She found the last one she remembered seeing: a ledger-style book covered in maroon fake leather with gold embossed lines and squiggles. Her father had taped pieces of paper to the cover and spine that said *1994.*

If her father left any clues on how he truly felt about managing people's problems, this is where they would be. It had been a hard year, one of Ramsbolt's worst. If he'd left a written record for posterity of what people wanted and what he couldn't provide, how he felt about it and how he handled the pressure, it would be within those pages. The journal in her hands was the closest she could come to sitting across the kitchen table and asking him how to win an election she hadn't wanted to run in to save a town she didn't deserve. It was the closest she could come to advice from her family, to comfort and encouragement from someone who knew the town and its problems and from someone who knew her, her abilities, her strengths and her faults. Holding his notebook, feeling the ridges of the spine in her hands and running her fingers over the embossed cover, she was a closer to her father than she'd been in years. The answers to her questions may not be written on the pages, but holding his words in her hands was a comfort.

Adelle had been a senior in high school in 1994. The town was getting smaller. It was contracting in on itself as farms closed and people moved on. There was a lot of hurt in those days, and it had hung in the air like smog that wouldn't lift with a strong breeze. While her parents talked in hushed tones and had sullen dinners, Adelle had been distracted with her boyfriend. As far as she was concerned, the sun rose and set on Tom. Everywhere she went during those days, people talked about when they were leaving, where they were going, what they'd be doing, how much they didn't have, and how very hard it would be, but Adelle was set for life. She had a steady job at the flower shop, a solid future running it, and with any luck, there'd be an affordable cottage somewhere in town that she and Tom would call home.

She'd been distracted by teenage infatuation at the time, but the effects on her family of the changes around them were visible in hindsight. Her father's journal gave no indication of it, though. The winter of that year, he'd left only bullet points from town meetings and fragmented thoughts about ways to resolve financial problems. Until April.

In a neatly written paragraph that filled half the page, her father laid out his frustration. For days he'd gone door to door, sitting with people, telling them about his plan for a small tax. It wasn't much, but it would save the town. It would ensure they could keep the lights on for the foreseeable future, anyway. He wasn't asking for much, and he promised not to waste it on newsletters and frivolous things, but no one cared. Not even if it meant they could get what they wanted.

Funny that she'd been so self-absorbed she hadn't noticed all that effort. Her father mentioned teas and coffees, gentle conversations on the plastic-covered floral sofas of the town's grandmothers and heated debates in garages with its fathers. He'd even hunted down some of her fellow students and begged them to stay, not to go to college, to open a store or take on a trade.

No one was willing to sacrifice a cent to improve their lot in life.

They were hanging on by a thread, too busy choking to hear what he was saying. Some listened, some thanked him for his hard work, and others changed the topic, turning to strange requests to settle disputes or build fancy amenities with money he didn't have. But no one heard the pain, how badly the town needed a tax to solve their problems. Instead, on Wednesday, May 3 of 1994, he went to the Andersons' to talk about the town's debts, but they were far more interested in the Conway house, with its barking dog and the untrimmed tree that was going to take out their shed if someone didn't do something.

Her father was exasperated. *The* Titanic *is sinking, and they're picking ice cubes out of the ocean for their drinks,* he wrote. And then he bought a chainsaw and trimmed the Conway's tree.

She laid the book in her lap.

All that time, she thought he'd fought to keep the town just as it was. That he clawed his way through and won every dispute with a town that demanded change because his vision, his life's work, was to preserve the best of Ramsbolt. She thought Ramsbolt's current economic misery was just another turning of the screw. She never knew he'd wanted a tax, that he'd wanted the progress she fought against.

*Maybe I should stomp my feet and scream at the top of my lungs,* he wrote. *Scream that they can have what they want if they can find a few dollars a year. They don't even know how truly bad things really are. I stand up there at every meeting and tell them about every bill and liability. They don't want to chip in. I can't make people care.*

How horrible it must have felt, to do all that work, carry all that stress, and feel like no one cared at all. Thinking back, it was around that time her father stopped trying. There were no more teas and coffees. No more late nights at the counter beneath the lamp, running his hands through his hair. It was around that time he started to get more sleep and seemed to embrace his role as a mediator in the town's bickerings and quibbles. Something within him must have snapped. And that must have been what drove Meldrick to challenge him. If Meldrick hadn't been so heavy handed, and the two men had seen eye to eye, maybe some real progress could have been made.

Adelle had opened his journal hoping to find an answer to her heartache, but she found the source of his instead. In the end, busying himself with the whining and complaining was his coping mechanism for not being able to tackle the town's larger problems. And now those problems were even bigger. So big they risked being absorbed by a town that was everything her father hated and run by a man he couldn't stand.

After all those years of thinking of her father as the great town protector, it turns out he tried to change it and failed.

The blue ink and yellowed pages faded behind her tears. She stood, her body aching from sitting on the floor too long, and carried the book to the counter where she plopped onto the stool and pulled it closer. Far too much had happened in her life, and she'd weathered enough storms to know that nothing good could come from asking *what if*. But with his intentions laid out before her, and his own regrets scrawled out like that, it was hard to choke back the rise of anger. If he'd done what he knew he should, regardless of the social consequences, she might not be stuck with the aftermath. So who was really to blame?

She wiped her sweaty hand on her knee and turned the page. Tucked deep in the binding was one of her clovers. She'd found so many over the years. She'd probably left it lying on the counter as she ran from the back garden to the street. Just another treasure that she had a knack for finding and hadn't valued in the moment.

She grasped the clover, tissue thin and delicate, between two fingernails, and held it to the light. A faint glow passed through five dried, muted green petals.

The past clamped down on her heart, squeezing within her chest, and her breath hitched in her throat. She hadn't thought about those five little leaves in years.

That hot summer day in 1994 seemed like a lifetime ago, sitting with Tom in the back of his dad's truck. Tom in his nineties grunge shorts, hair plastered to his head with sweat, beads of it running down her back like a river. It had been the hottest June she'd ever experienced, until this last one when the air conditioner broke. What ever happened to Tom and that old truck?

She'd found that clover down by the creek, traced the stem to the ground and pinched it off with her finger. Then she'd carried it home like it meant the world to her, the rarest thing she could hope to find on the worst day of her life. But on the way home the luck faded. The five-leaf clover hadn't been enough to mend her broken heart. Swept up in the firestorm of teenage emotion, she'd thrown it away and stormed up the stairs to her room. She never dreamed the luck was for her father. For Ramsbolt.

She spun the clover by the stem and planted it on the counter while she caught her breath and turned the page.

Her father had never been an artist. He'd never been one for whimsy, but he'd sketched the clover in green colored pencil and above, he'd written the word *HOPE* in all caps, each letter adorned with little serif feet and wings.

Hope.

Beneath the drawing, he wrote:

*I was about to give up and call that Waldon guy with the state to have them come and offer some solutions. I was putting together our profit and loss for the last few years when Dell runs through the shop and slams her bedroom door. She left this five-leaf clover by the sink. Maybe it means nothing to her, but it gives me hope. Ramsbolt needs a leap of faith. If I don't believe in this town, no one will.*

Anger simmered, and she slammed the journal shut. She wiped her clammy palms on her jeans. He'd been so close to saving the town. There were three times as many people in Ramsbolt back then. A tax wouldn't have hurt nearly as much as it would now. And he'd had options with the state worth exploring? Options that didn't include abandoning their heritage? And his idea of hope had been to do nothing at all?

If he'd pushed through a tax anyway, he could have saved the town. She wouldn't be sitting on her grandfather's stool next to a broken air conditioner, staring out the window at a bunch of closed up stores. People might have stayed. He could have avoided the fight with Meldrick, saved himself the stroke, and lived longer than he did. He could have saved himself another nineteen years of dealing with people's personal problems. Almost two decades of playing therapist and personal assistant to a bunch of entitled whiny people, all because his idea of hope was to give up and becoming the town's personal assistant instead.

Now, it was too late. There were too few people to shoulder the financial burden. And if they had to answer to Adler, there'd be a thousand new laws to follow, traffic cops, a fifteen percent tax, and impossible red tape to cut through in order to get anything done. And it would be her father's fault.

Ramsbolt wouldn't survive all that, and because her father couldn't pull off a solution, she had to stand in front of an angry town that demanded far more than silence from barking dogs. She had nothing to give them to ease the pain.

"Damn it, Dad." She slammed the journal into the box. "Why did you have to let Meldrick be right?"

He'd always seemed so deliberate, as if he was steered by some ethic or creed, and every decision pointed him, straight as an arrow, toward the right answer. She'd only skimmed a bunch of receipts and part of one journal, but the truth couldn't be any clearer.

She squeezed the box until the lid fit, and slid the boxes with her foot, one by one, back under the stairs. Then she grabbed the handle of the little red wagon and flung it back where it belonged, putting her father's history out of sight and out of mind.

The cart hit the wall with a satisfying thud, and she plopped onto the stool. Tiny terra-cotta pots and clumps of soil were strewn across the counter, debris from repotting aloe plants. She pushed them aside. There'd been enough chaos for one day.

Outside, the sun had just started its dip below the horizon, painting the street in hues of gold. Adelle had seen a countless number of those sunsets. As a kid, she'd soaked in it, packing empty baskets into the back of the old pickup truck. She'd rehashed the slam of the tailgate bouncing off the buildings so many times that it was branded into her, part of her DNA. Her mother had a noisy grace, offering an endless narration as they closed the store. Counting down the drawer. Stashing money in her purse. Did Adelle have her book bag. Where was her homework. Her father was a stone-faced stoic soldier in those moments, watering plants and tending the flowers, making sure petals and stems were comfortable for the night. With the metallic tumble of the key in the lock and the slamming of the tailgate, they'd bounce out of town and into the farmland.

The sunset limned the street a dark pink, and Adelle sat at the counter like a stone, waiting for time to erode the sharp edges of misery. Her eyes were fixed on the pavement outside, the coming darkness as much a deadline as the ticking election clock. She had too many things to figure out. How had her father become such a failure? How was she going to fix it? She needed a plan that didn't involve taxing the town, but no idea where to get one.

A familiar ache twisted within her. A deep want she hadn't felt it in a very long time. Closing her eyes tight, she could smell the earthy hint of chrysanthemums. Shuffling footsteps in the hall as her mother gathered their things. The crescendo of street sounds as her father opened and closed the door, dragging in plants, hauling out baskets. She thirsted to hear the slam of that tailgate one more time, the hunger to have it all back—her parents, the farm, the tire swing, the neighbors, the lively street with shoppers and kids on bikes and the slamming tailgate—it swelled within her and welled in her throat.

When she opened her eyes, it all fizzled away. The color had faded from the scene, leaving everything a dull gray.

She swallowed it back and hopped off the stool. As much as she liked the quiet of being alone, sometimes she needed the company.

# CHAPTER NINETEEN

Adelle wound her new scarf around her neck and stomped to Helen's Tavern. She paused at the little bridge and peered down at the creek. The patches of clover had grown wider since her teenage years. It was almost dark, too dark to stop and explore, but it smelled like damp earth, like being six years old, wading in water up to her ankles and looking for frogs.

She shoved her hands in her jacket pockets, pulled it down around her hips, and walked into the tavern. The door closed behind her with a solid thud, and her eyes strained in the darkened room.

Dan and Bern turned to face her. They worked for farms outside of town and dressed like characters in a Maine-drawn play, clad in flannel plaid and dusty denim. Dan had a beard down to his chest and a thirst for quiet, and Bern was a string bean of a man with no patience. She waved. They waved back and returned to their beers.

Penny and Nate sat by the taps. Arvil commanded a far corner, out of the light, his nose in a newspaper. Everyone there was in search of something. Quiet. Peace. A night out of the house. And night out of the fields. Adelle needed to soothe the rage that boiled in her stomach and simmered beneath her skin. She needed everything and nothing at once, and she couldn't ask for any of it. She had to wear her father's mask and pretend to be the stoic, capable one who had all the answers. The truth was, she had nothing but questions and a giant secret heaped on her shoulders.

None of these people knew. They had no idea the town paid taxes on empty properties and the more homes and stores emptied, the worse things got. They had no idea that every time the sun set, they were one step closer to being forcibly taken over by a man who wanted to do who knew what with their town. And she had no desire to tell them. The facts of their financial catastrophe weren't hers to tell.

It felt like mudslinging no matter how she phrased it in her mind. Morgan and her father would wear the shame. She'd be giving credence to Meldrick's argument that her father had been a bad town manager. The town's strongest argument in her favor was that she'd learned by osmosis. If they thought she'd learned the wrong things, her efforts to save the town would be wasted, and she'd only succeed at painting her father as a fraud. It would only make annexation seem more attractive.

Her legs went to jelly, and she felt ten times heavier than her bathroom scale suggested. She dropped onto a barstool next to Penny, nodded at Logan, and ordered a glass of white wine, hoping it would calm her temper.

"That town hall went great." Penny reached across the bar and grabbed a napkin for Adelle's drink.

"If a disaster is your idea of great, then it was marvelous." Adelle offered a weak half smile to Logan and accepted the glass. Her stomach tumbled and her hands shook just thinking about the next town meeting. "There's an election in four weeks, and it was a disaster."

"I don't think it was a disaster." Logan wiped a corner of the bar with a white rag. "Of course, you know I'm a city girl with a short fuse, so I tend to stand my ground. But someone needs to tell these people they can't have it both ways. You can't have police and code enforcement officers and big government and also have this small-town charm. I'm not saying it's impossible, but it's not easy to change and stay who you are at the same time. Trust me. I didn't have a choice, but I did it anyway, and it hurt like hell."

No one knew change better than Logan. She'd been heir to one of the country's biggest fortunes before losing it all and moving to Ramsbolt. If anyone could teach lessons in change, it was her.

"I never realized how much you and Ramsbolt have in common." Tiny beads of condensation formed on Adelle's glass. She wiped them away with a thin paper napkin.

"It's not lost on me," Penny said. "Logan's some kind of economic superhero. At least I had a choice. I could have found a way to ditch my grandmother's stuff and go back to school if I really wanted to."

Logan laughed. "I don't know about economic superhero. If I were, I'd have my money back, and I'd be on a plane to London instead of behind this bar. If I had that money back, I would give it all to Ramsbolt if it would fix anything."

Adelle swallowed a sweet sip of wine. If Logan knew how much it would take to fix crumbling Ramsbolt, she probably wouldn't offer. Even hypothetically. "That's a really kind thing to say. But, half of what the town needs is totally out of reach, and the other half looks easy on paper, but there's just no money for it."

Logan threw a glance at Arvil and leaned closer, across the bar, as if wanting in on her secret. "Have you *seen* the finances? Is it bad? I mean, it has to be bad if they can't fix a pothole."

Adelle shrugged and spun the napkin on the bar with the heel of her wine glass. Part of her wanted to throw it all out on the bar, spread her arms over the mess and scream "See! This is it. Aren't you proud of the mess we've all made?" But the wiser part of her wanted to keep it to herself, to keep her dreams and her father's legacy safe for as long as she could.

She grasped the truth a little tighter, holding on a little longer. "Maybe that's why I'm so frustrated. I don't even want to get out of bed these days. I should be happy, right? Running around with a huge smile like politicians on television? When I don't feel angry, I just feel miserable."

Logan rubbed at a shoulder as if it ached. "I'm no expert on getting through the tough times, but I know it's a hell of a lot harder when you hide in your apartment and wallow in what you lost. I tried that. It sucked. You just have to show the town that better stuff is out there. We just have to get up, get moving, and grab it. I think Ramsbolt is in a wallowing phase. We know things suck, but we're not ready to do the work yet."

Penny nodded. "She's got a point. There's gotta be a way. If people want things fixed that badly, they're going to have to accept a tough solution to a hard reality. I guess you just have to figure out what that solution will be."

"That's the tough part." Adelle tried to crack her neck, but it was too stiff to oblige. "You saw what went down in there. They don't want big picture changes. They don't want to choose between becoming a part of a larger town, with all its oppressive rules and procedures, and oppressing ourselves with a tax we can't afford to pay. Yeah, I did a terrible job of making that clear, but no one before me did any better. I don't think it would change anything, anyway. They don't want to deal with the big picture."

"You think the meeting was a wake-up call?" Penny asked.

"I don't think it was enough of one." Logan slung the bar rag from her shoulder and wiped at another spot on the bar. "If it were, there'd be a lot more people in here talking about it."

"Good point. Also, bad point." Adelle let out a sigh. It did nothing to relieve the tension in her chest. She gripped the edge of the bar. "And don't get me started about being annexed. Adler and those stupid signs. I don't know what he's trying to pull, but he's too quiet. It's scaring the crap out of me. I need a plan. I need to show people how bad it is. How do I show them life won't stay as it is unless we make some changes. I just don't know what the changes are. It's hard when all this other emotional stuff is in the mix. Even if we had a miracle and everything suddenly worked out fine, I still wouldn't get to leave the past behind. I'll have to answer to it while everybody throws it in my face."

Logan pulled a corner of the bar rag through her belt loop and threw her hands on her hips. "Ah. So this is about your dad. I don't think anybody is going to blame you for what he did or didn't do."

"Oh, how wrong you are." Adelle's eyebrows pinched. The scents of yeasty beer and salty bar snacks coated her lungs. "Meldrick will make sure they do. Even if by some miracle it never occurs to anyone that I grew up around all his faults, I will blame my dad."

Penny turned to her. "Why? Maybe he didn't do all he could in hindsight, but he did the best he could at the time."

Adelle shook her head. "Nope. I went through his old files today. I always thought he had no choice, and things were irreversibly bad all the time, but it turns out that wasn't the case. He had the opportunity to make things better, and he didn't follow through with it."

Penny shuffled in her seat. "But still, he—"

"No." Adelle tore a napkin to tiny shreds. "He appeased everybody in this town who wanted him to putz around with their frivolous crap. Instead of doing the hard work, he took the easy way out and focused on their petty bullshit. They treated him like he was their servant. He chose those little victories instead of the big important one, and it killed him."

"This is good, this rant." Logan folded her arms. "I think you should probably get this out now, before the election really ramps up."

Penny bumped Adelle's knee with her own. "It's totally normal to feel that way about everything that happened. I mean, I wasn't here, but maybe that's the point. A lot of things have changed since then. Maybe people are ready to do the hard work."

"Did you see what happened back there?" Adelle set her glass down a little too hard. "Do you know how bad it really is? We can't pay the bills. Not even the ten bucks a month we owe Arvil to store old parade supplies in his basement. If we don't start taxing ourselves, then we have to give up. That's it. No options."

"Sounds like the start of a plan to me." Logan caught a nod from Dan and pulled a beer from the cooler. She popped the top off and slid it down the bar. "I'm not gonna say a tax won't hurt, but I promise not to get pissed at you if that's what you have to do. Of course, a funny thing happens when people run out of money. They always seem to find enough to drown the sorrow at the bar."

"Yeah, but they stop spending money on silly things like flowers." Adelle folded the corners of her napkin around the base of her glass. "A tax would destroy just about everyone in Ramsbolt. See what I mean?

We can't win. If my dad had started one back when he should have, we wouldn't be in this mess. Now it's too late."

"Oh, hon." Logan grabbed the bottle of wine and poured her another glass. "It doesn't mean he did a bad job or that he was unlikeable. Penny's right. He just did the best he could in the moment. That's all any of us can do."

Adelle's anger at the past grew, feeding on her fear for the future. It all surged within her, bowling her over in a giant wave. She ran her hands through her hair and clutched her scarf.

"It's a losing battle. I either bankrupt everyone or sell them out to the highest bidder. We're going down either way. This will turn into a ghost town. It will destroy people's lives, and my quiet, happy hometown will be gone forever. What if no one has faith in me? What if they do, and I do the best I can, and I become the Big Bad Government, and everybody hates me for it? Ramsbolt is the only home I've ever known. If I make myself unwelcome here, I'll have nothing left. And I still have another town hall meeting to go to."

Penny frowned, her eyebrows furrowed. She spun her glass around on her napkin, making little wet circles. "Faith is really hard for me. I lost my mom when I was young, and she had this dream for me that I'd be a surgeon. When I gave up on that dream, I felt like I was letting her down. I know she'd say that she loved me anyway, and it didn't matter as long as I did my best and was happy, but sometimes I really wish she was here to say it out loud. Your dad will love you no matter what. And you'll keep on living, just like me and just like Logan, no matter what tough choices you have to make."

"I know you're right," she said. "It hurts all the same."

Adelle had relied on the status quo for so long, needing things to stay the same, but time and again the worst happened, spinning her out of control. They lost the farm and moved to a tiny house that smelled like mothballs. Then they lost their house and moved into the tiny rooms above the flower shop. Relying on faith alone to get through the hard times hadn't been easy, and things just kept getting harder. She hadn't learned to deal with it on her own, let alone guide a whole town through it.

"Thanks for listening. And for the advice." She dug a ten from her back pocket and tossed it on the bar.

Logan scooped it up. "Need change?"

"Nah. Keep it." It was a generous tip, but she couldn't bring herself to ask for change. Bad times were coming. They'd be worse than anyone could predict, and Logan had already been through enough. Adelle slid from her stool. "It's really great to be able to talk to you two."

Penny gave her a knowing smile. "I'm grateful for you, too. Glad to see you rocking that scarf. It looks great on you."

Adelle stepped out onto the sidewalk, around the building and back toward home, beneath a cicada serenade.

Something about a walk through town in the crisp, late summer air had always cleared her head. Seeing the same old trees and hearing the same bugs put things in perspective. The cicadas would still be screaming, and water would still be rushing over those rocks long after her troubles were over.

With each step, her anger ebbed and flowed, from her father to the town to Meldrick and Morgan. To herself. This would be the last time she showed a lack of confidence in public. It would be the last time she let cowardice ooze through the cracks. She was the only one in this town with the nerve to stand up for it, so if anyone deserved to wear the tenacity, it was her.

At the shop, she pushed through the door and into the chill air. The air conditioner had kicked on for a change. She pulled her jacket tight around her and hovered over the counter where she'd left the remains of her crafts. Decorative accents for the Blackwood's arrangement had scattered in the gust of air.

Her five-leaf clover had wafted onto silver backing to a necklace charm. She plucked the clover from the cabochon holder.

The petals were still intact. All the details she'd forgotten of the day came to her in a head rush.

It had been one of the saddest of her life. Her future had been so certain before then. Tom would propose. There'd be a white picket fence around a cottage somewhere across town. The future was supposed to be perfect, but it cracked that day. Everything shattered, and she was never the same again.

She placed the clover on the counter and traced the stem with her finger. It probably hadn't seen the sun since that June day in 1994. It stayed safe between the pages while she'd weathered so much.

She took the scarf off and let it fall to the counter.

The universe had thrown a lot of clovers her way lately. The scarf, then this. It had to mean something. Five simple leaves had given hope to her father, a reason to have a little faith. Perhaps it was a talisman sent from the past to tell her the future would be okay. If so, there had to be a way to hold onto that, to capture it and keep it with her.

She rushed to a shelf of craft supplies in the hall and grabbed bottles of epoxy resin and decoupage sealing medium. With a gentle brush, she coated the clover in the sealant. It only took a few minutes to dry. Then she sealed it in epoxy on the silver, oval cabochon holder. Sealed forever.

If she could find a five-leaf clover in a patch of weeds on the worst day of her life, then the power to find good might not be so far away. It might be inside her already.

<h1 style="text-align:center">CHAPTER TWENTY</h1>

"Christ. I don't think it's ever been this hot in June before."

Adelle dripped with sweat. The truck creaked and rocked when she shifted her weight in search of comfort. With high school graduation a week away, nothing was comfortable, and the heat wasn't the worst of it. She was distracted, antsy, eager to rush to the next thing, and she couldn't wait to get on with it. Her whole future was stacked in front of her like hurdles in gym class. Take her last final, pick up her cap and gown, go to graduation. Then she'd work in the store full time. It's where she was happiest, after all.

In the year since her mother died, her father had lost energy for the shop. Adelle had taken over most of the work, though there hadn't been much need for flowers in the ever-smaller town. There'd been enough interest in their plants to put food on the table and keep her on her toes, though. And with less weight on his shoulders he'd been animated lately, cleaning and arranging plants in the window displays that he'd ignored for a year. He was happy to take a step back, and Adelle was eager to keep him relaxed and happy. She needed to learn as much as she could from him before she took over the store next year. But sometimes it was hard to tear his focus away from being the town manager. Something about jumping and running for everyone else seemed to give him the sense of purpose he'd lost at the shop.

Running the flower shop had always been her dream. Seeing that hurdle on the horizon, jumping it, and landing on her feet would solve all their problems.

And then there was Tom. They talked about getting married all the time, getting a puppy and buying a little house of their own on the other side of town, maybe not so close to the cemetery.

Sitting in Tom's dad's pickup truck in the middle of a field of grain in the hottest part of the day, though, wasn't a dream come true. Her sweat-soaked denim shorts stuck to her thighs. Tom sweltered beside her. The top of her legs were burnt to a crisp by the sun, and her bottom was stuck to the hot bed of the truck. She leaned back. With a tool bag of gloves and rags as a pillow, she shut her eyes against the early summer glare and inched farther from Tom. As much as she wanted to make out in the back of his dad's truck, she couldn't stand the heat.

"Tom, it is hot as shit out here. Let's ride out to the woods for some shade?"

"I brought you out here for a reason."

Adelle sat up, her weight on one aching elbow. She shielded her eyes with one hand. Tom's hair stuck to his forehead in wet streaks, but otherwise no emotion lined his face.

*Not like this*, she thought.

It was the perfect spot, though. Cutting through that field as little kids, chasing each other down to the creek, she'd tripped on her own feet. Everyone kept going, farther and farther through the grasses, but Tom's hand had reached through and pulled her up, yanked her forward.

He'd been pulling her along ever since. She was barely fourteen when they had their first kiss in that field. By the time Tom had his driver's license, the bramble by the road was tall enough to hide the truck when they parked in the tall grass to make out.

*It's the perfect spot, though.* Her heart was already beating fast, straining against the heat and the sun. She wiped the adrenaline rush from her forehead with her arm. He gave nothing away. No sly grin, no wink. Maybe it was the heat. He wanted that future as much as she did. They talked about it from time to time. He wanted a puppy and a tiny house and a fresh future all their own. She glanced out across the field, at the hints of golden yellow. The timing was right, and the location was perfect. Maybe the heat or nerves were just too much for him to smile about it.

Tom sat up, wiped his palms on his cargo shorts.

"What is it? What's the reason? Why can't we find some shade?" She hated when he made her wait for things.

*What will I do? Cry? Laugh? Spin the ring around my finger and look at it adoringly?*

Tom scooted back, resting against the truck window. "You remember those college applications I filled out?"

"What does that have to do with anything?" *What does that have to do with getting married?*

"Remember how I got on that waiting list for U Maine? I got off the waiting list."

"Well, that's great. I mean, it's nice to know, isn't it? That you're not waiting around for them to give you an answer. There's always another school. Try again next year." It would just mean a change of plans, that's all. Instead of spending a year apart until she could get to Orono, they'd spend the year together. He could work, and they'd put money away toward a house. Then they could both go. She could hire someone to run the flower shop and follow Tom to college. He'd graduate and run a newspaper in town, like he dreamed of. Lying in the bed of the truck, beneath blankets of stars, that's all they'd talked about, building that future together. That's what she had wished for when she saw those shooting stars.

He'd want to propose so they could get married before he went to school. And it made perfect sense to do it here, in this field, even under this blazing hot sun. Butterflies flittered in her stomach when the bliss rose up. It felt like a ride at the state fair. She clenched her hands over her belly to hold the happy vertigo.

Sweat dripped from Tom's hair down to his ear. Adelle reached out and brushed it away. She wanted to remember everything about the moment, from the stray thread from her cutoff jeans itching her thigh to the spots of rust in the back of the truck. She wanted to be able to relive the moment he proposed to her over and over. So she could tell their kids someday how it happened.

"Dell, I'm sorry. I got in. I'm leaving in August."

Adelle pulled her feet in and sat cross-legged. She pulled on the stray thread of her shorts, but it wouldn't budge. It wasn't loose enough to come free. Her insides went to jelly. It wasn't what she was expecting to hear, but she could salvage the mood. "That's okay. It's great news. We can go to Otley, get an apartment together. I'll get a job and—"

"You can't."

"No, I can. I just have to talk to my dad."

Tom shook his head, and beads of sweat dripped to the rusted red bed of the truck. "You need to run the flower shop. It's all you've ever talked about."

"And getting married. We talk about it all the time."

She sought his eyes, but they were fixed on the measuring tape he'd pulled from his father's tool bag.

"This is the damn hardest thing I've ever had to do," he said.

All her insides squeezed. It was like her internal organs all bunched together in a black hole, and she was hollow inside. The world started to spin. The red truck, Tom's sweat-drenched hair, the blue measuring tape in his hand, the swishing gold grain, it all spun and spiraled like she'd had too much Boone's Farm and not enough to eat.

Where she got the strength to stand, she didn't know, but all the sudden she was standing, the thin soles of her Keds doing their best to keep her shaking legs straight and balanced.

"Then don't. Don't say it. Don't even bother, Tom." She spit her words, short and sharp, so he wouldn't hear her tremble. She grasped the tailgate, the chrome edge searing her hand. It felt good. Real. She stepped onto the black tread on the rear bumper.

A thousand times she'd put her foot there. She could do it in her sleep. And this was the last time. She'd never hop down from that truck again. She hit the ground with a shaky thud, her hands on her hips, and memorized the shape of the tread, like little etched diamonds filled with dried mud. She wanted to remember every detail and make them a part of herself.

"Talk to me, Dell. Let me explain. I just want to see the world. I need change. I don't want to live in Ramsbolt anymore. I want to see the world. What if there are other people out there? Other experiences?"

She put up a hand, surprised that it wasn't shaking like a stop sign in a thunderstorm. "Stop. I don't need to hear it. If I'm not good enough for you anymore… Just forget it."

One last look. The freckles that bridged his nose. The way he cocked one shoulder when he apologized. She burned them into her memory and spun on her heel. She kept to one rutted wheel path, tall grain to her left. If she could make it to the turn, hide in the grain, he wouldn't see her when she broke down and lost it. She had to hold it together. One step at a time.

"Dell," Tom called after her. "Don't go. Don't let it end like this."

The hollow space in her chest flared white hot, and the sadness went up in flames of outrage. She turned back to him, dust whirled onto her white shoes. "Don't you dare. Don't you tell me how this will end. I didn't ask you to abandon me. I didn't ask you to want some stupid stagnant life. If you think Ramsbolt is so small there's no room for you here, then maybe your head's too goddamn big. If you want something you can't get with me, go and get it. But don't you dare for one second think I'm gonna shed a tear for you. You're no loss. You hear me? No loss."

*Piece of shit.* She broke into a run. She would never again let somebody else dictate what made her happy. Everybody left. Her mother left. Her father checked out. Her friends packed up and moved away. *Screw them. Screw all of them.*

It was a good two miles to get to town, with no water to drink and a blazing sun. She raced through the grains, her feet pounding the hard dry earth until the flames of rage died down and sorrow took its place. Forget hiding in the grain. She wanted to get home as fast as she could, away from that heartache. Tears streamed down her cheeks, hot and salty. She swore they were the last she'd shed over somebody who didn't care about her.

She reached the street and rubbed her nose, smearing grit on her upper lip. Dusty dirt was glued to her legs by sweat. Bugs in her hair. There was no traffic on the road—there never was—so she crossed the street and cut between houses, slinking along wild blueberry bushes.

Behind the homes, the field dipped down where a stream crossed, and she stopped to wash her hands and throw some water on her face. It was ten degrees cooler in the shade of the sweet birch trees, so she rested on the cool rocks and watched the water pass her by. It swept summer leaves and twigs into little pools between rocks where they swirled and twirled, doing a little ballet on their way downstream. Where the creek began and where it ended, she'd never thought about, and frankly, she didn't care. She had a life to build. On her own. She had her own dreams to make; she didn't need anyone turning them off.

The future had been so close. It was supposed to be a little house with a fence and a dog and a few kids. It was supposed to be love. Now it was just a giant, scary darkness on the other side of this big brick wall of graduation and loneliness she'd been slammed into.

She planted her left hand on the soft, shaded earth, ready to stand. There, at the tip of her pinkie finger was a five-leaf clover.

She followed the stem down to the ground, as far as she could, and she broke it off where it met the earth.

"If a four-leaf clover means good luck, I'm not letting you out of my sight."

# CHAPTER TWENTY-ONE

Adelle set her morning coffee on the counter. The epoxy hadn't set on the cabochon yet, but she threaded a length of green ribbon from her craft supplies through the loop at the top. She held it up to her neck and admired it in the mirror, smoothing the ribbon against her collarbone. It looked a little silly against her fuzzy gray bathrobe, but she smiled all the same.

"I hope this thing helps me come up with a plan, because I am running out of time."

"Adelle?"

She jumped at the voice in the doorway, her heart in her throat, and spun to face Penny.

"I left the door unlocked again, didn't I?"

Penny stood by the flower cooler, an old pewter soup tureen in her hands. Her eyebrows pinched and forehead creased, apology spread across her face. "I saw the light on and figured you were open. I'm sorry. I didn't mean to startle you."

Adelle placed the pendant back on the shelf to finish curing. "Don't worry about it. I don't know why I'm so jumpy. A lot on my mind lately.

What's that thing?"

Penny set the unadorned urn on the counter. "Mr. Blackwood is slick. He was in yesterday and bought this while his wife's back was turned. He asked if I could bring it over. I'm out of the loop on the rest. Sorry I forgot to mention it last night. And for scaring you half to death."

"No, it's okay." She waved a hand and peered into the tureen. "It's for an arrangement for their anniversary. He asked for silver accents. He must want me to put the arrangement in this. She collects pewter things, and she'll love this."

"Good to know. I'll give him a call when pewter ends up in the shop. What was that necklace?"

Adelle grabbed a block of green floral foam from the shelf beneath the counter and eyed it up to see if it would fit in the tureen. "I found a five-leaf clover the day my high school sweetheart dumped me. Found it in Dad's old files. I turned it into a necklace."

Penny leaned against the cooler. "A five-leaf clover. I didn't know that was a thing."

"Yeah. It's still not set, so don't touch the epoxy, but here. Take a look." Adelle nudged the necklace across the counter, and Penny leaned over it. It felt silly all of a sudden, turning it into a charm, like it would bring her luck. It seemed so logical in a wine stupor to think it had been sent by the universe to give her some kind of skill or courage, but presenting it that way to Penny while wearing a poofy bathrobe seemed a little juvenile. "Anyway, I figured I'd preserve it. They're rare."

"Maybe it'll bring you some good fortune." Penny leaned on the counter and winked. "Or a man."

"Not this again." Adelle laughed and returned the pendant to its safe spot on the shelf. "Ever since you and Nate hooked up, it's like you want the whole world to fall in love."

"Not the whole world. Just you."

Adelle tugged her robe tighter and scanned the shop for her coffee cup. She found it by the sink, the coffee growing cold. "I'm a loner. It's just who I am."

"You're an introvert, but you're not a loner. If you were a loner, you wouldn't have come to the bar last night looking for some answers. Being an introvert doesn't mean you have to be single forever, either. Come on, you never date. What about Dan?"

"Dan?"

Dan was ten years her senior and light-years away when it came to interests. Other than working outside, playing with the multitool he clipped to his belt, and wearing flannel all year long, she didn't know much about him. He did like quiet at the end of the day, so they did have that in common, but she had no interest in Dan. She had no interest in anyone.

"He's not my type, Penny. No one's my type."

"Are you bisexual, maybe? Pansexual? Asexual? Demi? I'm not trying to pry or offend you by trying to fix you up with someone. I just...."

Adelle sat on the stool, cold coffee in her hands. "No. There's nothing wrong with any of those things. I just haven't met a guy I like enough for that, I guess. And Dan might be gay, for all I know. I just haven't had any interest in anyone." She cocked one eyebrow in mock interrogation. "The real question here is why do you want me to be in a relationship that badly?"

Penny laughed. "Maybe because I don't want you to feel like a third wheel."

"You and Nate?" Adelle gave up on the cold coffee and set it by the pewter urn. "Nah. I'm happy for you two. Nate's a good guy. Definitely has more energy now that he's with you. He's happy. You guys are good for each other. I'm not jealous of that."

If she was honest with herself, she was jealous. A little. Not that she ever had feelings for Nate, but she did sometimes wonder why she was still alone. That was part of the hazard of staying in a small town. She'd always be Tom's girl to the people who stayed, and no one who interested her ever moved to town. If finding love had been a higher priority when she was younger, leaving town would have been the only way to find it. Being alone wasn't something she wanted or planned for.

"Okay, I'm going to pry. Do you ever get lonely?"

Adelle stood, and the stool grated against the floor. "I really don't want to talk about this. It's nobody's business." She grabbed the mug and dumped the contents into the sink. "My coffee got cold."

Penny took a step back, toward the door. "I'm sorry. I didn't mean to. I had good intentions. Forget I said anything? Forgive me? I won't mention it again."

"I'm not mad." A sigh was all she could muster. She was mad. She was lonely. She did sometimes feel like a third wheel, even though she was happy for them. She lived an isolated life, and it wasn't because she wanted to; it was because she got used to it. Every friend she ever had left. The things she liked and the life she wanted to live in Ramsbolt weren't good enough for anybody else, so they all left. Penny and Logan might be an exception, but they sure as hell weren't the rule. And she wasn't going to waste her time on another guy who would run off because the grass was greener in some other town. Everyone she ever cared for left her behind just like they did the random crap that wouldn't fit in their car on the way out. She didn't mean anything more to them than some old CDs.

It wasn't Penny's fault, though. Just because she was angry at the people who left didn't mean she had the right to take it out the people who chose to show up. "I'm sorry. I'm just tired and frustrated. I can't shake this worry that something is going on out there, that Adler didn't put those signs up just so people could take them down. It's in the back of my mind all the time. I know you're just being nice. Look, I'm just not interested. Maybe if the right person came along one day. But—" She shook her head. "Just forget it. Okay?"

Penny's knowing smile said her outburst was forgiven. "Don't worry about it. Sorry. All my fault. Like it never happened."

"Thanks for bringing this over. It'll be perfect for the arrangement."

"Roses?"

"A few. Cream colored. Gardenia. A little white hydrangea. Some green filler. Maybe a splash of pink in there. Pink flowers always look nice with cream roses."

"That sounds romantic. Show it to me when you're done?"

"Of course. You should take a picture of it for your website. Show people what they can do with found containers from your store."

"You're so smart with these things. You'll be great as town manager. I was thinking about what you said last night, how you felt bad about yelling at the town meeting. I don't think you should feel bad at all. You did the one thing nobody else has. You finally told them the truth. Being nice isn't getting this town anywhere. We need somebody to fix the problems. We need someone with balls." Penny checked the time on her phone and glanced over her shoulder, across the street. "And that Adler thing. I wouldn't worry about it. Nothing's come up. Anyway, I gotta run. Nate and I are having breakfast at Marissa's. Want me to bring you anything?"

Adelle took a knife from the drawer and carved into the block of green floral foam, trimming it to fit into the urn. "No, thanks. I'm good. I'll swing by later when this is done."

Morning sun splashed the street, and Adelle sat at the counter, carving into the block of foam as pieces of frustration and anger fell away. The block trimmed, she soaked it in a solution of water and nutrients while thinking about gardenias, hydrangea buds, and cream roses. It left her more tranquil than she'd been for weeks.

There was a lightness to finding her way. Her heart was less heavy having found a purpose in her desire to stay when so many had left in search of something more. When she was younger, snared by the restlessness of youth, she'd been jealous of the people who went searching for that something more. Back then, she was sure they knew something she didn't. Jealous that their eyes were fixed on a distant spot on the horizon, and they had taken aim, but when she looked out there'd been nothing at all. Turns out her purpose had been in Ramsbolt all along. Just like Penny and Logan. Now she had to prove to the town that she could be the change they needed. They didn't need Meldrick's charisma or her father's supportive intervention, and they certainly didn't need to be part of Bloomburg. They needed someone who would actually fix the real problems.

Outside, Penny and Nate crossed the street on their way to the bakery, arm in arm. Jake hopped into the window of Penny's Loft searching out a ray of sun. Adelle had worried about the cat after Penny's grandmother died. She'd worried the antique store would sit empty and fill up with mice. That Nate, who was just as allergic to cats as she was, would stop caring for the kitty and drop him off at a farm somewhere.

*Thank God Penny showed up and saved that cute little cat*, she thought. Some days Jake in the window across the street was her only company.

She never could have done what Penny did, showing up in some strange, small town, astute and persistent, adamant that she would not take on a mess she didn't ask for. Of course it had been hard to watch Penny throw everything onto the sidewalk like it didn't matter. Eliza's store had been full of memories, cast-off items no one wanted, things that had filled every house in town for generations. To see it all strewn along the street like common garbage had been a kick to the chest, and hearing Penny rant about how she had no interest in Ramsbolt hadn't helped either.

As timid as she felt about running the town, it made sense Penny would think she had the nerve to do the job. Looking back, she'd had no trouble at all sticking up for the town.

* * *

"You can't leave all this here." Adelle's hands were still wet from dethorning roses. She held the door open with one hand, leaned outside into the heat, and yelled at that Penny woman, Eliza's redheaded granddaughter who'd been making a mess of things and insulting the whole town with her *I have no intention of living here* attitude. "You can't litter the sidewalk like that. It's dangerous."

Penny spun and gave her a sarcastic sneer. "You're kidding me, right? Who walks here? No one walks here. Besides, there was already crap all over the place."

Of course there was crap all over the place. It was thrown out of car windows by careless people who drove through town, and there was only so much she could do to keep an entire street clean by herself.

"You're making this place ugly. Maybe you don't give a crap about Ramsbolt, but the rest of us do, and we don't want that stuff all over the sidewalk. Just leave it alone."

The defiant young lady who didn't even want to be in Ramsbolt threw her hands on her hips as if anything she had to say was going to make Adelle want to see all of Ramsbolt's history thrown out onto the sidewalk like it held all the meaning of a used cigarette butt.

"If Ramsbolt had cared enough about all this stuff and this stupid store, I wouldn't be here trying to sell it all back to you."

Adelle had to admit she had a point, but making the street look like a landfill wasn't going to solve anybody's problems. If the woman tried to sell it instead of throwing it in people's faces, she might make a few friends. Instead, Penny ran around insulting the town, gloating about how she had to get back to medical school, how she was too good for this place, and looking down her nose at their way of life.

"It's not my fault you're disorganized and can't figure out how to run an antique store. I shouldn't have to look at this all day because of your chaos. You come in here and act like we can't take care of our own."

Penny threw her head back. "My chaos? Your own what? It's not my fault my grandmother didn't sort her shit. I didn't even know the woman because she tried to raise her own daughter in so much mess that she ran off screaming. If you all want this stuff so badly, come get it! If Ramsbolt had taken care of its own chaos, I wouldn't be here doing it for you. If you love the way things are so much, why don't you buy it from me so you can run it the way you want? I didn't ask for this. I'm just trying to sort it out as best I can."

A thousand arguments came to mind, none of them worth the words. Yelling across the street at this transient who had no interest in sticking around was a waste of her time. She had roses to dethorn. Besides, she never really knew Penny's mother or why she left town. She just assumed the woman abandoned her family and went in search of grandeur like everyone else. Eliza had been a perfect neighbor, though. It was a shame she was gone.

She gave the door a nudge and caught it when it swung back. "This better be temporary. You've been nothing but a mess since you got here."

"Tell me about it!" Penny threw her hands in the air. "And stop saying that. I'm not a mess. I'm here to fix this shit and go home, and this whole town is a giant roadblock."

*Trust me. Nobody's standing in your way,* she thought. But it wasn't worth saying out loud. *And how dare she.* "Ramsbolt doesn't like getting involved in other people's affairs. We don't need change, and we don't need you." Adelle stormed inside, the door slamming behind her.

* * *

Adelle had apologized a hundred times for how she'd treated Penny in those early days. She'd tried to make up for it by being a good neighbor and supporting her business. It wasn't Penny's fault she hadn't formed a great first impression. The way she tried to discard of Ramsbolt's past with such disregard had touched a raw nerve in Adelle that was pinched in a vice of eternal, churning change. All she wanted was a little calm air, a little stability, and Penny was a tornado.

Adelle lifted the block of green floral foam from the pot of water. It was saturated. She dropped it into the pewter urn, and it fit like a glove.

Turned out Penny was just what Ramsbolt needed. The town could do with more people like her, hell-bent on making their own change.

What if they could? What if she could find a way to engage the town, make a whole pack of Pennys? They could build a future together, so it wasn't all on her shoulders. She had to make them see how dire the situation was, to get them invested in their own solutions. With that kind of spirit, they could overcome anything Adler might throw their way. Suddenly the next town hall meeting seemed a lot less worrisome, and winning the election seemed a lot more possible.

Adelle pulled a length of packing paper from the roll she kept at her feet. Three feet wide and the length of her counter, it gave her plenty of room to draw.

# CHAPTER TWENTY-TWO

Adelle hunched over the length of brown paper, black marker in her hand. She drew a big circle to show where the park should be and scribbled a poor excuse for the sailor statue and little benches where they sat. Radiating out from the park, she drew lines for Main Street, little squares and rectangles where the buildings were, and the church at the end with its wide stairs and pointy steeple.

She drew Levering to the left, a road wide enough for a trolley that never came to be, the failure of an administration older than her father's. She sketched little alleys from memory, where they ran between buildings and traced yards. At the end of the road, where it faded into farmlands, she added the cemetery and the little houses that framed it. To the right, she drew the cottages that lined the road heading east. And she scribbled little trees and shrubs along the creek, beside the bridge that led to Helen's Tavern.

Deep in the back of the drawer, she found the broken stub of a red colored pencil. She colored in the empty buildings that Morgan said the town owned. With her black marker, she put a dollar sign inside their vacant walls.

More than half the town's commercial properties sat vacant, sucking the town dry. Leaning back to take it all in, she saw a lot of red. Each one of those dollar signs was costing the town money. Seeing it laid out like that made her angry. Why hadn't her father changed the rules or made a new law or organized a town board to do something about it, like Penny did when they needed approval for the festival?

And no one knew the town owned those properties. Her father. Meldrick, maybe. Morgan. And her.

Every few months, the state sent a subsidy to cover the cost of roads, schools, and things their tiny town couldn't handle on their own. And every so often, the state sent tax bill for all the vacant properties. After paying the teachers and the electric bill, Ramsbolt returned what was left. Then they went to bed at night, hoping no one else left town.

If she could turn those vacant properties into profit, if she could use that real estate to give people the power to change their own fate, the town might be able to avoid charging people a tax. Instead of becoming subjects to some other man's rule, they could work together and bring back some of what was lost. The festival had been a great first step to brightening the town. Together, they could shine a beacon to draw in more people. And with the right incentives, maybe people would stay.

She opened her email on her phone and found the attachment Morgan had sent, the one that had the properties and how much they hemorrhaged in taxes. Beneath each dollar sign, she wrote what the empty property cost the town each year.

If they could rent out those properties for twice that amount, or even more, they could make a profit and avoid implementing a tax. They would need patience, not a miracle, to fix the streets and broken sewers, to upgrade the lights and get the clock working again. It all started to seem so possible.

She flipped the brown paper map over and scribbled ideas in her fractured shorthand. If people started small businesses and opened little stores, if they renovated second-floor apartments for new residents looking for a fresh start like Logan did, the whole town could prosper.

Resting her hand on her chin, her eyes wandered across the street, not truly seeing the buildings or the trees beyond them. She was fixated by the chances wasted between the empty walls.

Miller's General Store was long gone, and with it, the magic of orange creamsicles, but if Ramsbolt could make those same memories for a new generation of kids, maybe they wouldn't want to leave so badly. And if people saw a return on their investment in the town, they might be motivated to solve some of their own problems, too.

It wouldn't be easy. Starting a new business was hard enough, even in a big city. People would need an incentive, some help to get them through the early lean years. She drew a box around her notes and off to the side, she worked backward, figuring out a five year rent escalation that would give them a break and help them succeed while the town still made a profit. There would have to be a contract, encouraging them to fix up the properties and take care of them. Rent to own options that, once fulfilled, left the town with fewer burdens. And with a stronger economy, a tiny tax wouldn't be so hard to swallow. But that was all for the future.

She slammed the pencil on the counter and paced the store, treading the worn footpath from the front door down the hall. The ties of her fluffy gray housecoat swung by her sides. In her pink Nyan Cat pajamas, she rushed out the front door, crossed the street, and slammed into the locked door of Penny's Loft. Of course. They were out to breakfast.

She paced the sidewalk, wringing her hands to burn out the electric current that crackled within her.

Back across the street again in her bedroom slippers, she flung open the door and spun to face her father's picture. She wiped a layer of dust from the frame. Dad grinned back at her, his arms full of flowers that faded long ago.

"Dad. I did it. Goddamn it. I figured it out!" Her breath hitched in her throat, and her eyes welled with tears. "You'd be so proud of me. I'm sorry I got mad at you for abandoning the tax thing; it could have changed everything. But none of that matters now. We are where we are, and I figured out how to get where we need to go. It all worked out the way it was supposed to."

She fell back onto the stool and dragged the paper close. With the stub of her pencil she jotted a note.

*Town board.*

The town still had the board that they voted on before Penny's art festival. They never voted to dissolve it.

*Application process.*

The town could take rental applications, and the board could vote on them.

*Rules.*

There'd have to be rules. Rules about rent escalations and things she couldn't even conceive of yet, but the board could help with them. Arvil was on the board, and he was on her side. He knew more about real estate than anyone else she knew. It might be a source of contention with him, if cheaper retail space in town would compete with his high rents, but he knew the stakes, and he'd been reasonable so far. If she could show him, on paper, how dire things were, she was sure they could come to an agreement.

*Explain all of this to the town. All of it.*

The plan looked great on paper, in her bullet points and scribbled notes, but she'd have to explain it with facts and figures and prove to everyone that it was their best chance at survival. She only had a few days before the next town hall.

This time, she couldn't let them lead with questions. She had to take control right from the start. She needed big posters to show them how bad the finances were. And more big posters with detailed plans that showed how much money they could make. She wasn't much of an artist, but if she could draw a decent enough map, people might get excited about where the stores could go.

Glancing across the street at the old General Store, her electricity fizzled just a little.

"It'll mean a lot of change, Dad. The kind we both hated. A lot of things will go away. Like the ice cream cooler and the candy table."

It would mean an end to a lot of things. No more longing looks across the street at the empty General Store, pretending someday someone would revive the past. People would come, paint the shutters, put up new signs and cover over the past. But that didn't mean she had to stop wishing it would all go back to the way it used to be. That was just the result of growing up in Ramsbolt.

She wouldn't be able to control what history stayed and what history was replaced by a cell phone store. But she couldn't deny that they really could use a cell phone store.

# CHAPTER TWENTY-THREE

The sun set red on Adelle's end of Ramsbolt. Stuart would be coming soon, with his worn leather messenger bag and his tattered notebook. He took his job as the town journalist seriously, even if the hardest hitting piece of news in Ramsbolt was a new flavor of frozen yogurt at the market. That, and the way her father had been treated by the town's only newspaper, had kept her from being a reader. But that was before Stuart took over. He only had a few months of work under his belt, and she regretted not having read any of it. She couldn't even say "Oh, I liked your story about the cat in the tree."

She glanced at her watch. Five minutes. Definitely not time to run to the newspaper box outside the market to grab a copy. Instead, she cleaned. She flipped the light on and swept plant clippings from the counter into the trash. Her drinking glasses full of coleus were growing little white roots. She lifted one to the light.

"You're doing such a great job. You're almost ready for dirt, I think. But for now, you go up here." She placed the glass on the shelf, where green ribbon curled from her clover necklace and dangled off the ledge. She slipped it from the shelf, tied a knot in the ribbon, and slipped it over her head. It was a little long, but she could always shorten it later.

She tugged the neck of her T-shirt and let it fall against her skin. It was safer there. Hidden. No one would mock her for it or flash a condescending smile because they thought it unsophisticated. It was her very own invisible, mysterious charm.

She filled the shelf with glasses of coleus.

"What do lucky charms do, anyway? Bring you money? Give you strength? Either way, I'll take all the help I can get." She patted her shirt and turned to the window just as Stuart stepped into view.

*Thank God he didn't catch me talking to myself,* she thought. She sat on the stool then stood again. *No, don't sit. Greet him. Go to the door.*

But Stuart was already through it and into the store. She reached out her hand to greet him, but Stuart's head was down. Brown hair sweeping into his hazel eyes, a pencil behind his ear, Stuart could have been from any town that grew corn and male actors, but he'd shown up wiry, underfed, and reclusive just a few months before Logan arrived. Rumors had swirled at the time about the young man in his late twenties, who'd blown in with the wind. For being such a recluse, it was a shock to Ramsbolt when he started a newspaper.

She retracted her extended hand and a torrent of worry swirled within her like a tornado, picking up her father's history, bits of the past, and all of the peril—the risk of not winning the election, her fear of saying the wrong thing—and dashing it against the walls of her brain.

He wasn't looking. She wiped her sweaty palm on her jeans.

"Thank you for coming." Her voice croaked out of her. It didn't sound like her at all.

Stuart rummaged through his bag. "Sorry if I'm running late. I got stuck taking a picture of the park for the story. Just a little 'Adelle is responsible for beautification of the park after volunteering' kind of thing. It looked nice with the sunset. Not that anyone will see it. It's a black-and-white newspaper. But still."

Stuart yanked his hand of his messenger bag, and Adelle grasped it. But he wasn't trying to shake at all. Instead of his hand, she grappled a tape recorder.

She let go and sputtered an awkward laugh. "I'm sorry. Here I am being all thumbs. I don't mean to be so—"

Stuart waved the recorder. "Don't worry about it. This is new. I still make notes, but this frees me up. And everybody gets nervous." He dropped the recorder on the counter. His smile was disarming. "Shall we?"

She took a grateful seat at the counter, across from Stuart, the recorder resting like a ticking bomb between them. Could the recorder tell that her mouth was dry? What if she couldn't speak at all?

He dug through his bag for a green steno pad and slipped his pen from his shirt pocket. When he clicked the pen and poised it over the pad, her head went dark. Every thought she'd had about fixing the town disappeared.

But Stuart flashed that likable smile, and it didn't matter whether she remembered the plan or not. All she had to do was answer the questions and remind people to vote.

"So." Stuart leaned forward and clicked the record button. Little wheels in the recorder went round and round as the tape cataloged their chat. "First, I apologize for not getting here sooner. The town has been so busy the last few weeks."

"Think nothing of it." Not getting there sooner? Part of her wishes he'd never come at all. "Anything exciting?"

She wanted to ask about the mysterious posters promoting annexation that Arvil had ripped off the store windows but thought better of it. No sense shining light on something people may have already forgotten.

Stuart scribbled a line on his steno pad. "Nothing exciting. But this election, huh? What made you run?"

It wouldn't serve her very well to say that she hadn't wanted to at all. Outside, behind Stuart, a flock of crows landed in the street. They picked at pebbles and stray bits of litter. Adelle's eyes fell on the picture of her father, his arms full of flowers.

"The past, I guess. For generations my family has lived in Ramsbolt. Three generations of us have run this flower shop."

"And you have no kids, right? No siblings? So you would be the last generation to run a flower shop here." Pen poised over paper, Stuart's narrowed look begged for more. "Did that play a role in your decision to run for office?"

Adelle shook her head. "Did not having kids impact my decision to run for town manager? No."

"Sorry, I could have worded that better. Rather, does having more time on your hands afford you more opportunities to help the town? Without a family or significant other, you'd be more emotionally free, right?"

Had he been talking to Penny? Why all this focus on her lonely life? "Look, there's nothing lonely about my life, if that's what you're getting at. I have a churning tide of blooming flowers and plants to tend to, and I enjoy it very much. None of them cry or complain. Whether I have more or less time and energy than anyone else didn't factor into my decision to run for office."

A crow pecked at the window, begging for an offering. He fluttered at his own reflection and hopped back to the street.

Stuart tapped his pen on the pad. "You said the past is what drove you to run. Can you expand on that?"

What did he want her to say? That she'd been stuck in old patterns, rehashing the past for so long that she was destined to relive them? That she blamed Meldrick for her father's failures, and her decision to run was a rash one, based on her intense desire to spite the man?

She took a deep breath and held in the hint of gardenia blooms. Maybe Penny had a point. If she had someone else in her life, they'd keep her from doing stupid things like running for office. There'd be more present to her here and now. Maybe she'd be more passionate about the future, if she didn't cling so much to the shapes of the past. But she loved the past.

"The General Store," she said.

Stuart's head snapped up from his notes, one eyebrow arched. "The empty General Store encouraged you to run for office? How so?"

"I sit here every day and look out the window at the General Store. I loved going there when I was a kid. When I was little, we lived on a farm and coming into town for shopping was a big deal. My mom would drag me into the old fabric shop, and I would get tired of waiting for her to pick out what she wanted, so I'd beg her for a quarter. It was a battle of the wills: Mom holding onto every penny for the sake of the future, and me begging for relief from the present. If Mom failed to give in, I knew my grandfather would oblige. I'd slip away and cross the street, weave through his baskets of fruits and veggies, and I'd come in here, into the shop where he'd dig a shiny quarter from behind my ear. Then I'd run back to the General Store. I'd weave through the forest of legs and arms and all those tall adults, and I'd buy a creamsicle."

Across the street, the last of the sunset echoed off the General Store windows. Inside she could see the corner of the old cooler. It had defrosted well over a decade before, and the sun had faded its lettering, but the words *Ice Cream* in red script font still evoked the sting of nostalgia. She could still feel the lid, its handle cool to the touch on the hottest summer day. The sound of the door sliding in its metal track. The rush of icy air as she leaned in, hand straining to reach an orange creamsicle. She could still get them in the market where they were sold in boxes of twelve, but it wasn't the same.

The crows took off in unison, leaving the street deserted.

"A lot has changed since I was a kid, but the feeling of Ramsbolt is still here. I think we need to do everything we can to preserve the best of us while doing better for the future. That's why I'm running."

Stuart nodded. "This is good stuff. Thanks. Next question, then. How does the past inspire your view of the future?"

She blinked at coleus on the shelf, at its wispy roots. "I guess everything I know about life I learned here. Thinking about the old General Store, that's where I learned to make my hardest childhood decisions. I'd step up to that candy table with a dollar in my hand, and I'd have to count down the money I'd spent and tally up the sugar rush. I learned hard lessons about budgeting when it came to Swedish fish. It's not just the places that are precious to me and the truths about life that they taught me, but the fact that they've endured. We have to protect these things."

"But what about progress?"

"What about it? We can have both. Look at how great Penny has been for the community. When she came here and cleaned out Eliza's old store, I was pretty upset to see all that history strewn on the sidewalk. But it all worked out for the better. Growing pains are just that. They hurt for a moment, but we're bigger and stronger in the end." As if on cue, Jake jumped into the window of Penny's Loft and licked his paw.

"But what if Penny hadn't come here. What if it was a dry cleaner or a cell phone store instead?"

She couldn't bear to think of a dry cleaner moving into the General Store, tossing the cooler and candy table onto the street like garbage. It had been hard enough to see Penny, Eliza's own granddaughter, do it with random town relics. What *would* she do if a high-tech business moved in, installed neon lights and fancy screens? What was lost could never be replaced. Once all that history was out of sight, it would only be a matter of time before it was all forgotten. But they were barely more than artifacts now, lying unused in a vacant building waiting for archaeologists to discover them. The world had no need for general stores anymore, for penny candy or quarter ice cream. If someone came along who wanted to bring value, she would have to be the progressive voice the town needed and encourage them to stay, no matter how much her heart hurt with saying goodbye to the past.

"I doubt a dry cleaner would want to set up shop here. Not enough customers. And cell phone stores might find a lack of business, but if a modern high-tech company found its footing here, it would be for the better. We have to strike a balance between modernity and preservation. Look, we have to be practical. We need more businesses, more places for people to work, more opportunities. And no matter how much we love the character of these places, we need people to fix them up, care for them, and make their own mark on the town the way people like Logan and Penny have done. It might be hard to watch it happen. But seeing the history scraped into the trash and replaced with the unknown, however scary it might be, will be far better than watching the decay."

Stuart flipped to a new page of his notepad. "You seem to be talking about a new era for Ramsbolt. What uniquely suits you to be the person to usher it in?"

Her dad smiled at her from his place beside the door. She returned the smile, and Stuart spun to follow her line of sight. He pointed with his pen. "That's your dad, right?"

She nodded. "Yeah. He was before your time here, I think."

"He was. I never met him. But people say you're the best one for the job because you saw him do it for so long. Do you plan to follow in his footsteps in the town manager role and run the town the way he did?"

Adelle leaned back. "Emphatically, no. The town has changed since then. Our needs have changed, and there are things he tried to do that... Back in the 90s, more people lived here, and we were better off. We'd just experienced a steep decline in our economy after a big box store moved in half an hour from here. Dad wanted to put through a tax, just a small one, but everyone opposed it. It wouldn't have hurt the town nearly as much as it would today. If he had gone through with it, the town might be in better shape now. It's arguable. But no one ever makes progress by spending all their time in the past. Dad learned that town culture was very important to the people of Ramsbolt, that's why the plan I'm unveiling at the town meeting aims to keep our culture intact without putting through a tax. It's important we learn from the past without getting stuck in it."

The door swished open, and Penny stepped in, a glass of white wine in her hand. Stuart spun to face her.

Penny walked back. "I'm so sorry. I didn't know you were doing an interview. Hi, Stuart."

Stuart nodded and tucked his pen in his shirt pocket. "It's no problem. I have to run anyway. Tight deadline tonight." He reached for the recorder and paused. "One more question, though. You said you're unveiling a plan at the meeting. There's no chance I can get you to spill some details, can I?"

Adelle shook her head. Stuart was nice, and everyone trusted him, but she wasn't giving up control of her message that easily. "Not a chance. It's a surprise."

Stuart shoved his steno pad and recorder back in his bag. "I didn't think so. It's the perfect hook to get people to go to the meeting, anyway." He slung his bag over his shoulder and stepped out the door. "Thanks for your time."

"You, too. Thanks."

Penny plopped down in Stuart's empty seat. She propped her chin in her hand. "Plan? You have a plan?"

Adelle folded her hands on the counter and smiled. "Yeah, I do."

"I came to tell you that Nate's grilling burgers out back. We're drinking wine out of a box. You should come and tell us about this plan."

Adelle glanced over her shoulder at her ancient laptop, where it charged on a shelf. "It's a great offer, but I shouldn't. I have a lot of work to do to prepare for the town hall meeting."

"Fair enough. But I still want to know about this plan!" Penny's eyes were wide. She slapped a hand on the counter and wine swished in her glass. "Come on. This is great news, and you're so calm about it. Tell me the details."

"I am calm. I don't know why. Maybe because I was panicked for so long about whether I'd be good at the job or if people would treat me the way they did Dad. Having a plan helps." She pointed across the street. "Know all that empty real estate out there? The town owns it, and I have a plan to lease it out."

Penny took a sip of her wine and gulped a beat too early. She wiped her lower lip with the back of her hand. "The town owns all that? I had no idea." A slow realization spread across Penny's face. "And you want to lease it out. So you would charge less than Arvil?"

"Dirt cheap. We get a subsidy from the state because we're small and poor. But we have to give it right back to pay property tax on those empty buildings. If we charged more for rent than we have to pay in taxes, that would go in our pocket."

"I get it. Then we could make small improvements."

"Exactly. We can fix the sewer and the roads, improve the quality of life for the people here, so they would see an immediate result. And it would make starting a business here more attractive."

"If I wanted to start a small business, and I had a few towns to choose from, an incentive like that would draw me in."

Adelle let out a sigh. "Maybe not every business owner, but the kind of people who like to be invested in the town where they live, sure. And since all our flaws are out in the open, we won't set unrealistic expectations. We'd be attractive to just the right types of businesses."

"I'm sold." Penny swirled wine in her glass. "How do you convince the rest of the town?"

"Arvil may not go for it." Adelle threw her elbows on the counter and picked at a hangnail. "Meldrick will be impossible to convince."

"Only because he's an impossible person. We'll be there, at the meeting. And Logan. And Grey. We can clap really loud and ask leading questions so you can get your plan across, if that helps."

"It might. It definitely helps to see a friendly face. Especially after last time. But showing them the plan is the easy part. Telling them why we need it is something else. I don't think people know we own this stuff or how bad the finances really are. Even people who think they know how much we struggle don't really know the jeopardy we're in. And I'm afraid they'll turn on Morgan or blame my dad."

"Wait. Do you mean that nobody here knows what the town's finances look like? I don't, but I'm not a political person or anything." Penny arched an eyebrow. "I remember when I lived in Otley, they put out a little magazine every year with the budget in it. It wasn't interesting, but it had some pretty pictures of the parks."

"Right." Adelle stuck her hands in her back pockets. Guilt swelled within her, even though the poor communication wasn't her fault. "Well, I guess nobody felt the need to ask. Nobody ever cared. It's not like we can afford a glossy magazine, and finances are a pretty dry topic. But the town needs to know, so that has to change."

"Oof. I see what you mean about awkward. With Morgan standing right there, trying to explain why the town has no money? He'll understand that people have to know, and I don't think anybody will be mad at him."

"They were pretty brutal last week."

Penny took a sip of wine and squinted into her emptying glass. "True. But he's young, and everyone likes him. I think people will forgive him."

"I hope so. Ramsbolt has always been a hands-off kind of place. That's a good thing sometimes, but transparency is important. It doesn't matter if you can trust the town manager or not. It's…I guess it's about personal responsibility. We all need to be invested."

Penny put a hand on Adelle's arm. "You're doing what no one here has done before. It might not be easy, but it'll be worth it. I gotta run. Dinner. But don't you dare back down on this. This is a great idea."

The door clicked to a close behind Penny, and Adelle was left alone with her plants and her plan. A slow car went by, its headlights shining off the windows of empty storefronts. If she got her way, their days of isolation were numbered. Penny, Adelle, and Nate would have neighbors. People would move in with their own agendas, their own ideas about what Ramsbolt should be, and they could very well throw all their keepsakes in the trash. It would be their right to start fresh and build new. The cooler, the candy table, all laid to ruin.

Adelle's eyes welled with tears, and she let them fall. She was finally free to be the sentimental fool her heart always steered her to be.

Saying goodbye to the past was hard enough. She'd said goodbye to so much of it over the years, most of the time she'd been kicking and screaming. Now she had to embrace it, encourage the rest of the town to want it as much as she did. It was an unnatural leap, and it would be the first personal challenge of many, if they wanted her to have the job. Even with charts and graphics and hard numbers, the people of Ramsbolt might be too blind—too willfully blind—to hear what she had to say.

Adelle locked the door and settled back on her grandfather's stool. She cut a length of paper from the roll and started another sketch, however unrefined, preserving the town of her memories in blueprints of the past.

# CHAPTER TWENTY-FOUR

Adelle's hunt for poster board and markers was incomplete without coffee. She pushed open the door to Marissa's bakery. The air was thick with vanilla and spice but void of sound. The tables were empty, but it was in the morning and hardly time for bagels and cupcakes. She called out.

"Marissa? You here?" The door clicked to a close behind her. She stepped to the counter and slipped a paper cup from the stack. "I'm grabbing coffee!"

Marissa emerged from the back, a tray of sunflower cookies balanced in one hand. She slid them into the display. "Help yourself."

Adelle tossed her purse on the counter. "Large, please?"

Marissa pressed buttons on her register.

Adelle handed her three ones from her wallet. "Keep the change."

"People have been talking about that last town hall meeting like there's nothing else going on around here."

Coffee spurted into Adelle's cup from the carafe. She tore open a sugar packet with more force than she needed and white confetti sprayed across the counter. She brushed it into the trash.

She'd finally started to forget about how horrible she'd been at the meeting. Scribbling the first hints of a plan had soothed the aching shame, and she'd been more energized about being town manager than she'd been since she lost her temper in Meldrick's doorway.

*So much for that*, she thought.

Marissa hadn't meant to rip the wound open again, but there it was. She couldn't run from it, so she stirred what remained of the sugar into her cup with a thin piece of splintered wood and turned to face it.

"I really should apologize to everybody." She threw the stirrer in the trash.

"Why?" Marissa bit into a macaron.

"Losing my temper and screaming at the town doesn't make me very electable." She blew into the coffee. Steam swirled and lost itself in vanilla-thick air.

"Nah. I thought you were brilliant. There were a few Meldrick fans who believed what he said back in the day, but they're the people who feed on drama. It's a validation thing."

"What do you mean, validation thing?" The coffee was still too hot to drink.

"Meldrick didn't really care whether he got the job or not. He just needed validation for his outrage, so he ran around trying to convince people to join him in hating your dad. The more people he could convince, the better he felt about himself."

Adelle snorted. "What about all the people who believed him and jumped on the bandwagon? What do they get out of it?"

"It just gave them permission to express outrage. You've never been outraged about something after hearing one side of the story?" Marissa shrugged. "It's human nature. Meldrick stated a case, and asked them to take a side, so they did. Everybody does it about crap they read in the news every day. I was just pissed about something I saw on Twitter that wasn't even about me. But lots of people in here yesterday said they never trusted him again after he ran a hate campaign against your dad." She wrinkled her nose and shook her head. "I mean, who does that?"

"I've heard that line from people before, and I call bullshit." Adelle blew on her coffee. "What do they call it? Revisionist history? They say…Oh, I never believed him. But no one bothered to stick up for him. Not once."

Marissa cocked her head to the side and gave her a sympathetic half smile. "Your dad was so nice. Meldrick caused a bunch of unnecessary drama that wasn't founded on anything. He should have talked to your dad directly. You're right. If people really believed that, they should have said something at the time. Or voted for him instead of electing Meldrick to a job he didn't even want."

Instead, her father retreated from the world and died alone. Adelle took in a breath of sweet bakery air and let it out in a deep sigh. "I really need to stop thinking about it. It's been years, and it's hard to put this behind me." If she didn't, she could lose the election and Ramsbolt with it.

"I know it's hard from where you are, but people don't think about it as much as you do. Most people have forgotten it." She shrugged. "Maybe they didn't know what to say. They didn't know your dad was upset or that he needed support."

"Whatever they thought, he needed support and didn't get it. He needed a friend." And she'd needed people to show up for his funeral, but after everything that had happened, she wouldn't have wanted to see them there anyway with their fake sympathy.

Marissa dropped a blueberry muffin on the counter and nudged it with her fingertip. "It's all water under the bridge now. Treat?"

Adelle gave her a sad but grateful smile. "No thanks. I'm not sure it is water under the bridge, though. I keep thinking about those signs Adler put up. Where do you think that idea came from?"

Marissa shook her head and gave her a smile that was probably meant to be reassuring. She gestured toward the window. "I have no idea. Adler probably heard about it from some network of town managers. I haven't seen any since, though. They're all gone now. Disappeared before the dew was off the grass."

"Do you think Meldrick is behind it?"

"Dell, so what if he was. It's a new era. You have to put all that stuff behind you."

Adelle chewed on a jagged nail. "You're right. Whatever prompted it doesn't change my course."

Marissa leaned on the counter. "You *deserve* to put it behind you. You don't have to carry this forever. It seems heavy. You should put it down."

The coffee was finally cool enough to sip. Marissa had a point, it was too heavy. She'd love to put it down and walk away from it, but there was no instruction manual for letting go of things that stuck to her. Sometimes the anger and pain of it all felt like their own entity, feeding off her to stay alive.

"Well, the town didn't deserve for me to yell at them."

Marissa rolled her eyes. "Hell, yes, they did. They got what they deserved. Now you get the healing you deserve. Justice will be served when you win that election."

She wrapped her hands around the cup. "Thanks for the chat. I gotta run. Errands."

"No problem. I meant what I said. Don't you dare apologize."

Adelle tugged the door open. "That's good advice. I have a plan to fix all our problems and put money in our pockets, which is much better than an apology, anyway."

"A plan?" Marissa leaned forward, expectant, her eyes wide and jaw dropped. Adelle didn't give her time to beg for details. She waved goodbye, plunged onto the sidewalk and crossed the street. Outside the newsstand, her name caught her eye, red lettering on the white sign. There was something out-of-body and oddly adult about it. It really was real. She was running for office and had a plan to fix the town.

Warren kept his poster board in the back of the store, where it hung from angled racks. There were six pieces of white foam core, one with a dinged corner. She took them all and a jumbo box of magic markers up to the counter, where Mack and Lewis held court over Warren, change jingling and rattling keys in their pockets.

She threw everything on the counter.

"Warren. How are you today?" She dug in her purse for her wallet.

"Just fine." Warren drawled his vowels. "The sun came up, and I got out of bed with it. Best I can ask for."

"That's a great perspective." She handed over her debit card, and Warren swiped it through the machine.

"Those flowers for Jaleesa were quite nice," said Mack. "Brightened up the whole town."

Lewis' eyebrows were raised, his forehead lined. "I still can't mow my lawn for that fence all up in it."

Adelle accepted her bank card and receipt from Warren, who winked at her knowingly. There'd be no pleasing Lewis and Mack. "Seems to me you have a problem with your neighbor then, Lewis. We've all learned our lesson about addressing our problems with people, right? I bet if you talked to them directly, you'd see some forward momentum."

Mack hiked up his pants and smoothed his belt over his generous frame, his mouth twisted in a grin. "Lesson, huh? You teaching one at the school with your markers? Making posters?"

Lewis threw out an elbow and nudged him. "She's gonna save the town with arts and crafts."

The two men dissolved into giggles. She shoved the markers in her purse and threw the boards under her arm.

"I do have a plan. But it's got nothing to do with arts and crafts." She nodded at Warren. "Thanks. See you soon."

She paused on her way out the door to zip her purse. If Mack tried to lower his voice, his fading hearing got in the way. "She's not strong enough to be the town judge and jury. We need someone with gumption to throw down the gauntlet."

The bell rang out when she opened the door and stepped onto the sidewalk.

"You don't think I'm strong enough?" she said to herself. "Watch me."

# CHAPTER TWENTY-FIVE

Adelle flicked the switch, and light flooded the counter. Penny and Nate pushed a dozen little terra-cotta pots of coleus against the wall.

"Thanks for helping me with this." She shuffled the foam core signs, plucked out one with a hand-drawn map, and dropped it on the counter.

Penny dumped the box of markers next to it, and Nate snagged the green one as it rolled his way.

"Perfect." He pulled off the cap, and the sour smell of ink saturated the air. "Reminds me of childhood. I can't remember the last time I used these things."

"Me either." Adelle grabbed a red marker and jammed the cap onto the end. She colored in a vacant building. "They still smell the same, though."

Penny yanked the cap off a brown marker and colored in the church. "Some things never change."

"Do you have an extra poster board lying around?" Nate highlighted the edges of the park and drew squiggles where the trees lived. "I could do a rendering to show what Main Street could look like if all the stores were full. You know, like those real estate things you see in the paper with cars, and trendy shoppers carrying thirty bags."

"I do have an extra. That would be really neat! Is there enough time, though? The town hall meeting is tomorrow." Adelle exchanged her red marker for a black one and outlined an empty store.

"It may not be elaborate, but it would give me something to do this afternoon."

Penny leaned over the board, shading in shops on Main Street. "It would get their attention, too. If they're busy processing visuals, they'll be less likely to come up with reasons to object. How are you, though? Nervous?"

"A lot less nervous than I was before I had a plan. It's the election I'm worried about." Adelle filled the hardware store with brown ink. Worried was an understatement, but she couldn't find strong enough words to explain the constant churning in her stomach. It didn't help that she'd been awake all night, cleaning every inch of the store, wondering how long she could hang onto the shop, her home, and life as she knew it if she lost the election.

The door flew open, and Logan stepped in, Grey behind her. A duffle bag fell from her shoulder to the floor with a thud, and she walked the counter.

"Got the urgent text and looked around my place. I don't have any markers, but I'm here to help." With narrowed eyes, her head tilted, she looked down at the poster. "What's going on? I just didn't realize we'd be working on our senior year science fair project."

Penny brushed red hair from her eyes. She tapped another brown marker, and it rolled Logan's way. "We're helping with posters for the town hall tomorrow. All these buildings with brown dots get colored in."

Logan caught the marker before it rolled off the counter. "Thank

God. Because I'm definitely the wrong girl to help with anything related to the endocrine system."

Adelle shuffled to the side, making room for Grey and Logan. "Thanks for your help, guys. I'd never get all these done on my own."

Grey stepped up to the counter. "So what is all this?"

"Since you're all here." Adelle stood and stretched. "This is my plan to save the town. All these buildings with red dots are vacant."

Grey leaned further over the poster and put a finger on a red dot. "Yeah. This place was a shoe store. It's been empty since I was in middle school."

"The town owns it now." Adelle snagged a red marker and handed it to Grey. "All those red dots are owned by the town. And we have to colored them in."

"Wait. The town owns these properties? The Griffins owned it forever. They lived upstairs. I think I was eleven when he passed away, then she went to a retirement place in Colby. How does the town own it?"

Adelle brushed hair behind her ear. "Anything abandoned becomes property of the town after five years. The state sends us the tax bill, and we turn around and pay it from the subsidies we get."

"So basically we could have school lunches and buses and everything we want, if we don't have to pay all that property tax," said Penny.

"Technically. Eventually. It would take a while to go from debt to income, but yeah." Those were other hills to climb, and they were for another day.

"I wouldn't know where to start." Nate shifted around the poster and added trees to the cemetery. He nodded to the stack of posters leaning against the wall. "I saw the prices and everything. The rent escalations, you called it? How are you going to get businesses to take over these places?"

Adelle's late-night crash courses in real estate and economic development had given her a lot of ideas. She traded her brown marker for a red one and colored in an empty store. "I hope people from Ramsbolt will want to start their own businesses. We'll definitely have to advertise outside town, too. There are plenty of places to do that. And the state promotes incentives to businesses looking to expand. Marketing the shops and the town will be pretty easy, I think. A lot of people will find us attractive, as a place to get in on the ground floor."

Other than making a general plan, she tried not to think about the what-ifs and why-nots. What worried her most were the inevitable squabbles once the town had money in the bank. Some things would be easy to prioritize; Diane needed the sewer fixed a year ago. But the rest would be a balancing act, managing the expectations of restless neighbors.

"It's fun to dream, isn't it?" Logan colored in the outdoor store. "I'd love to have a bunch of stores here. Not that I can afford to shop in any of them."

"But maybe you would if more people spent money on things." Grey bit the cap of his red marker, leaned on his elbows, and colored in the old shoe store. "I would love to have an appliance shop around. Every time there's a water heater emergency, I either have to make people wait while I order a new one or I have to drive way out of town."

"I want a craft store," Adelle said. "Sometimes I just need the right kind of glue or a little decorative thing for an arrangement, and I don't want to order it online and wait for it. I want to walk down the street, browse some shelves, and pick something."

"I was never very crafty." Penny shook her marker and tackled another square. "But Lord, I want a restaurant. Nothing fancy. Just a place to get some comfort food. Mac and cheese, meatloaf, lobster rolls, chowder."

"Nachos," Logan said. "I want nachos."

"A real coffee shop." Nate didn't look up from the garden he drew behind the tea shop. "Not that Marissa isn't awesome, but a real coffee shop with shelves of books and bags of coffee beans and rows of mismatched mugs so you'd have a favorite. And wood tables that are never quite level, so they wobble, but you never touch them because you're busy with a book or a newspaper. That's what I want."

Penny nudged his elbow. "You should open one."

"No way," he said. "Too much work. There are all those food service rules and health inspectors. Toy stores are super easy. You just sell what kids like and parents will buy."

"I would love to open a store." Logan shuffled around the poster to color in vacant buildings along Levering. "Maybe a liquor store."

Penny shifted to give her room. "That's a great idea."

Logan capped her marker and tucked it behind her ear. She scanned the map and tapped an empty shop between the market and the tea house. "Right here. It's the perfect spot."

"You should do it," said Grey. "How much rent are you talking about, Adelle?"

"I could never afford it." Logan pulled the marker from behind her ear and colored her way down Main Street.

Adelle went to the stack of finished posters and found the one with the prices. She leaned it on the counter, against the wall. "Here ya go.

The column on the left is how much the state charges us in property tax. To the right is an estimate of what we'd charge in rent for a year. Every year after, that rent goes up a little. This column shows how much profit the town would get the first year it's rented out. It's all just estimates, and there would be increases over time. Every building is different. Some need more work than others. And different types so businesses tend to pay different types of rent. All of that would be factored in."

"What do you mean?" asked Grey. "Sorry, I've never had to pay rent like that."

"She means that some businesses pay per square foot, some pay a low flat rental rate plus a percentage of their profit. That kind of thing." Logan looked up at the board. "I learned a lot from listening to my dad over the years. Hey, that little shop by the tea house would be six hundred dollars a month. I could swing that. Not right now, but someday. I'd have to save up some money, and I'd have to make enough profit to pay an employee to help with it, so I don't have to quit the tavern."

"Would it cut into profit at the tavern if we had a liquor store?" Adelle asked.

"Nah. We only sell beer to go. That's all beer, though. If I opened a store that sold wine and liquor, I'd have all the markets cornered."

Penny stood and stretched. "People will always want to go out for drinks. We enjoy the walk, and it's nice to see people. Even Arvil goes to the bar, and he hates people. Man, it's hard hunching over that counter. I don't know how you do it all day."

"Luckily, I don't stand like this often," said Adelle. "You know, Logan, you could always find an investor to help you get started."

Grey tapped his temple with the end of his marker. "That's along the lines I was thinking. We could always move in together to help you save some money, too.”

“For real, Grey?” Logan’s smile was sarcastic. She cocked an eyebrow. “That’s how you want to take our relationship to another level? A totally unromantic, casual gesture that’s entirely financially motivated.” She shrugged. “I’d consider it.”

“Seriously. I could help you with the store rent and be an investor. Think about it. If you weren’t paying Warren for that apartment, you’d have your rent money right there.”

“Then I’d have to buy inventory to stock the shelves.”

“You could get a small business loan,” said Nate. “Everybody at the bank knows you.”

“You guys are making this sound doable.” Logan stood and looked down at the poster. “I could do this. I would definitely pay you back, Grey. And I’ll think about that moving in together thing.”

“Looks like Warren’s about to lose some rental income.” Penny shot a coy smile at Nate.

Adelle put the finishing touches on the rectangle that used to be the General Store. “I bet it won’t sit empty for long. Not if there are more jobs and opportunities in town to be had. There’ll always be a need for Warren’s little penthouse suite.”

# CHAPTER TWENTY-SIX

Adelle patted her back pocket to be sure the notecards with her talking points were still there. If she lost those she'd be…lost. The posters were safe in the black portfolio case she borrowed from Nate. They banged against her leg as she trudged to the library.

With her head down, she slipped past cliques of residents on the sidewalk. It was hard enough to focus on what she had to say. The last thing she needed was to be dragged into a casual conversation and lose her concentration. She'd end up standing on stage, staring blankly at the back wall, wishing someone would put her out of her misery.

The door was open and a warm, orange light spilled out onto the porch. Inside, Sandy rested behind her desk.

"Hi, Adelle." Sandy stood. "You look nervous. Are you nervous? I would be."

Adelle painted on a smile. It felt shaky. "To be honest, I am. I think it's just general public speaking anxiety."

Her anxiety was anything but general. There were a hundred specifics. Fear of ridicule. Fear that people would blame her father for the debt, for not acting when he had the chance. Fear that they'd turn on

Morgan, who had done his best with a tough situation. The shame of having yelled at the town during the last meeting. The only way to rise above it was to keep things positive and stick to her plan.

"You'll get over that with time. A few more of these and you'll be great." Sandy held out a slip of yellow paper. "Would you like a list of our events for this autumn? We have a lot going on. Marissa and I are working on an apple pie contest for October."

"Um, sure." She slipped the paper into her pocket. Movement caught her eye; Penny and Nate waving by the stairs. "You're probably right about the nerves. Once I get set up, I'll feel better."

"You will. Oh, and if you could mention those events, it would be a huge help. People just aren't as into the library as they used to be. I'm hoping apple pie will help. Outside of course, on the porch. Pie and books are a bad combination." Sandy drew a line across her throat. "Anyway, Morgan always mentions the events."

Adelle patted her back pocket. "Got it. I'll try to remember."

Penny and Nate were gone when she turned to the stairs. She descended alone.

The familiar smell of damp concrete and cheap coffee hurled her backward thirty years. She'd always be that shy little girl who'd rather be reading but was dragged instead to her father's meetings to sit with her hands folded in her lap. Now the roles had reversed. It was her turn to cradle the facts in her hands, to offer them up like communion, and hope the people cared enough about their souls to bite. What she wouldn't give to see her father in the crowd, hands folded in his lap.

She wound through clumps of people, the portfolio at her side. Her fingers found the necklace beneath her white button-down shirt. She needed all the comfort she could get.

*Stupid charm*, she thought to herself. *Not much help in the bravery department.*

She found a chair in the front row, on the end, and dropped her purse on the floor.

*Debt, income, prosperity. Debt, income, prosperity. That's all you have to remember.* She patted her back pocket. *Just read the notecards.*

"You look relaxed." Logan slid into the seat next to her. Penny and Nate inched down the second row to sit behind her, Styrofoam cups of steaming coffee in their hands.

"If I look relaxed, it's because I'm succeeding at faking it. Have you seen an easel?" She scanned the front of the room. "Morgan said there'd be an easel. I can't mess it up too badly, can I? The election's tomorrow, so there's only so much time for people to parse everything." Her eyes fell on the easel behind the lectern, collapsed. She unfolded it. "Should mention Bloomburg and the threat of being turned over to another town? I should."

"Don't you dare. It'll sound like fear-mongering. It'll remind them that they have a quick fix." Logan unzipped the portfolio and extracted Nate's rendering of Main Street. In it, a woman in jeans and a sweater, her arms covered in bags and her hair flowing in the breeze, stepped out of a store beneath an awning that shaded cafe tables on the sidewalk. She held it out to Adelle. "Like we talked about. Keep it positive. Anyway, I meant that you look relaxed despite the buttons."

"What buttons?" She placed the rendering on the display.

Logan handed her the rest of the sorted posters. Adelle sorted them, looking for the one with very large numbers that showed the very small numbers Ramsbolt had in its checking account. She placed it facing outward. There was no use saving the truth for the right moment. The more time she had for it to sink in, the better.

"Whoa." Logan stood back, her arms folded. "I never thought I'd have more money in my bank account than Ramsbolt does. Anyway, what I was saying about the buttons? You need to look around."

Adelle scanned the room. People chatted in little clusters. Some sipped coffee, others sought chairs or leaned against the walls, holding bottles of water. Half of them, maybe more, were wearing blue and white buttons. Glossy buttons about two inches in diameter. Renee Sommerwill fell into a seat in the second row, beside Nate, a button affixed to her Guns N' Roses T-shirt. Adelle returned her faint neighborly smile and tried not to stare but caught enough letters to make it all out. *Meldrick for Manager.*

A bitter bile rose in her throat, and her hands began to sweat. Her vision clouded. She turned her head and faced the empty lectern to hide her shock. Surely Meldrick was in the crowd, waiting for her reaction.

She should have known he'd pull some trick, stick some well-used knife in her back and publicly humiliate her. Was Adler in the crowd? Was he behind this?

Sour acid churned in her stomach, a boil of ire. A rush of heat came over her, but she couldn't let anyone see her sweat. She lowered herself into the seat next to Logan and clutched her notecards to keep her hand still.

She'd spent years preparing for the shock of Meldrick Lacey, avoiding him on the streets and in the stores. But nothing could prepare her for the shock of half the town supporting that man for a second time, after what he did to her father to get the job he then abandoned.

She straightened her shoulders and reasoned with her shaky insides. Meldrick was entitled to run for the job. Anyone was. There was nothing she could do about it. She would just have to let her message speak for itself.

Beside her, Logan leaned in. "You have tons of support. Penny and Nate are here. Grey is running late, but he's on his way. Warren and Jaleesa are in the back. Even Arvil was here early. Everyone who matters is here to support you. Just...stick to your plan. Show them the money and what you want to do."

Adelle nodded. "I got this." Her eyes felt hot. Why did her eyes feel hot?

The room grew quiet around her. What was the worst that could happen? Meldrick would call her names? Make jokes about her posters? She felt for the necklace, seeking solace in its warmth.

Morgan stepped up to the lectern. "Hey, everybody. We had a second candidate join the race this week. My dad. Meldrick, I mean. Adelle will speak first, since she threw her hat in the ring first. Before we get started, just a reminder that voting is from eight to eight tomorrow in the church. Heather is packing a lunch this year so she won't have to lock up for an hour in the afternoon. The winner will be announced in the town park at nine, so everybody meet at the sailor statue. Okay? Adelle, you ready?"

Her heart snapped like a broken rubber band, and all the heat and sour fell away. It didn't matter anymore. If the town wanted Meldrick as its manager, they could have him, but this was the last moment the button-wearing Meldrick fans who spread gossip about her father would be able to rest easy without the knowledge that she was about to drop. If she only had one moment to avenge her father's memory and plead her own case, then she was going to use it to tell them the truth. Without emotion or affect.

"Thanks, Morgan." Her voice was loud and crisp. She stepped up to the lectern and pointed to her first sign. "This number? This is our current bank balance."

Small gasps and murmurs broke out in the crowd, but Adelle didn't give them time to interrupt. She flipped to the next sign.

"Here's why. This chart shows how much money Ramsbolt makes each year. It's not much. This red line is money going out. We owe more to the state each year than we get from them in subsidies. Something needs to change if you want to avoid an income tax."

She flipped to the map of empty stores, with Grey's childhood shoe store shaded red and the town park colored green by Nate. She glanced Penny's way and mirrored her smile.

"But I have a plan. Ramsbolt has gone through a lot of changes over the years. If you're old enough to recall the jewelry store, the old sewing machine repair place, or the luncheonette, you're probably old enough to remember when we weren't in such disrepair. All those stores are empty now. You may not know that the town owns these properties." She flipped to the next sign. "And these numbers? This is what we owe the state just for having empty real estate. And then there's the danger of falling shutters and ancient windows covered in lead paint, liabilities the town must shoulder."

She caught Arvil's eye, and he winked.

"The subsidies we get should stay here in Ramsbolt. We shouldn't be handing back the money they intend for our kids and streets and improvements. More of our neighbors should be successful. We should have tenants living in these apartments and shops that we want to visit. We should be able to fix these streets, add new streetlights, and buy a lawn mower to maintain the park. We deserve infrastructure and a savings account to fix what breaks. And if we don't do this for our town and our future, we'll have no one to blame but ourselves when another town has to take over, because we never tried to save ourselves."

She defied Logan's advice, proud of herself for stating the stakes. She dropped the sign to the floor. The next showed a list of the properties, the amount of tax charged by the state, the rent they could charge, and how much the town could profit.

"We may not be able to fend off a town tax forever, but we can make it less painful if our economy improves. I propose renting out these town-owned properties to generate some profit. A lot of them need work. We'll make arrangements with tenants on a case-by-case basis, to reward them for the improvements they make. The town board we elected to help with the festival can help with the application process, and in the end, the town will have income, we can afford some of the initiatives you've proposed over the years, and our kids will be able to thrive here. They can start their own businesses with the support of the whole town."

She scanned the faces, looking for hints of support. Arvil wore the faintest of smiles, but pleasing Arvil didn't mean she'd pleased the town. She dreaded to ask, but she had to.

"Does anyone have any questions?"

"I have a comment." Carol stood. "I never knew the town owned these properties. All the time Diane has needed the sewer fixed and no one thought to offload this? Renting it out makes more sense than sitting on it. I would be willing to offer a discount from the hardware store to new tenants, to help with the cost of some materials if it means we can get some actual work done around here."

Adelle warmed at the first words of support. "That's really nice of you, Carol. I'm sure we can work something out so you aren't stretched too thin."

Grey raised his hand. "This might sound kinda dumb, but now that we all know the situation, we have to take some responsibility for it, right? Like Carol just did. I'm just a plumber, but I can flush the lines for free and remove any old tanks if it helps get some of these places back into shape. I can do a discount on some labor costs, too."

"Thank you, Grey."

Arvil cleared his throat and every head snapped to attention. He wagged his finger at Adelle. "You can already see the secondary benefit to your plan. People are already more invested in the town's success. I'm on that committee, and I take very seriously the role I will play in shaping what the town will look like in the future."

A man in the front row spun in his seat to face Arvil. "Isn't this a competition for you? Shouldn't you recuse yourself from the committee?"

Arvil snarled. "Renting out retail spaces next to mine at a fraction of the cost does compete with my business interests. Maybe you think I should step down, but I'm smarter than you think I am. If Ramsbolt doesn't survive, my real estate won't have any value. We're hardly competition. Renters who don't want to put in the sweat equity are welcome to rent from me." Arvil scanned the crowd. "Marissa!"

Marissa turned in her seat, her eyes wide and back stiff with alarm.

"You'll benefit from this," said Arvil. "You and Diane with the tea. Stores will want grand openings."

Marissa relaxed and nodded, relief washing the worry from her face. "That's true. I absolutely support this plan. I look across the street at an empty store every day, and I swear some of those bricks are loose. I didn't know we had all that liability. Some stranger could come in on their way through town and stop to use the bathroom and BAM." She clapped, and people jumped. In the front row, Barbara clutched the neck of her white sweater. "We could be sued. This is bad, people."

Spurred on by their interest, especially from Arvil who was hard to please and always took the negative view, running it through his mental calculator and multiplying it, she stepped in front of the podium. "That's exactly right. Exactly. It's a huge liability. That's why we need to work as a team."

Morgan cleared his throat and tapped his watch. Her time was up.

She'd done it. She'd made her case and told the town the truth. It was up to them now, to take control of their own fate. Meldrick leaned against the wall, his arms folded, and a sarcastic sneer etched on his face. All the anger she'd felt toward him melted away, through the soles of her feet, into the floor, off to wherever anger went when it finally wore out its welcome. She basked in the lightness of it all: the meeting, her plan, and the buoyancy of not caring about Meldrick.

"Morgan says my time is up. Thanks for listening. Oh." She dug Sandy's slip of paper from her pocket and waved it. "Sandy asked me to tell you about the fall events. There's an apple pie thing in October. Anyway, I'm out of time, but check out the bulletin board on your way out."

She could have slammed Meldrick for his role in the past. She could have made promises she'd rather not keep. But she took her seat knowing her father would be proud, that she held herself to her own standards. And if it wasn't good enough for the town, at least she would know that she had done her best.

Logan patted her knee. She watched without animosity as her enemy stepped up to do battle, for she'd already won the war.

"Thanks, Kid." Meldrick gripped the podium. "Look, this plan she cooked up is ridiculous. The board wasn't elected for that purpose. They were elected to vote on an art festival so people could stop and look at crap on their way through town. You can't expect the guy who bags your groceries to know what's best for the town."

"Hey!" Sean bolted upright in his seat. "I would do it. I would serve on that committee. I want a music shop. I want to buy records, and I want a place to teach guitar lessons."

Helen leaned forward on her cane. She'd owned a diner for most of her life and converted it to a tavern when the economy tanked. Now she owned the pub that Logan ran and enjoyed a retirement that was easy on her knees. She waved a finger at Meldrick from her first-row seat, and the town fell silent. "Look here, young man. Only two new people have moved here in years: Logan, who chose Ramsbolt because it was so dang small, and Penny who was financially handcuffed to her grandmother's store. Kids leave as fast as they can."

Adelle leaned toward Logan. "What's she doing? She's interrupting."

Logan winked. "She's not interrupting. She's filibustering. He only has ten minutes."

"Your own son is running out of town," Helen continued. "And he already has a great job doing the one you should have done. Every couple that gets engaged here ties the knot and heads for the hills."

"You're proving my point, Helen." Meldrick folded his arms. "No one here spends enough money to support new stores."

Helen stood, her weight on her shaky cane. "Penny's festival proved you wrong. People stop here when there's a reason."

Meldrick threw his arms in the air. "Who's gonna show up here in the dead of winter to buy a used record?”

“Riley? You say something, huh? Speak up.” Helen patted the postman’s shoulder. When he stood, he seemed ten feet tall.

“Meldrick, you gotta trust this town to grow. I don’t wanna leave, but I’ll have to if some other town takes over. And when I go, one less person will be buying from the market or Marissa’s bakery. I can’t buy cement from Carol to fix my sidewalk if I live in Vermont.”

“If we have a tax, I’ll have to go.” Grey shook his head, and his dark curly hair bobbed. “I’ll take Logan with me if she’ll come. She can tend a bar anywhere.”

“See what you’d do?” Helen tilted her cane in Meldrick’s direction. “You’d put a poor old woman back behind a bar that has less patrons than ever in it. What kind of great plan do you have? Other than folding your arms and leering at people?”

Meldrick held up his hands, asking for calm. “There are options we haven’t even explored that could increase property values and make Ramsbolt a better place.”

Arvil stood. “Is that the smart idea you had with those signs?”

Meldrick shaded his hands with his eyes, as if Arvil were a mile away and the light too bright. “What signs?”

“Don’t play coy with me. You put signs around town. About annexation. Caught you on a camera. You think I don’t know how to connect a camera to Wi-Fi? You hung up those posters. Your idea of an option is making Ramsbolt disappear.”

“Dad.” Morgan tapped his watch. “Time is up.”

Meldrick shooed his son away. “No, you’ve got it wrong, old man. I did put up those signs, but only because handing this town to another Faulkner is the fastest way to tank it.”

Morgan stepped up to the lectern and pushed his father aside. "Time is up for our candidates, guys."

"Just one more thing I gotta say about letting her run the town. Her father could have fixed all this back when—"

"Dad. I gotta be fair." Morgan gave his father a nudge. "Time is up. Good meeting, huh? Okay. We need a volunteer to count ballots with Heather tomorrow after eight o'clock."

Grey raised his hand. "I'll do it. I'll be down that end of Main Street anyway."

"Thanks, Grey. See you all tomorrow."

Adelle's legs were glued to the chair. Of course he'd take one last swing. She swallowed the lump in her throat and let it glance off her. She stuffed her notecards into her back pocket.

Logan nudged her knee. "You did it. Great job!"

"Thanks. Now I get to rehash every syllable."

The finality of the moment that sat in her like a lead weight. There was nothing else she could do, nothing more she could say that would convince them all to look up at the coming storm and build a shelter.

Morgan, however, looked light as a feather. He grabbed his messenger bag from the floor and moved through the crowd and up the stairs. Adelle couldn't get away that easily. She could barely stand.

Penny stepped beside her, Riley at her heels. "This went so well. I mean, last time it was good, but this was great!"

Adelle stood. "I never expected Meldrick to run."

"Don't worry about that." Penny grabbed her elbow. "You can't do anything about that right now."

"But all those buttons. He has a lot of support."

Logan hoisted her duffle bag over her shoulder. "You have to be seen tomorrow. Walk down to the stores in the afternoon, when people are out at lunch, and make sure you point out that Meldrick gave up the job once before. And we wouldn't be in this position if he'd fixed it himself. If he wasn't capable then, he's not capable now." She inched toward the stairs. "I gotta run and open the bar. You should come and get a drink. I bet half of these people will stop in on their way home."

The last thing she wanted to do was have conversations she hadn't planned for. She'd sit awake all night, mulling over every word, building a case against herself. But a beer sounded good. And she'd be awake anyway. At least she'd be in good company. "Yeah. I'll come by. That's a good idea."

Riley ran a hand through his hair. "I got an early morning, so I'm gonna skip out on the bar. But I'll be glad to scowl if I see Meldrick supporters tomorrow. I can't campaign on the job, but maybe I can remind them that their mail might be slower if it has to come from out of town." He winked and made for the door.

Cheryl reached a perfectly manicured hand through the crowd. "Adelle, it was a great presentation. Thanks."

Adelle couldn't help but notice the Meldrick for Manager button, overhead tube lights reflecting off its glossy sheen.

"You're welcome. Thanks for listening."

The woman was gone in a whirl of sleek black hair.

Adelle cracked her knuckles. "There are so many buttons, Penny. What if I lose."

Penny rolled her eyes. "People put those on before they heard the truth. Ramsbolt wouldn't be in this situation if Meldrick did his job. You don't have to say it. We will."

"People only took those buttons because Meldrick wasn't proposing change. Or they took them because he handed it to them, just to be nice." Logan stepped toward the stairs. "But worse change will happen if they don't believe you. Come on. We'll talk it up at the bar. I don't have any rules about campaigning at work."

CHAPTER TWENTY-SEVEN

The letters had faded from the sign above the flower shop long before Adelle was born. Only faint outlines remained, the words themselves lost to time. She would glance at it on her way home from the store with bags in her arms or when dusk shaded her door, but she was always too busy, too laden to borrow a ladder, buy some paint, and fill in the word *Florist* above her door.

A helplessness, a restless ache that only lifted when she moved her hands, sent her rushing from the store at the hint of dawn. She wandered the streets until the hardware store opened. Carol promised her the small can of green paint would suffice. As soon as the lights came on in Penny's Loft, she borrowed an ancient wooden ladder and climbed it with an old paint brush to recolor what her grandfather had painted two generations before.

Unsteady on her feet, she clutched the paint can in one hand, the brush in the other, and prayed she wouldn't fall.

*It's a good thing plants grow in the ground, because I am not good with heights.* Her legs and shoulders hurt from bracing herself, trying to balance, hold the can, and not drop the brush. She'd never liked to paint. With the curve of the brush, she finished the last petal of a five-leaf clover. Her fingers ached from trying to be precise. She put the lid back on the can.

"This is a surprise." Nate held the ladder while she climbed down. He wore a white oval sticker with a red swoosh and the words *I Voted* in vibrant blue. "Looks great."

"Thanks. I was up early. Kinda restless. I figured I'd do something productive, since there's nothing to do but wait for the day to go by. All that talk about fixing up the town. I figured I could use all this energy to lead by example. Was it busy at the church?"

Nate waved a hand. "Nah. It never is. Not in the morning anyway. It's busier at lunch."

"That's what Helen said, that lunch was the busiest time. Logan suggested I go to vote when it's busiest, so I can be seen."

"She's a smart one, that Logan." Nate stood back, head tilted, considering the sight. "You know, I'm a little sad to see that old sign change. It's been like that as long as I can remember. What's with the five-leaf clover?"

Adelle traced the ribbon around her neck to the pendant and held out the necklace. "A bit of good luck from the past. Found one on a bad day when I was a teenager. I've been wearing it for luck. Not that I believe in all that. It was just for fun."

"That's a cool talisman you got there. You made that?"

"A little epoxy. It was easy." She tucked it back inside her shirt. "I know it's cheesy, but I found it in some old books, and it felt like an omen or something."

"It's not cheesy. Positivity is a good thing. I have a little basket of painted stones by the register, and every time a kid comes in, I let them pick one to take home. I tell them it's for good luck, to protect them on their adventures, but it doesn't really make you brave. You were already. It just gave you a reminder."

She'd like to think that he was right, that she'd been brave and faced down Meldrick and the town's worst challenges on her own, but she'd always tied bravery to success, and she hadn't experienced any yet. So far all it could prove was her folly. She tucked the necklace under the ancient T-shirt of her father's that she wore to save her clothes from the paint.

"Speaking of positivity, I'm afraid to ask, but are there signs of support out there or is everybody wearing Meldrick buttons?"

Nate wrinkled his nose. "There are some signs for Meldrick out there. I saw a couple on lawns back behind the cemetery when I went out for a walk this morning. Nothing on Main Street, though. You have signs in every window there already, so I guess he didn't feel welcome."

"But still. All those buttons. I wonder if talking to people at the bar helped at all."

"I suspect the Meldrick supporters are fewer in number than they appeared. You convinced a lot of people with that presentation. Don't sell yourself short. Oh! I ran into Warren."

"What did Warren have to say? He's friendly with Meldrick, isn't he?"

"He is, but he said he's not voting for him because he gave the job up once before, and he has no kids left to hawk it off on. Said you were the first person willing to do it for the right reasons in a very long time. Some of the old men in there are voting for you, too."

"That's good news. Very good news." Mack and Lewis were the

squeaky wheels that Ramsbolt tended to grease. It was easier to fall in line than to listen to them complain. If they were voting for her and being vocal about it, they might sway some undecided voters.

Nate's gaze wandered to the end of Main Street, toward the park. "What's up with Morgan?"

Adelle followed his stare. Morgan shuffled up the sidewalk, his head was down, hands in his pockets. He was the very picture of dejection.

"He looks so sad." It couldn't have anything to do with the election; it was far too early to tally the votes and most people wouldn't vote until lunch time.

"I wonder if he's just bummed about passing the baton," Nate said.

She shrugged. "I dunno. He seemed excited about it before. He leaves for college in a few days. Maybe he's just sad about all the change."

"Maybe that's it. You done with the ladder? I can drag it back to Penny for you."

Adelle glanced up at her work. The ghosts of old letters had been a great template. *Florist.* Once painted black, the sign was now a deep forest green. A five-leaf clover at each end of the sign gave it some style. Her grandfather may not have approved of the change, but it wasn't his store anymore. It wasn't his town anymore, either. The time had come for hard change. Inevitable change. And the time had come for some voluntary changes, too.

"Sure. I think I'm done."

Nate collapsed the ladder and lugged it across the street, dragging one leg on the pavement. The scrape of wood on rutted tarmac echoed between the buildings. Someday there'd be more of that, more hammers and power tools and ladders on the sidewalk. Adelle enjoyed the quiet most days, but some sounds of progress would be nice.

By the time Nate propped the ladder by the door to Penny's Loft, Morgan was within earshot.

"What's got you so down?" Adelle and Nate bridged the distance, and the three of them met in front of an empty store.

"My girlfriend broke up with me. I know, it's kid stuff. She doesn't want a long-distance relationship, and she's already jealous of college girls that don't exist yet." Morgan stuffed his hands in his pockets.

If it hadn't been for her own heartbreak, she wouldn't have a five-leaf clover and hope after the storm, even if had been short lived at the time. "Change can hurt like hell sometimes. But it heals, too. You get stronger in the broken places."

"That's what they say. I'm here about something else, though. Bad news. Worst ever." Morgan motioned toward the recessed doorway. "In here. I'm serious. It's bad."

What could be worse than the town falling apart? Was half of it on fire? Her hands went clammy, and her heart raced as she tried to picture what it could be. She shot a nervous glance at Nate and stepped into the doorway. Nate shrugged and followed.

"Why are we hiding?" Nate asked.

"A guy in a fancy suit is here from the state finance department. He's talking with my dad right now."

Nate peeked around the corner. "That must be why Meldrick wasn't around. I figured he'd be out campaigning."

"This is really bad, you guys." Morgan's forehead was lined with worry. "The state still has his name on file as town manager. He's using his official role to start the transition of merging Ramsbolt with Bloomburg."

"What!" The blood drained from Adelle's face. She felt colder than the last days of summer allowed for. Her hands shook, and she shoved them in her pockets. "He can't do this. We're having an election. Right now. At the church. He can't do this. There has to be a way to stop him. Is Adler with him?"

Morgan shook his head. "No. It's just the guy from the state."

Nate put a hand on Adelle's shoulder. "There's got to be something we can do. Don't let him get the better of you."

She wrapped her fingers around the clover pendant. It warmed in her hand.

Morgan peeked his head around the corner, peering to the end of the street. "They're coming this way. My dad's been giving this guy a tour of all the vacant properties. I don't know what's going on, but it can't be good. I really don't want to lose my hometown. I grew up here. I don't hate my dad, but I sure don't agree with him. You've gotta help me stop him."

Nate balled his hands into fists. "Turns out Meldrick wanted change after all. He just wants big city change. That's not what Ramsbolt wants. He's acting against the town's wishes."

"That's it. I've had it." Adelle took off her father's old T-shirt, brushed green with paint, and threw it on the sidewalk. "I'm done with this. They're coming this way?"

Morgan nodded, his eyes wide. "What are you going to do?"

Running a town wasn't all about rainbows. There wasn't any glitter, and she'd never seen a unicorn stroll past the store. She knew it required a certain toughness, a willingness to put one's passion aside and stand up for things with a diplomacy that belied the rage beneath. Her father had been far too kind, making him vulnerable to men like Meldrick. She had no intention of being a victim to that man's gambit or sitting helpless while the worst kinds of change plowed her over.

There was no way to avoid confronting situations like this. She would have to address men like Meldrick on their level if she intended to fight for the kind of change that was right for Ramsbolt.

She smiled. "Thanks for the heads-up, Morgan. I'm gonna go say hello."

# CHAPTER TWENTY-EIGHT

Morgan scampered behind Adelle, trying to keep up with her long stride. "What are you going to do? Are you going to say something?"

Adelle strode toward the end of the street, her back straight and chin lifted. "Tell me everything you know in ten seconds or less."

Morgan reached her side, out of breath, with Nate at his heels. "Um. The guy asked for our financial history and property records. He wants them in a week. Seven days."

Adelle scowled and shook her head. "That's after the election. Did your dad sign any papers?"

"There were papers all over the table when I got in. I think he did, but I don't know for sure. I don't know what they were."

What had Meldrick done? It was one thing to be an unworthy opponent who'd given up on the job once before. It was something else to slander her father. But dragging the town into a worse situation was a level of spite she never thought he'd stoop to.

A few doors up, Meldrick rounded the corner from Main Street. Beside him, strolled a middle-aged man, tall and proper, with greasy hair that held the tooth marks from his comb like Marissa's royal frosting. He wore a dark suit and shiny black shoes. Adelle didn't wave; there wasn't time. The two men ducked into the first empty store.

"Jesus." Nate finally caught up. "Wait, Adelle. What are you going to say?"

She came to a halt and gave Morgan and Nate her best smile. She flipped a strand of brown hair over her shoulder. "Why, I'm just the friendly neighborhood florist here to see why there's activity in this here empty store. You never know. There could be vagrants. Or squatters. Common thievery."

She spun on her heel and walked into the dark dusty space that once was a video store. Back in the eighties, she could rent VHS tapes there for three dollars. There had been little bricks of microwave popcorn by the register and a rack of candy—Red Vines and Skittles and Fun Dip—by the door. The last thing she remembered renting was *Beetlejuice*. Now the store sat empty, like the rest. The Sheetrock walls were faded and peeling, ceiling tiles smashed on the floor. She cleared her throat, and the two men whirled to face her.

She put a hand to her heart, the pendant pressed against her chest. "I'm so sorry. I didn't mean to scare you." She shoved her hand out for a shake. "Adelle. It's a pleasure to meet you."

The man in the suit accepted her grip. When she didn't let go quickly enough, a slow look of recognition spread across the man's face. "Adelle? You're the former town manager's daughter, right? Meldrick was telling me about you."

She let go of his hand, and he wiped it on a handkerchief from his pocket. He turned his back to her and ambled across the room, stepping over fallen debris and piles of dusty plaster. He walked through that debris like a man terrified of dirt.

"I didn't realize anyone still used handkerchiefs. That's charming." Adelle aimed a broad smile at Meldrick. "You know, I was just up the street there, outside my store, and I noticed commotion down this way. I figured I'd see what was happening. Make sure we didn't have any burglars running around trying to steal from our cute little town."

She glanced over her shoulder. Morgan and Nate hadn't followed her. Cowards.

"We're just tending to some town business." Meldrick tilted his head back and looked down his nose at her, as if she were a child and none of this were her personal concern.

"As a citizen, I'd like to know a few details, if you don't mind." Her nose wrinkled when she smiled.

Meldrick sneered, one lip curled in a savage grin. "You can file a Freedom of Information Act request if you'd like to know. It'll take forever to get the paperwork together, though, so you might just want to wait for the next town meeting. Plus, it's really complicated. You have to write a letter and send it in the mail."

She locked eyes with Meldrick, ice running through her veins. "Oh, gosh. A letter. Well, I don't have any kids at home I can convince to do these things for me, so I'll have to figure it out all on my own." She turned to the man in the suit. Head back, he squinted up at the ceiling, into a hole left by a departed ceiling tile. "What did you say your name was, sir? You're from the state, is that right?"

"Charles," he said without looking her way. "Charles Anthony. Deputy Chief of Finance."

"Well, it's very nice to meet you. I'm a candidate for town manager. Today's the election. You may have seen the signs. The ones with my name on them all over Main Street."

"You're hardly a candidate." Meldrick ran a hand across his forehead, peeling away a layer of sweat. He raised his voice. "She's just the flower girl."

Hands on her hips, Adelle glanced at her feet but knew better than to appear weak. She lifted her chin. "I know more about what Ramsbolt needs than a man who had to pay his son to do the job for five years. I believe in thoughtful deliberation and doing what's right for the town. I suspect Charles Anthony here doesn't know that the town is unaware of your plan. I'd like to know what papers you signed and how to stop this process."

"Here." Charles strode across the room. He pulled out his cell phone and swiped at the screen. Standing next to her, he held the phone out. "I was called about three weeks ago to initiate the annexation process. Most of the paperwork has been filed, and we're onto the third stage now, valuing properties and assessing your debts."

Weeks ago. And he hadn't told the town at the meeting. She clenched her hands into fists and ground her teeth to keep her rage in check. She looked down at a tiny spreadsheet with dates and numbers and a column of things like Letter of Intent and Due Diligence. "Agreements have been signed?"

"The initial items. There are still a few steps go to yet. Next we'll identify duplicate services, set up a budget moving forward, and we'll all meet in Augusta to sign the papers."

She handed the phone back. "We?"

Charles tucked the phone in his pocket and wandered to the window. "Ramsbolt, Bloomburg, and Augusta. Once the final agreement is signed, it's a tiered transition. It won't hurt much, and you'll get some help with repairs. Adler and the guys from Bloomburg will come by to draw up improvement plans. You'll be phased into a local tax while we phase out subsidies for the school and so on."

Adelle folded her arms. "And who specifically initiated this?"

Charles stepped into a ray of light that stretched across the floor. "Your current town manager. Meldrick, here. I don't want to get in the middle of small-town politics. It's hard enough working in big state politics."

Adelle offered him her most conciliatory smile. "Oh, there's no small-town politics here, is there Meldrick? None at all. All those power struggles and the ego stroking. It's tiring. No, we don't have the energy for all that. We're just a friendly group of neighbors. For the most part. Wouldn't you say, Meldrick?" She didn't give him time to blink. "Anyway, out of curiosity, what would happen if we *didn't* go through with it?"

Charles wiped his glasses with his handkerchief. "It would be highly unusual at this stage to not go through with it."

Adelle blinked at him. She'd hoped for an easy answer, like a tiny eraser or a blink-and-nod genie thing. No such luck. "Are you saying things are far along?"

"Somewhat."

"Well, Charles. If I may call you Charles? I'm sure this process is complicated, what with all the moving parts, but clearly you're not in any hurry to rush off. I hope you're able to stay until at least eight o'clock when the town plumber reads the election results in the park just over there."

"I don't think I can—"

"Because the town plumber is also on the town board." She waved a hand. "I know all these terms seem antiquated. It may seem silly that we don't have a town council like the guys in Bloomburg do. Our town board would be really interested in what Meldrick is doing, though, since they have no clue that he's put us up for sale, and we'll all be charged money for the privilege, instead of focusing on a plan that's better for our town. I do hope you can join us, but I absolutely understand if you'd rather head back to Augusta."

Adelle gave him her sweetest smile.

Charles checked his phone. "It feels like I've stepped into the middle of something, and we've done all we can do here today, anyway. Why don't I leave you all to it. We'll be in touch."

Meldrick's face was red, and his eyes bulged. His fury warmed her heart, and a joy swelled within her. She'd interrupted his little plan. She locked eyes with him again and grinned. "And Charles! Do stop by Marissa's bakery before you go and grab a blueberry muffin. They're the best you'll ever have. Local blueberries, even."

Once the finance guy with his fancy suit and dirty shoes had cleared the building, she spun on her heel and left Meldrick alone in the debris. She didn't care one bit for whatever witty retort he would conjure, whatever insult however thinly veiled. She had a paintbrush to clean.

She stepped onto the sidewalk and squinted against the sunlight. To her left Charles was heading to some distant car, probably one of those boring sedans with a state-owned plate. To her right, Nate and Morgan clung to the doorway of the empty shop next door.

"Well?" Nate blinked at her. "You were brilliant."

She checked her sneakers. Her white Keds were free of dust and dirt. "Thanks. But I haven't been brilliant yet. I'm just getting warmed up. You were right, Morgan. This is very bad, indeed."

She walked left, toward Main Street, Nate and Morgan in her wake.

"The process is already started. He said it would be highly unusual to call it off at this stage. And Meldrick could still win. Everything I worked for could mean nothing. If he's busy trying to sell us out, he might be confident. Maybe he talked to people and found out they don't want my type of change."

"What's next?" Morgan asked.

"I have to convince them."

She turned the corner and headed down Main. A woman loaded bags into the trunk of her car while a little boy clung to her side. Adelle stepped up beside her.

"Hi, ma'am." She stuck out her hand. "Have you heard about my plan to bring new businesses to Ramsbolt?"

# CHAPTER TWENTY-NINE

The park was chilly for a late August night. Couples held hands beneath the moon. People sat in lawn chairs and stretched out on the grass in pools of light while kids ran in a circle around the sailor statue in a game of tag that was older than Adelle. Ramsbolt was like any small town with its games of tag. Helen received the town matriarch role from Claire. Mack inherited the town grump task from Roscoe. Maybe it was her turn to be it, or maybe it wasn't. Either way, someone would be it just after nine o'clock, and everyone gathered, waiting for Grey to emerge from the church and walk down Main Street to tag the next town manager.

Adelle watched them all from a distance, from the path beside the sailor statue, her insides twisted into knots and her hair tied up in her clover scarf. She should be mingling or thanking people for their votes. But she was frozen to the sidewalk in a shadowed gap between pools of yellow light, clutching the five-leaf clover and praying it brought her some kind of strength or wisdom. At the very least she hoped it reminded her to smile if she lost and had to hear Meldrick's name called in front of all those people. She grabbed the knot and adjusted the ribbon around her neck.

The park seemed foreign, like a movie filmed in a familiar setting but from odd angles. All of the flaws seemed larger somehow. An uneven brick wobbled beneath her left heel, and crabgrass sprawled from between the bricks. The kids didn't care. Around and around they ran in a dizzying whirlwind. She pictured herself on a warm spring day, her momentum lost by knotted red tape, crawling through the park on her hands and knees, pulling plants from the cracks as if it were all she could do to hold the town together.

"I should be out there," she muttered. Beside her, Penny and Nate laughed with Logan about some small joke or witty observation. Adelle heard none of it.

"What was that?" Penny nudged her.

"I should be out there. Talking to people. I have no idea what to say, though."

Nate peered around the statue. "It doesn't look like anybody's looking to talk to the candidates. They're all doing their own thing. I don't see many Meldrick buttons either."

"See?" said Penny. "Relax. Besides campaigning is over. Nothing to do but wait."

"Easy for you to say." Adelle tapped her pockets, looking for her phone. "What time is it?"

"It's been two minutes since you asked." Penny poked at Logan's arm. "Text Grey and find out where he is."

Logan wrenched away. "He'll be here. I don't want to bother him. Appearance of impropriety or whatever."

Nate chuckled. "You'd know all about that."

"You're right. I do." She rolled her eyes and gave him a sarcastic sneer. "With a felon as a father, you learn a lot about indecency."

"I hadn't thought about that." Adelle's eyes scanned the crowd, looking for signs of support, hints of how people voted. Nothing. "It might be bad that Grey is the one bringing the message."

"Nah." Nate shook his head. "Heather's in charge of tallying the votes. No one will question her. She counts the change from the offering plates on Sundays for a reason. Most trustworthy person in town."

He elbowed Adelle. "Look. Meldrick showed up."

"God, look at him." Logan leaned against the marble base of the statue, her arms folded. "He's not even nice when he orders a drink. He left me fifteen cents as a tip once after ordering three beers. A dime and five pennies. That guy's such an ass."

Meldrick wore a broad smile and wove himself through the crowd, puffed up, clad in khakis and loafers with no socks and a polo shirt. He walked through clusters of people, slapping shoulders and shaking hands, like a man who had already schmoozed the crowd and won. Maybe he had. Maybe he knew something she didn't.

Just the sight of him made Adelle's pulse quicken, and not in a good way. He bent and shook the hand of a woman reclining on a beach towel. Before he turned, he tossed her a button.

"What a sleaze." Logan shifted her weight.

"He makes my skin crawl," Adelle said.

Meldrick circled the park and paused at a bench where a mom sat next to a stroller. Something white peeked out of his shirt pocket.

"Is that a notecard? You think he made a speech. Crap." Adelle turned her back to him and wrinkled her nose. "Maybe I should go out there and talk to people. Do you think I should have made a speech? Just in case? It's too late to come up with something now. Dammit. How is he so confident?"

Penny shrugged. "Who knows with him? What a weirdo. You still have time if you want to make one, though."

The last of the summer cicadas warmed up their tymbals and let out an evening wail.

"I didn't think to prepare anything." Panic rose within her and scattered all her thoughts. Her brow furrowed, she looked at her shoes. "I don't even know what I'd say. That's worse than winning, getting up there and saying something stupid. I don't want people to regret their votes that soon."

Logan grabbed her by the shoulders, a broad smile on her face. "Whoa. Don't melt down on us. All you have to do is fake it. It doesn't matter. See? Smile?"

"You think I'm gonna lose?"

Logan's arms fell to her sides. "No. No one will remember what you say. Just blurt out whatever you think another politician would say. Pretend you're in a movie."

Adelle slumped against the sailor's marble base. "I could talk about preserving history and culture while moving into a new era. How's that?"

Nate dug a mint from his pocket and wrung it from the wrapper. "That sounds good. Really good. You could mention what that new era would look like, too."

"How about... A new era with new stores and businesses, a stronger economy, and a working clock, so we know that time is working for us, and we aren't fighting to keep up with it."

"Ooh." Penny smiled and wagged a finger. "That's good. Remember that."

Logan nodded toward Main Street. "Here he comes."

Grey clutched an envelope and came down the church steps. He was such a tiny speck at that distance, but he carried her whole world: her flower shop, her family history, her friends, her hope, and her whole town.

Her breath caught in her throat. She should have gone to church more, to make her tiny prayer have more value. She begged God not to let her lose. Losing the election would mean losing everything. It would mean losing her plants and the worn-out floor and Jake in the window across the street. She would lose Marissa's blueberry muffins and her terrible coffee and making flowers for anniversaries. She would lose all the places she loved.

It was terrifying, watching him make that walk, not knowing what he knew. He was still too far away for her to analyze his features, or read anything into his expression, but she sent all her wishful thinking his way, and tried to fake a confident smile. She'd need it if she lost to Meldrick in front of all those people.

*Look up. Look at me. Wink. Nod. Smile. Wave your arms. Scream the results. Anything. Jesus, why is he slow? Sorry, God. I pray that Grey arrive as quickly and safely as you allow. Please. Thanks.*

Her eyes were glued to Grey's form as it faded and brightened in and out of the streetlights.

What if she'd failed? If the town didn't vote for her, it would mean the end of everything she loved. It would mean they chose the opposite, that they didn't want the same things for the only town she'd ever lived in and cared for. It would mean an end to her father's legacy, a certain end to the flower shop, and probably an end to the friendships she'd made there with Logan, Penny, Nate, and Grey.

If the town voted for Meldrick, it would mean her feelings about Ramsbolt were wrong. And she wouldn't belong here anymore.

Grey hopped the curb and climbed the hill to the top of the town park. He gave no indication, not even a glance at Logan, that Adelle could interpret. He pulled an envelope from his back pocket, jumped up on the bench in front of the statue, and ran a hand through his brown curls.

Adelle stepped around the statue to see better.

"Guys, I have the results. Heather and I each counted the votes twice, and we have a winner. Heather certified it." He waved the envelope. "This is the official winner of the election for town manager."

He opened the envelope and pulled out a slip of paper.

"I don't know why Heather wrote it down. It's not like I couldn't remember. But I guess it's, like, a rule or something."

"Grey," Logan barked. "Read it."

He unfolded the slip of paper.

"Our new town manager is Adelle Faulkner." Grey jumped from the bench.

A suffocating crowd formed around her. Hands reached for her shoulders. She sucked in a quick breath and caught Penny's eye. Words came out of her friend's mouth, but Adelle couldn't hear them. She couldn't hear Logan cheering beside her either. It was as if her heart stopped beating for a moment, and the world slowed down. The woman on the bench packed a bag of snacks into her stroller in slow motion. Some people started to leave for home, others crowded around her.

Hands clapped her shoulder and voices shouted their congratulations as the world came back into focus and returned to normal speed.

Nate nudged her. "Turns out that clover was more amulet than talisman."

"What's the difference?"

"A talisman gives you power or bravery or something you didn't already have. An amulet just protects you from the bad stuff." Nate nodded toward the back of the crowd.

From her tippy toes, Adelle could see Meldrick slip away, alone. Hands in his pockets and his shoulders back, he crossed the street and was gone. No speech or good wishes, he just dissolved among the buildings and streets. She had a twinge of pity for the man. If his intentions were truly for the town, and if he really thought that what he wanted was best for everyone, he would have earned that pity. But for most of her life she'd known him to be vindictive, demanding the removal of her father from society just because they didn't see eye to eye. She swallowed back her emotions. She could pardon him for the crime, but she didn't have to forget.

"You should say something." Logan pointed to the bench. "Hop up there."

She took Grey's spot on the bench before the statue and raised her hands, asking for quiet. It wasn't as rickety as it used to be, thanks to Carol's workmanship. And it was much more stable than Penny's old ladder. Looking out across the crowd of fifty or so, she couldn't help but be humbled. They had faith in her. They believed in her plan. And the hard work was just beginning.

"Everyone, thank you. I am honored by your vote, and I promise to do my best to earn the faith you've placed in me."

A late summer breeze pushed across the park, giving her goosebumps. The necklace felt cool against her skin. She pressed her hand over the clover pendant, warming it, keeping it safe.

"I figured I would say something about moving into a new era and starting a better economy, but all of that is for tomorrow. Tonight, I just want to say that we've all been through a lot. We lost jobs and homes and downsized over and over. There's not a person here who doesn't know that the best things in life are the little things, because sometimes it feels like that's all we've got left. That's what's so hard about change, isn't it? Little things are so easy to lose. It doesn't really matter what size house you have or how many things you cram inside of it. None of those things change who you are on the inside. No matter what we've faced, none of it challenged our beliefs about who we are and what Ramsbolt should be."

The crowd applauded. Logan gave her a thumbs-up.

Sandy was right. She was getting used to the public speaking thing.

"The real work begins tomorrow. I'm excited for the future, for ours and for Morgan's. Let's give him a round of thanks for everything he's done here."

While the crowd cheered for Morgan, Adelle stepped from the bench. Around her, people lifted bags, draped blankets over their arms, and headed for their homes. They radiated out from the park and into the streets.

"That was pretty good speech you gave there." Logan pulled her into a hug. "You're gonna be good at this. You sound like a pro at this change thing."

"I'm not very good at change, really." Moving from the farm as a kid had been hell. Living in the mothball house by the cemetery had been scary and small. She'd fought back every chance she could get, never settling in or letting anything get too familiar. Eventually it all just wore on her. She'd love to live somewhere other than the little rooms above the shop. She'd love more than anything to choose her own change this time around, rather than dwelling within the walls she'd been dealt. They were supposed to be temporary, anyway.

Adelle threw an arm around Logan. "What do you guys say? Celebration round?"

Penny linked arms with Nate. "We're in."

The group took off across the park, up the hill toward the tavern.

"I couldn't have done this without you guys, you know."

"Yeah, you would have," Grey said over his shoulder.

"You were the perfect person for the job." Penny gave her a smile. "Everybody tried to tell you."

# CHAPTER THIRTY

Penny's red Jeep grinded to halt at the curb. Adelle adjusted her necklace in the side view mirror. The clover charm looked perfect on the chain she bought, professional enough to go with her new pant suit. She hopped out of the passenger seat, and her feet hit the parking lot outside the law building in Augusta.

"Thanks for the ride." She collected her tote bag and smoothed her jacket. "Hopefully I won't be coming back to the capital too often."

"Any time. Don't worry about it." Penny's hand was poised on the shifter. "Text me when you're done. I'll be a few blocks down checking out antiques. We can grab lunch."

"Will do. This won't take long."

Adelle turned to face the imposing building, which was several stories taller than anything in Ramsbolt. Had her father ever been intimidated by the formality of it all, by the giant state seal on the building, by all the concrete and perfect landscaping? It was almost like a show. *Imagine how many people had to conspire to create a system, to build these buildings and this pristine parking lot. And imagine all the work we do inside.* There must have been a hundred windows.

Her heels clicked on the sidewalk. A blast of air too cool to balance the climate hit her when she opened the door. Inside, she signed her name in the visitor log and accepted an ID badge from a sweater-clad woman with a black headset. Adelle pinned the badge to her jacket.

"Your meeting is in conference room 209. On the second floor. Go up those stairs and take a left." She smiled and pushed a button on her headset and returned to a call about forms and faxes.

The staircase was broad, made of glass, and bordered by a thin metal handrail. She traced it to the second floor, following its wide curve, and counted the numbers on the door as she passed. 207. 208. She paused outside the door. The frosted glass wall gave no hint of the room within.

Laughter rang from inside the room. It sounded of businessmen. The way her father laughed at a joke that wasn't funny and bonded with people he had no care for. The Adelle from a year ago would have raised a hand and meekly knocked, but this Adelle let the tote bag fall from her shoulder as she pushed the door open.

A large oval table with a black top rested beneath a mirrored ceiling with accent lights. Thin black chairs on sleek metal frames surrounded it, each facing a dark gray blotter. Tall fake plants held up the corners of the room, to which she feigned not taking offense. Along one wall, a sideboard framed a tiny fridge, and on it were stacks of binders and folders.

She closed the door behind her.

Three men from the state were poised at the table like figures from modern fine art, pristine white shirts with iron folds in the sleeves. One slouched in his chair, one leaned back with arms folded, and Charles Anthony at the head of the table inspected his phone. Then there was Adler, draped in the chair as if this were his living room and everyone else a mere guest, for his whimsy.

"Charles. Nice to see you again." She chose the chair across from Adler, pulled her pen from her bag, and placed it on the blotter.

Charles nodded and set his phone to the side. His cufflink clicked against the black table. "Ms. Faulkner. If we're all here, we might as well get started."

A younger man rose and handed out binders and folders. She'd seen it all before, in PDFs emailed from the state. She'd read them a hundred times at the counter, late at night while the town slept. There was no need to rehash where they'd been or where they'd be going. There was no value in looking at the hows and the whens.

She set the binder to the side and opened the folder. There were dozens of forms in stapled sets to cancel services and start new ones, merge what they had with what Bloomburg offered. The important form was in the back. She removed it without disturbing the rest.

"Thank you so much for your help this week, getting this last bit of paperwork together," she said. "I apologize for the inconvenience, but we have definitely made our decision."

She initialed each of the four pages and signed her name at the bottom. Without a word, she added the date. Then she slid the Declination of Proposal form across the table to Charles, who promptly collected it and inspected her signature.

Adler beamed. He leaned in, propping his elbows on the table. "We won't need your little committee anymore, so you can tell them to disband today. We'll have a team out to Ramsbolt tomorrow to set up the office. We plan on using that old General Store space on Levering, right across from your flower shop."

He smirked. She wouldn't give him the satisfaction of seeing her shift in her seat, writhe in discomfort. She smiled down at the blotter instead and closed the folder.

Adler's seat creaked when he leaned back, folding his hands, and placing them behind his head. "I assume you can have that old ice cream cooler and that giant wood table thing out by morning. We won't need that junk."

Adelle gave him her kindest smile. Her father had always told her not to gloat, that what she thought gave her an advantage today would be her undoing tomorrow. There was no sympathy to draw upon, nor apathy for that matter. She was simply elated for Ramsbolt and proud of herself for coming so far.

"There's no need for you to swing by tomorrow, Adler. I dissolved the agreement. We aren't turning our town over to you."

Adler lowered his hands to his lap. He fiddled with his watch.

She owed him no explanation, but it gave her satisfaction to lay it on the line and hear herself say it out loud. "We have a solid economic development plan and plenty of interest from entrepreneurs inside and outside town to start their small businesses in Ramsbolt. We are committed to keeping our town independent."

She placed the binder and folder in her tote bag and stood, then pushed in her chair.

Adler shook his head and slammed his binder closed. "You're making a big mistake." He wagged a finger at her, but she wouldn't accept the scolding like a child. She lifted her chin and raised her eyebrows.

"I would ask you how so, Adler, but it's no longer relevant." She turned to the door. "Thank you for your time and effort, Charles."

"Those people in that town elected Meldrick because they wanted action, and they wanted change." Adler's voice boomed. "They want amenities and basic services that *your* father refused to give them. You should be ashamed of yourself. You're throwing away your only chance to deliver what they need, sealing your fate as the worst thing to happen since your father, and you're throwing that town to the wolves."

She paused with her hand on the doorknob. Adler was lashing out as she expected he would. She turned to face him but kept her hand on the door. "If Meldrick had truly wanted change, he should have created it, instead of paying his son to do the job for him. My father tried to give the town the positive changes it needed. He went to every single house, and every single person declined his proposal. They didn't understand the urgency then, but they do now. The only negligent person in Ramsbolt's history is Meldrick, and when people voted a month ago, they did so knowing the facts. They voted for my plan. Declining your offer today is my first step to fulfilling my campaign promises."

Adler folded his arms, his eyes fixed on the binder. All of those plans were laid to waste. "What you don't know, lady, is that running a town takes a lot more than one person. You're setting yourself up for failure if you think you can be some great hope that will make it all better."

She opened the door and stepped into the hall. "I have plenty of support from my town. Good luck, Adler. And thanks again, Charles."

# CHAPTER THIRTY-ONE

Adelle tucked a pale pink rose between gardenia stems and spun the lazy susan, checking the arrangement from all angles.

"Not bad," she said, mostly to the leggy coleus that tumbled toward the counter from the shelf above. "You're growing like a weed. Anyway, Logan will love it. Grey has great taste in flowers for a plumber."

She checked the clock. Kyle, the guy coming to look at the old General Store space, was running late, but he'd said he might. The long commute between wherever he lived and his farm job outside Ramsbolt was a big reason he wanted to open a shop of his own. She trimmed another gardenia stem and nested it in the vase. It was almost too full, but it was an important arrangement, after all. Grey wanted the first day they lived together to be special.

"Now it's perfect," she said, spinning the lazy susan again. "What do you think, Dad?"

He would have approved.

She tucked the vase on the top shelf of the cooler, right at eye level where she could admire them as she worked. Outside, kids flew by on their bikes, barely disturbing the heat that sizzled off the street in summer's last gasp. It was scorching for the end of September.

A small sedan followed the bikes, old enough to be a classic and young enough to make Adelle feel bad for the poor thing. Its green paint chipped and cracked, revealing the yellow plastic bumper beneath. The car pulled down the narrow alley that led to parking across the street, behind the buildings. That had to be him.

She checked her pocket for the key and shivered. Ever since she'd had the air conditioner repaired, she'd kept it indulgently cool inside the shop, but she turned it down anyway. No sense wasting money she didn't have. She grabbed the manila folder from her counter as her phone buzzed with a text. She unlocked the screen.

*I'm here! Sorry I'm late.*

*No problem! Meet you around front.*

She didn't really want to leave her shop to go out into the heat, but she pushed the door open and stepped out into a wall of hot air. It was like standing on the surface of the sun. The key warmed in her hand as she skipped across the street.

"Lord, I hope it's cooler in the shade."

The recessed door of the old General Store was flanked by glass display windows. When she was a kid, Mrs. Miller would change it with the seasons. She'd have giant Easter baskets full of crocheted eggs, a big Christmas tree covered in glass ornaments. And every summer she'd fill a blue plastic kiddie pool with sand and buckets and little kid shovels. It may never be the same again, but at least it wouldn't be empty. She had no clue what the guy intended to do with the space, but she'd be happy to see something in there other than peeling paint and broken sheetrock.

The air was a little cooler in the entry. The cracked hexagon tiles in black and white shaded from the sun. Footsteps scrambled on the sidewalk behind her, and she turned to face Kyle. He was her age, maybe a little older, his face lined by the sun. He had kind eyes, dark hair speckled gray, and an easy smile. He extended his hand. At his feet, at the end of a leash, a puppy tumbled and wagged its body.

"Puppy!" Adelle dropped to her knees and tousled the dogs ears. He yipped and slobbered her hand. "What's your dog's name?"

"This is Jacques. Like Jacques Pepin." Dark brown eyes peered down at her. His wavy hair brushed against his eyebrows. He wore gray plastic-framed glasses and had a kind crooked smile. In another world, he could be a late-night talk show host.

"I loved watching cooking shows as a kid," he said.

"Me, too." She stood and brushed the dirt from her knees.

"Sorry I'm late." He shuffled the dog leash and stuck out a hand. "And sorry for the dog. I didn't want to leave him in the car. Is it okay if I bring him in?"

"Of course! Don't worry about it!" She shook his hand and stuck the key in the lock. "The lock sticks. It's old. You have to jiggle it a bit, and it'll open right up."

She pushed the door open, and a wall of pulpy air hit them, thick with dust. She held the door open and followed him inside where flecks streamed through ribbons of light that pierced the shadows. Jacques bumbled in, undeterred, nose to the floor as he searched for something to chase.

"The store is a blank slate, really." She leaned against the old ice cream cooler. "What do you think you want to do with it?"

His eyes scanned the ceiling, the walls. A hopeful, gentle smile spread across his face, as if he could see the future there among the cobwebs and old tin ceiling tiles. Jacques yipped and jumped. He left circles of footprints in the dust.

"I always liked to cook," Kyle said. "There's something about soup that's so comforting. Anyway, I want to open a kitchen supply shop. Colorful dutch ovens, toasters, cast iron pans, nice dishes, utensils. That kind of thing. Specialty things like coffee bean grinders. And someday, when I do well enough and can afford to put some ovens in, I'll have some cooking classes."

"That would be fun." She walked to the old candy table, covered in white dirt like powdered sugar. She ran a finger through one of the troughs and dark wood the color of chocolate frosting showed through.

"What was that thing?" he asked.

"Candy was in here. Penny candy."

He nodded and turned away, walking along the far wall. "Maybe I can use it for something."

"You know, thinking about cooking classes. If you get that off the ground, maybe we can even collaborate sometime."

"Yeah?" He raised an eyebrow while Jacques nipped at her shoelaces.

"Sure. If you do a class on cooking with local veggies, I could hop in and teach them about growing kitchen herbs. Something like that. I dunno. Just a thought."

"It's a good one." Kyle opened a door to an old bathroom. "This place could use some cleaning, but it's a nice space. And the price is great. I looked for a place in Bloomburg once. A long time ago. But it was so expensive. I thought I'd never be able to chase this dream."

She'd tried to play it cool, but she couldn't hold in the smile. "It is a little rough around the edges. It's been empty for a long time, but it is a lot cheaper than Bloomburg, that's for sure." She folded back the cover of the manila folder. "I've got a contract here for you to look over."

She held it out, and he took it with a shaking hand. "This is a super simple process. The rental fees are really cheap. And it doesn't kick in for six months. You do have to fix it up, though, and all the terms are in here. You can do the work yourself, but it has to pass inspection before it opens. You call Martin for that, and his number's in there. There's a list of vendors and phone numbers, too, to help you out."

He didn't look up from the pages. There were only four of them, but the type was small enough to intimidate anyone. "I know Martin. He comes by the farm sometimes. I've run into him at Carol's."

"Good! She can help with paint and drywall at the hardware store, if you need it. She even has some discounted items to help people opening up new shops."

"No rent for six months, huh? Even if I open before then?"

"The town board put together a really nice plan for this space. The six months help get you on your feet. After that, rent kicks in, and it's really cheap for the first two years. After that, it increases a bit every few years. It's all laid out in here."

"This is really cheap. I could never afford to open a shop like this if it weren't for this deal. I've been wanting to open a little store for years. It's been my dream not to have to work for someone else." He flipped the pages over, pulled a pen from his shirt pocket, and leaned on the old counter, where Mrs. Miller's register once sat, to sign it.

"You're the first town tenant. It'll be nice to have a new neighbor."

"I bet you're tired of looking out the window at all these empty buildings." He clicked his pen closed and dropped it back into his pocket.

Tired? No. She'd clung to the nostalgia for so long it was like an old friend. But she was ready to let it go.

"This was a dry goods store in my great-granddad's time. They sold hats and ribbon and plain paper until about fifty years ago. Then it became a General Store. That cooler over there had popsicles in it. When I was a kid, I'd sneak a quarter from the register at my granddad's shop and buy a creamsicle, the frozen orange filled with cream. I would hide around the corner in the alley and eat it."

"I loved those as a kid." His eyes landed on the cooler. "We never came in here when I was little. Couldn't afford to. Maybe I can get this one up and running. That might be a nice touch."

Adelle shook her head and wrinkled her nose. "I doubt you'd want to. It's been sitting there empty since the nineties, I guess."

He shrugged and leaned against the counter. "I could get a new one. I'd probably need one anyway for frozen foods."

"You grew up here?" She studied him with a narrowed gaze. "I don't remember you. When did you go to school?"

Kyle smiled as he bent down and ruffled Jacques' head. The puppy gnawed at his hand. "I remember you. You were a few years younger than me. We lived outside town and didn't come this way often. I left to go to college and came back a few years ago. I do maintenance and help manage the books for farm out that way." He nodded toward the town park. I wish we'd spent more time downtown when I was a kid. I don't have many memories of what it used to be like.

Adelle waved a hand and dust glittered in the air. "It's changed a lot. For the better, in the grand scheme of things. Growing pains are extra hard on little towns like ours, but there's a strong sense of place here, and people really care about the future of it."

"I can tell. Everyone's really nice." He stood and grabbed the folder, revealing a clean swath of wood counter where his elbow had been.

"We do like newcomers. Gives us someone new to talk to." She accepted the signed contract. Jacques jumped at her ankles, and she bent to pet him goodbye. "I'll leave you to it. You probably want to measure everything and start making lists of what you need. I'll get this to the committee for a vote, and I should have an answer for you next week, at the latest. It's entirely up to them, of course, but I'd say your chances are really good."

"Thanks. You don't mind if I take my time?"

She paused, the old brass doorknob cool in her hands despite the humid swelter. "Not at all. I have a guy picking up an arrangement for his girlfriend soon, so I have to run. I'm excited to see what you do with the place. Let me know if you need anything."

She turned the knob and tugged at the door. It gave way with a crack as the old paint let go.

"Adelle! I meant to ask! What about colors? Are there rules about what colors I can paint the outside trim? I know it's historic."

When she was a kid, the trim had been a deep forest green. The brass doorknob had shined in the sun. Since then, the paint had chipped away, revealing white layers and wood beneath, and the brass had tarnished to a spotty, flat brown. But there wasn't any point in reliving the past.

"Any color you want. She's all yours now. Well, almost." She waved the folder.

"And this is gonna sound strange." He gestured to her necklace. "Is that a real five-leaf clover? I saw one on your shop sign, too, so I had to ask."

She raised a hand to the pendant. "It is. I found this when I was eighteen."

"That's funny." His eyes wrinkled at the corners when he smiled.

Adelle's cheeks burned. She tore her eyes away and looked at her feet. "They're really rare. I found one myself when I was a kid. I have it tucked in an old copy of *Treasure Island*. Kept all my clovers in there."

"I kept most of my clovers in *Anne of Green Gables*. Except for this one." She grasped the charm that dangled from the chain around her neck. It was still cool from her day in the air conditioning.

"They say each leaf stands for something different."

"Faith and hope." She shook her head. It had been ages since she'd heard it. "I can't remember the rest."

He counted them on his fingers. "Love, luck, and wealth. That's the five."

Adelle let go of the charm and pushed the door open. A blast of early autumn pushed in. Jacques yipped a goodbye and wagged his body with his tail. "Well, four out of five's not bad."

"There's hope for us yet," he said.

# ABOUT THE AUTHOR

A Maryland native and Pennsylvanian at heart, Jennifer M. Lane holds a bachelor's degree in philosophy from Barton College and a master's in liberal arts with a focus on museum studies from the University of Delaware, where she wrote her thesis on the material culture of roadside memorials. She resides with her partner Matt and a tuxedo cat named Penny.

**Receive free prequel stories, news about upcoming releases and more by signing up for the author newsletter at** jennifermlanewrites.com

OTHER WORKS BY THE AUTHOR INCLUDE

*Of Metal and Earth*
*Stick Figures from Rockport*
*and*
*The Collected Stories of Ramsbolt Books:*
*Blood and Sand*
*Penny's Loft*
*Hope for Us Yet*